NO ESCAPE!

Jack, with an exclamation of dismay, felt his horse flounder into a laboring trot through the muck, and leaning to the side, he peered ahead to make out how far the field extended. The moon-haze was thick before him, but in the little distance he could make out the outlines of a fence. Toward this, then, he pressed on, and glancing back over his shoulder he saw the posses tearing across the field in pursuit and gaining now at a fearful rate.

Well, let them run as they pleased. When they reached the ploughed ground it would stop them more effectually than a wall of stone. Brown Susan, stepping more than fetlock deep, struggled on toward the fence, stepped onto a strip of firmer going just beside it, leaped the obstacle like a cat, and landed on deeper and newer ploughed ground just beyond!

That was the meaning, then, of the triumphant shouting behind him and to the sides. They understood that he had run into a trap from which there was no exit. No, he was helpless, for looking to the side, he saw a group of riders spurring down some undiscovered lane to skirt around and gain the front of him. There, hemmed in on all sides, they would shoot him to death from a safe distance.

Already they were opening fire.

DUST ACROSS THE RANGE/ THE CROSS BRAND

LEISURE BOOKS NEW YORK CITY

A LEISURE BOOK®

July 2000

Published by special arragement with Golden West Literary Agency.

Dorchester Publishing Co., Inc.
276 Fifth Avenue
New York, NY 10001

ISBN 0-8439-4743-8

DUST ACROSS THE RANGE

ONE

Off the high, level plateau of the range, cattle trails dip like crooked runlets of white water into the valley of the Chappany. Louise Miller, bound for home on her best horse, came off the level like a ski jumper from the take-off mound. She had come back to the ranch to celebrate her twenty-first birthday and take over the management of the 40,000-acre spread while her father embarked on a two-year drifting voyage through the Old World.

She had brought home in her pocket, so to speak, two specimens of man between whom she was to select a husband, because, as her father warned her, 'ranch days can be kind of long,' and she had ridden out alone on this day to think over the two of them and make her choice. She had made her decision and, having arrived at it, she was homebound, hell-bent, to tell big Frederick

Wilson that in the pinch he was man enough to suit her.

That was why she took the second downward bend of the trail so fast that Hampton skidded under her. Then the danger flashed in her eyes in the form of a three-stranded barbed-wire fence, as new and bright as a sword out of a sheath. She sat Hampton down on his hocks and skidded him to a halt a yard or so from the wire.

A hundred yards away nine men were building a second line of fence, stretching and nailing wire, or tamping new posts in place, or screwing augers into the hard ground. Eight of them were CCC men, she knew, donated by the government to help make the Hancock ranch an example of soil-conservation methods to the entire range. The ninth man, pinch-bellied and gaunt-ribbed from labor, was undoubtedly the fellow to blame for this pair of insane fences which cut the old trail like a pair of knives. He worked with a thirty-pound crowbar, breaking the hardpan.

That was Harry Mortimer, who for two years had been at work trying to make the Hancock place pay real money. He had a one-third share in the property and came out of the East with a brain crammed full of college-bred agricultural theory and an odd missionary desire to teach the ranchers new ways with the old range.

His family had spent long generations wearing down the soil of a New England farm until the bones of the earth showed through. Mortimer's father left the farm, went into business that prospered, but left his son the old yearning to return to the soil. That was why agriculture had been his study in college, but when he looked for a sphere to work in after graduation, the rocky little New England farms seemed too small a field. That was why he had gone to the West to exploit his inherited share in the Hancock place.

Whatever the bookish idiocy that suggested this pair of fences to him, Louise Miller wanted to get to him fast and tell him what she thought of the idea. So she hurried Hampton around the lower end of the fence. But here the ground chopped into an ugly 'badlands' of little gullies and gravel ridges. Hampton began to go up and down over them like a small boat in a choppy sea. He slipped on loose soil. And the next instant Louise Miller was sailing toward the far horizon.

It never would have happened except that she was thinking about steering the chestnut, not keeping her seat. Her only thought was to damn everything, including her own folly and Harry Mortimer. Then she was sitting up, with the landscape settling back from a dizzy whirl. Sweating men were lifting her by the armpits, but Harry Mortimer was not among them. He had let this chip fall where it might while he climbed on one of the mules that grazed near the wagonload of posts and wire, and trotted off in pursuit of

Hampton.

Vaguely she heard the CCC men speaking words of concern and comfort and felt their hands brushing her off carefully, but she was mainly concerned with wishing Hampton would kick a pair of holes through Mortimer. Instead, the thoroughbred stood near the fence like a lamb and allowed himself to be caught and brought back at the mildest of dogtrots. Harry Mortimer dismounted from his mule and handed the girl the reins.

'I thought for a minute you might have a long walk home,' he said.

It was hard for her to answer, so she looked him over and pretended to be catching her breath. He worked stripped to the waist, with a rag of old straw sombrero on his head. The sun had bronzed him; sweat had polished the bronze. He had the light stance of a sprinter, but around his shoulders the strength was layered and drawn down in long fingers over his arms. The pain of labor and the edge of many responsibilities seamed his face, but above all he had the look of one who knows how to endure, and then strike hard.

At last she was able to say, 'Sorry you ran out of places where fences are needed. This is just some practice work for you and your men, I suppose? Or did you think it would be fun to block the trail and cut up the livestock on your barbed wire?'

He picked up the thirty-pound crowbar and tossed it lightly from hand to hand.

'While you're thinking up an answer,' said Louise Miller, 'I'd suggest that there's lots of fence to put up on my place, and where it will do good.... Where does the fun come in, Harry? Digging the holes or seeing the pretty wire flash in the sun?'

The CCC men laughed, heartily. She understood that they lived in almost religious awe of their boss, but they stood back and laughed with deep enjoyment.

'Talk it up to her, Chief,' they called. 'Don't lay down in the first round.'

'You have to give a lady the first hold, boys,' said Mortimer, grinning at them. Then he added, 'Any sore places from that fall, or are you just feeling sour?'

'Not at all,' said the girl, laughing with pure excess of hate. 'I'm simply asking a few questions.'

'Want me to answer pretty Lou Miller?' he asked. 'Or am I talking to the manager of the John Miller ranch?'

'I'm going to manage it, all right,' she nodded.

'D'you know enough to?' he demanded.... 'You fellows get back to that fence-line, will you?'

They departed, their grinning faces turned to watch the comedy.

'Every Miller who ever was born knows enough to run a cattle ranch,' she answered.

'By divine right, or something like that?' said Mortimer. 'Then why don't you know why I'm running these fences?'

'I do know. It's for exercise, isn't it?'

He jabbed the crowbar into the ground and leaned on it, smiling. But she knew that if she had been a man his fist would have been in her face.

'How long has the trail run over this ground?' he asked.

'Two or three years.'

'Where was it before?'

'Over there,' she answered, proud of her exact knowledge. 'Over there where those gullies are opening up.'

'Was there a trail before that one?'

'Yes. It traveled along that big arroyo.'

'What made the gullies and what started the big arroyo washing?' he asked her.

'Why, God, I suppose,' said the girl. 'God, and the rain He sent. What else?'

'It was the trail,' said Mortimer. 'It wore down through the grass and down through the topsoil till it was a trench, and the first heavy rains began to wash the trench deeper. I'm building these fences to turn the downdrift and the updrift of the cattle from the tanks. I'm making them wear new trails.'

She saw the justice of what he said. She saw it so deeply she was angered to the heart because she could find no good retort.

'The point is that the old range and the old range ways aren't good enough for you, Harry. Isn't that the point?'

12

She waved her hand across the valley of the Chappany to the house of her father and the green lake of trees that washed around it, and to the miles of level ground that spread beyond.

'The other generations didn't know. Is that it?' she asked, sharpening her malice with a smile.

He considered her for a moment, as though he doubted the value of making an answer. Then he pointed.

'See the edge of that thousand acres of hay your father planted?' he asked. 'And, spilling into the valley below it, you see the silt that's flowed onto the low ground? That silt spoils fifty acres of good river-bottom that's fit for the plow. Know how it comes to be there?'

'Wash from a heavy rain, I suppose?' she answered gloomily.

'Yes. Your father ripped up a thousand acres of virgin range land. His plow cut through the roots of the grass of the topsoil that's been accumulating for a million years. The rain came on the loose ground and washed the cream of it away. The first dry season and hard wind that comes along, and that thousand acres will blow away like feathers; and the earth will have a million years of work to do all over again.'

'Father had to have extra hay,' said the girl. 'That's why he planted. What else was he to do?'

'Look down the Chappany along the Hancock land,' said Mortimer.

'It looks like a crazy quilt,' she answered.

'Because it's strip-plowed to leave a percentage of holding grass; and it's contour-plowed in other places to keep the soil from washing. Those brush tangles in the gullies are dams that will keep the gullies from deepening. Every slope of more than twenty per cent is planted to trees; every slope of more than twelve goes to permanent grass. In another year or so I'll have every acre of the Hancock place buttoned down to the ground with grass or trees, so that it *can't* blow.'

'I understand,' she said. 'You've been reading the silly newspapers about dust storms. Do you happen to know that there's never been a dust storm on this range?'

'There *will* be, some day,' he answered. 'Look at the mountains, yonder. That blowing mist isn't clouds. It's dust. It's ten thousand acres going to hell this minute!'

She stared toward the horizon and, above the blue of the mountains, saw a smudging darkness in the air. Mortimer was saying, 'That's the Curtis Valley blowing up in smoke. A dry season and a strong wind.... Here's the dry season with us, well enough. The Chappany has stopped flowing, though it's only May. Realize that? Only May, and the range is bone-dry.'

She glanced down the slope at the lakes in the bottom of the valley. There were five of them extended by old dams. Three lay on her land; two belonged to the Hancock place. As a rule the Chappany ran for eleven months in the year, only ceasing in August, and during that month the cattle came in from miles off the dry back of the range. This year, to be sure, was very different, for as the little river ceased flowing, the water holes on the farther range also were drying up and the cows had already commenced to voyage to the valley for drink. Little wind-puffs of white spotted the tableland and drifted down into the valley as parched cattle came at a trot or a lope for the water. Scores of them even now stood shoulder deep in the lakes, and the throngs were lying on the dry shore waiting to drink again, and again, before they started the trek toward the back country and the better grass again.

Mortimer was pointing again. 'A dry season, and a hard wind,' he said. 'That thousand acres your father plowed is a gun pointed at the head of the entire country. If that starts blowing, the top-soil all over the range is apt to peel off like skin.... I tell you, every plow furrow on the range is like a knife cut; it may let out the life and leave you worthless dry bones. The whole range – beautiful damned miles of it – go up in smoke. My land lies right under the gun.'

Her brain rocked as she listened and felt conviction strike her as with hands. If she could not argue, at least she could hate. Her father hated this man, and she would have felt herself untrue to her name if she did not hate him in turn.

'And that was why you tried to stab Father in the back?' she asked.

'I complained to the government and the soil-conservation authorities,' he said. 'I did it after I'd tried a thousand times to talk sense to John Miller.... And they would have *made* him toe the line, except he knew the right political wires to pull.'

She laughed through her teeth. 'Wire-pulling? That's better than rope-pulling, Harry!' she said.

'You mean your father would like to see me lynched?' he answered. 'I suppose he would ... he hates me. I despise him.... But I'll tell you what I'd do. If I thought I could change his mind, I'd crawl a hundred miles on my hands and knees and kiss his feet. I'd sit up and beg like a dog ... because he's the king of the range and, until he wakes up, the whole range will remain asleep ... and one night it'll blow away.'

She swung suddenly into the saddle. This strange, savage humility troubled and stirred her so that it was hard to find in her heart the chord of hatred on which she had been strumming. The only answer she found was to say, 'Why not try him again, Harry? This evening, for instance. There's going to be a barbecue, and perhaps he'd be glad to see you. I'm sure the *boys* would be glad.

And so would I!' She laughed again, put some of her anger into her spurs, and made beautiful Hampton race like a long-gaited rabbit, scurrying down the slope....

Into the wagon Mortimer loaded his eight men at noon and drove the wagon back to the Hancock ranch house. He had been a fool, he told himself, to talk to the girl with a frank sternness, as though she were a man. He could not force a young wildcat like her to see the truth, but he might have tried to flatter her into a new point of view.

A dangerous expedient suggested itself to him now, and in that light of danger he began to see again the faces and the souls of the eight men in the wagon behind him. Every one of them had been with him at least a year and a half. Every man of them was like another right hand to Mortimer. They had come to him as a surly, unwilling, random collection which he had begged, borrowed, and stolen from the CCC camp at Poplar Springs, justified by his intention of making the Hancock ranch an exemplar in soil conservation to the entire range; but the entire eight had remained like members of a family. He gave them his time like water and they gave him back their ungrudging affection. He knew the worst that was in them and they understood his affection. They understood his ultimate purpose, also, which was far more than simply to put the

Hancock ranch on a high-paying basis: He wanted to reform the ranching methods of the entire range and widen the margin of security which old-fashioned methods constantly diminished.

Each one of the eight had some useful quality, some weakness. Baldy Inman was the most docile of all, but when he went on a binge, once a month, Mortimer sat with him night after night and brought him home again to sobriety. Bud McGee loved battle, and twice Mortimer had dragged him out of saloon brawls at the risk of both their necks. George Masters loved poker and knew all too well how to deal. Chip Ellis and Dink Waller were always about to start for the gold lands of Alaska and talked up the beauties of far countries till the rest of the boys were on edge. Lefty Parkman had been in the ring and he helped on Sundays teaching the boys to box. He had beaten Mortimer to a pulp, in spite of his lighter weight, Sunday after Sunday, until sheer dint of pain taught Mortimer the science and gave him a deadly left of his own. Pudge Major supplied music and noisy jokes.

Jan Erickson, the giant of the crew, had once broken away and followed the old call of the underworld as far as Denver, where Mortimer overtook him and brought him home again. Mortimer returned from that journey with an eye which changed gradually from black to purple to green, and Erickson's face was swollen for a month, but they never referred to what happened in Denver and remained as brothers together in the times of need.

It was while he thought of his crew, one by one, that the determination to take the great chance came strongly home in Mortimer. He stopped the wagon in front of the big shed which had been turned into a barracks for the CCC workers. Shorty, the cook, was already in the doorway banging a tin pan and yelling to them to come and get it. Mortimer, instead of going in with them to sit at the long table, passed into the Hancock house.

As usual, he found Charlie Hancock stretched on the couch in the parlor with the limes, the sugar, the Jamaica rum, and the hot-water jug conveniently on the table beside him. Because of the heat of the day he was dressed in trunks and slippers only, and he had a volume of Boswell's *Johnson* propped on the fat of his paunch. His glasses, his prematurely aged face, and his short gray mustache gave him the air of a country gentleman reposing in a Turkish bath.

This posture of reading had become hardly more than a posture recently, for, since Mortimer had appeared and was willing to take charge of the ranch, Charles Hancock had sunk into a long and vicious decline. A fine education had given edge to one of the clearest minds Mortimer had ever met; it was also the most vicious brain he

19

knew. The main direction of the ranch work had been left to Mortimer, but there still remained on the place half a dozen haphazard cowpunchers whom Hancock picked up, not so much because they knew cows as because they shot straight and were devoted to him. Aside from rum and books, guns were the main preoccupation of Hancock. If he left his rum bottle, it was generally to go hunting with some of his harum-scarum hired men. They did not mix with the CCC men.

'Wang!' called Hancock. 'Bring another glass for Mr. Mortimer, and some more hot water.'

The Chinaman appeared in the kitchen doorway, bowed, and trotted off.

'I'm not drinking,' said Mortimer.

'Still a slave to conscience, Harry?' said Hancock.

Mortimer began to pace the room, on one side staring out a window that looked up the valley of the Chappany where he had worked so hard during the two years, on the other looking vacantly at the photograph of old Jim Hancock, who had retired from the ranch to live in a cottage in Poplar Springs. On $50 a month he kept himself happy with frijoles and whisky and let the world wag on its way. The literal arrangement was that the income from the ranch should be split three ways, one to old Jim, one to his son Charles, one to Mortimer; but as a matter of fact Charlie managed to use most of his father's portion besides his own.

'Yes,' said Charles Hancock, answering his own

question, 'a slave to the conscience that forces you to make the world a better place to live in. You see nothing but green, Harry. You want nothing but a big range and nothing but green on it. What is there you wouldn't do for it?'

'I've been wondering,' said Mortimer, vague with thought.

'Grass for cows, grass for cows!' said Hancock, laughing. 'And yet you'd die to give it to 'em.'

'It's something else,' answered Mortimer, shaking his head. 'It's the idea of a living country instead of a dying one.... Tell me, Charlie: What would happen if I showed my face at the Miller barbecue this evening?'

Hancock sat bolt upright, then slowly lowered himself back to the prone position. He took a deep swallow of punch. 'Nothing,' he said. 'Nothing ... at first.'

'And then?' asked Mortimer.

'At first,' said Hancock, smiling as he enlarged his thought, 'there would be a dash of surprise. Old John Miller wouldn't faint, but he'd come close to it. And his cowpunchers would have to remember that the whole range had been asked to see Lou Miller's twenty-first birthday.... Afterward, when the drink began to soak through their systems and got into their brains ... that would be different. I don't know just how it would happen. Someone would stumble against you, or trip over your foot, or find you laughing in his face and take a word for an insult, or misunderstand the way you lifted an eyebrow … and presently you'd be stuck full of knives and drilled full of bullet holes!'

'You think Miller wants me dead as badly as that?' asked Mortimer.

'Think? I know! You bring down a damned commission on top of him. It rides over his land. It finds that the great John Miller has been overstocking his acres, destroying the grass with too many hoofs. The commission is about to put a supervisor in charge of the Miller ranch and cause all the Millers to rise in their graves. Only by getting a governor and a couple of senators out of bed in the middle of the night is he able to stop the commission.… And he owes all that trouble to you. Trouble, shame, and all. Wants you dead? Why, John Miller's father would have gone gunning for you in person, with a grudge like that. And John Miller's grandfather would simply have sent half a dozen of his Mexican cowboys to cut your throat. These Millers have been kings, Harry, and don't forget it.'

'Kings … kings,' said Mortimer absently. 'The girl will be running the place in a few days. And she's as hard as her father.'

'Soften her then,' said Hancock.

'She challenged me to come to the barbecue,' said Mortimer. 'If I come … will that soften her?'

'Of course it will,' answered Hancock. 'And the guns will soften *you*, later on. Are you going to be fool enough to go?'

'If I win her over,' said Mortimer, 'I win over the whole range. If the Miller place uses my ideas, all the small fellows will follow along. If I go to the silly barbecue, maybe it will make her think I'm half a man, at least. You don't hate a thing you can even partly respect.'

'Ah,' said Hancock. 'He's a noble fellow. Ready to die for his cause, and all that … You bore me, Harry. Mind leaving me to my rum punch?'

Mortimer went out into the shed that housed the CCC men and passed through the room where the eight sat with a platter of thin fried steaks rapidly disappearing from their ken.

'Hi, Chief,' said Pudge Major. 'Are you giving me your share?'

'He can't eat … the Miller gal fed him up to the teeth,' suggested Chip Ellis.

'He's lovesick,' shouted Bud McGee. 'You can't eat when you're lovesick!'

They all were shouting with laughter as he passed them and entered the kitchen, where Shorty was stubbing about on his wooden leg, laying out his own meal on a table covered with heavy white oilcloth.

'Hi, Chief,' he said. 'Can't you chew a way through one of those steaks?'

'What's the lowest a man can be?' asked Mortimer, sitting on the window sill.

'Cabin boy on a South Seas tramp,' answered

Shorty instantly.

'How about a man who tells a girl he loves her? Makes love and doesn't mean it?'

'You take it with gals, and the rules are all different,' said Shorty. 'Now, over there in Japan ...'

'A white girl, Shorty, as straight as a ruled line, even if she's as mean as a cat.'

'Why, if a gal is straight and a gent makes her crooked ... why, they got a special place in hell for them, Chief,' said Shorty.

'Reasons wouldn't count, would they Shorty?' asked Mortimer.

'There ain't any reasons for spoiling a clean deck of cards,' said Shorty.

Mortimer went back into the dining-room and took his place at the head of the table. He speared a steak and dropped it on his plate. 'There's no work this afternoon,' he said.

'Quit it, Chief!' protested huge Jan Erickson. 'You mean you declare a holiday?'

'I'm going to a party, myself,' said Mortimer, 'and I've never asked you to work when I was off playing, have I?'

'Where's the party?' asked Pudge.

'Over the hills and far away,' said Mortimer....

He spent the early afternoon preparing himself with a scrubbing in cold water; then he dressed in rather battered whites, climbed into the one-ton truck, and prepared to deliver himself at the barbecue.

Charles Hancock appeared unexpectedly in the doorway of the ranch house, a fat, red, wavering figure. He called out, 'If you want to take that Miller girl into camp, you'd better slick yourself up with a five-thousand dollar automobile. You can't go fast enough in that contraption. She'll keep seeing your dust.'

Mortimer looked at his partner for a moment in silent disgust and silent wonder; then he drove off through the white heat of the afternoon.

When he bumped across the bridge and finally rolled up the trail onto Miller land, he felt that he had crossed the most important Rubicon of his life. Others were coming in swaying automobiles, in carts and buggies, and above all on mustangs which had cruised from the farthest limits of the range, but he knew that he would be the most unexpected guest at the carnival. Halfway up the slope the swinging music of a band reached him. He felt, in fact, like a soldier going into battle as he reached the great arch of evergreens which had been built over the entrance to the Miller grounds.

Sam Pearson, the Miller foreman, ranged up and down by the gate giving the first welcome to the new arrivals, and the first drink out of a huge punchbowl which was cooled in a packing of dry ice. When he saw Mortimer, the foreman came to a pause on a ready-made speech of welcome and stood agape with the dripping glass of punch in his hand. Then he came slowly up to the side of the truck and narrowed his eyes at Mortimer as though he were searching for game in a distant horizon.

'What kind of legs have you got to stand on, Mortimer?' he asked. 'What you think is gunna hold you up all through the day?'

'Beginner's luck,' said Mortimer.

The foreman suddenly held out the glass. 'Have this on me,' he said. 'You got so much nerve I wish I liked you.'

Mortimer drove on into the space reserved for parking, between the corrals behind the house. There he climbed slowly down to the ground and went on toward the Miller residence, with a sense that his last bridge, his last way of retreat had been broken behind him.

The crowd gave him some comfort in the feeling that he might lose himself among the numbers who drifted beneath the trees surrounding the ranch house. Throngs of colored lanterns swung from the lower branches and the gala air helped a sense of security, also. But he was noticed at once. A rumor ran ahead of him on invisible feet. A whisper spread, and heads were continually turning, amazed eyes were staring at him.

He put on an air of unconcern, but the weight of a man-sized automatic under his coat was the sort of companionship he wanted then.

It was Louise Miller whom he kept an eye for as he wandered casually through the crowd. He went down by the big open-air dance floor, where the band played and where a ring had been built for the wrestling and boxing which were to be part of the entertainment; but she was not there. He passed back to the open glade, where a huge steer was turning on a great spit against a backing of burning logs. For three generations the Millers had barbecued their meat in this manner for their friends, but roast beef was only one dish among many, for in enormous iron pots chickens and ducks were simmering, and in scores of Dutch ovens there were geese, saddles of venison, and young pigs roasting. There were kegs of beer and ale, kegs of whisky, incredible bowls of rosy punch, and such an air of plenty as Mortimer had never looked on before.

He lingered in the central scene of the barbecue too long and as he turned away he saw a pair of big cowpunchers, dressed up as gaily as Mexicans, solidly barring his way and offering fight as clearly as boys ever offered it in a schoolyard. Mortimer side-stepped them without shame, and went on, with their insulting laughter in his ears. He knew without turning his head that they were following him. Men began to be aware of him from both sides and from in front. He heard derisive voices calling out: 'The land doctor!' 'Give him a start home!' 'Help him on his way!'

He shrugged his shoulders to get the chill out of his spinal marrow. He made himself walk slowly to maintain a casual dignity, but he felt his neck muscles stiffening. When he stumbled on an uneven place, an instant guffaw sounded about him, and he felt as though a great beast were breathing at his shoulder. It was in the crisis of that moment that he saw a girl coming swiftly through the crowd, and saw Louise Miller panting with haste as she came up to him.

'Are you crazy – coming here?' she demanded.

'I thought you asked me,' said Mortimer.

'Come back to the house with me. I've got to talk with you and get you away,' she said. 'I've never heard of anything so idiotic. Didn't you see them closing in around you like wolves for a kill?'

'Just a lot of big, harmless, happy boys,' said Mortimer, and she glanced up sharply to see the irony of his smile.

They came through the trees to the wide front of the old house, and then through the Spanish patio, under the clumsy arches, and so into the house. She led him into a library. A vague, indecipherable murmur of voices sounded through the wall from the next room, but the girl was too intent on him to notice the sound.

'Sit down here,' she commanded. 'I'll walk around. I can't sit still.... Harry Mortimer, listen to me!'

He lighted a cigarette as he leaned back in the

chair and watched her excitement.

'It isn't my fault that you've come, is it?' she asked. 'You know it wasn't a real invitation, didn't you? Ask you up here into a den of wildcats? You knew that I didn't intend that!'

'What *did* you intend, then?' he asked.

She pulled up a chair opposite him, suddenly, and sat down on it, with her chin on her fist, staring at him. The billowing skirt of her dress slowly settled around her. 'You know,' she said. 'Those fences … the silly fall I took … and then I wasn't making very good sense when I argued; and it was a sort of crazy malice, to have the last word, and leave a challenge behind me. Ah, but I'm sorry!'

The lowering and softening of her voice let him look at her deeply for an instant.

'I'm not sorry,' he told her. 'D'you see? I'm here in the castle of the baron – right in the middle of his life. Perhaps he'll listen to reason now.'

'Because he can see that you're ready to die for your cause? No, he'll never listen! He's as set as an old army mule, and as savage as a hungry grizzly. He's in there now, Harry, and I've got to get you away before he –'

Here the door at the side of the room opened and the deep, booming voice of John Miller sounded through the room, saying, 'We'll announce Lou's engagement to you before the evening's over, Fred.'

29

'But, Mr. Miller, if we hurry her ...' said a big, handsome fellow in the doorway, as blond as Norway and built like a football tackle.

'She's made up her mind, and that's enough for me,' declared John Miller, leading the way into the library.

His daughter and Mortimer were already on their feet. In her first panic she had touched his arm to draw him away, but he refused to avoid the issue; the two of them stood now as though to face gunfire. It opened at once. John Miller, when he made out the face of Mortimer, ran a hand back through the silver of his long hair and grew inches taller with rage. He actually made a quick step or two toward Mortimer before another thought stopped him and he remembered that no matter who the man might be, he was a guest in the Miller house. He had the blue eyes of a boy and they were shining with a pair of bright, twin devils when he came up and took the hand of Mortimer.

'Mr. Frederick Wilson, Mr. Mortimer,' he said. 'I am happy ... a day when everyone ... I see, in fact, that you and Louise are old friends?'

He was in a sweat of white anger, though he kept himself smiling. Frederick Wilson, who could not help seeing that something was very wrong, looked quizzically from his fiancée to Mortimer.

'I'm sorry that I was here when you wanted to be private,' said Mortimer, withdrawing.

'Ah, about that!' exclaimed Miller. 'But I can trust you not to spread the word in the crowd? I want to save it as a surprise.'

Mortimer was already close to the door and, as he turned to go through it, he heard the girl exclaiming, 'But an announcement!'

'Have you two minds or one?' answered her father. 'If you have only one, it's already made up.... Now, what in the devil is the meaning of Mortimer here in my house, when the poisonous rat has been doing everything he can to ...'

Mortimer was already out of earshot and walking slowly down the hall, through the patio, and once more into the woods of the carnival, with the music of the band roaring and booming in his ear.

He was not noticed immediately, and he tried to interest himself in the variety of the people who had come to the barbecue, for they included every type, from tough old-timers whose overalls were grease-hardened around the knees, to roaring cowpunchers from all over the range and white-class citizens of Poplar Springs.

Near the glade where the roasting ox hissed and spat above the fire, he saw a compacted group that moved through the crowd like a boat through the sea, and a moment later he recognized the lofty, blond head of Jan Erickson! They were there, all eight of them, and they gathered around him now with a shout and a rush.

He took Pudge Major by the lapels of his coat and shook him. 'You're behind this, Pudge,' he said. 'You're the only one who could have guessed where I was coming. Now, you take the rest of 'em and get out of here. D'you know that every man jack in this crowd is heeled? And if trouble starts they'll shoot you boys into fertilizer.'

'And what about you?' asked Pudge.

'I'm having a little game,' said Mortimer.

'Yeah, and when you're tagged, you'll stay "it",' answered Dink Waller. 'We'll just hang around and make a kind of a background so's people will be able to see you better.'

'Listen to me. I'm ordering you back to the Hancock place,' commanded Mortimer.

This seemed to end the argument. They were looking wistfully at their chief when George Masters exclaimed, 'This is time off. Your orders ain't worth a damn this afternoon, Chief. We're where we want to be, and we're going to stay.'

With a half-grinning and a half-guilty resolution they confronted Mortimer, and he surrendered the struggle with a shrug of the shoulders; but already he felt, suddenly, as though he had walked with eight sticks of dynamite into the center of a fire.

A thundering loud-speaker called the guests to the platform entertainment, a moment later, and that invitation called off the dogs of war from Mortimer and his men. They drifted with the others toward the dance floor, and from the convenient slope Mortimer looked on with anxious, half-seeing eyes at dancers doing the buck and wing, at a competition in rope tricks, at a pair of slick magicians, at wrestlers, at a flashy bit of lightweight boxing, at an old fellow who demonstrated how Colts with their triggers filed off were handled in the old days. And still he was wondering how he could roll his eight sticks of dynamite out of the fire, when a huge, black-chested cowpuncher got into the ring to box three rounds with a fellow almost as tall and robed from head to foot with a beautiful coverage of muscles. The blond head of the second man meant something to Mortimer and, when the fellow turned, he recognized the handsome face of Frederick Wilson, smiling and at ease with the world.

The reason for his confidence appeared as soon as the gong was struck and the two went into action.

'He's got a left, is what that Wilson's got,' said Lefty Parkman. 'He's got an educated left, and look at him tie it onto Blackie's whiskers!'

The big cowpuncher, full of the best will in the world, rushed in to use both hands, as he had done many a time in saloon brawls, always to bump his face against a snapping jab. When he stood still to think the matter over, he lowered his guard a trifle, and through the opening Frederick Wilson

33

cracked a hammer-hard right hand that sagged the knees of the man from the range.

'What a sock!' said Lefty Parkman, rubbing his greedy hands together. 'But Blackie don't know how to fall!'

The cowboy, though his brains were adrift, still tried to fight, while Frederick Wilson, with a cruelly smiling patience, followed him, measured him, and then flattened him with a very accurate one-two that bumped the head of Blackie soundly on the canvas. Friends carried him away, while the crowd groaned loudly. Only a few applauded with vigor. Big John Miller, standing up from his chair on the special dais, with his silver hair blowing and shining, clapped his hands furiously; but Lou Miller merely smiled and waved, and then turned her head. That sort of fighting was not to her taste, it appeared.

Frederick Wilson, in the meantime, had discovered that the fight did not please the crowd, so he stood at the ropes and lifted a gloved hand for silence. When the quiet came, he called in a good, ringing bass voice: 'My friends, I'm sorry that was over so soon. If anybody else will step up, I'll try to please you more the next time.'

Some wit sang out, 'Paging Jack Dempsey!' and the crowd roared.

Then Mortimer found himself getting to his feet.

Lefty Parkman tried to pull him back. 'You're

crazy,' groaned Lefty. 'He's got twenty pounds on you. You can fight, but he can *box*. He'll spear you like a salmon. He'll hold you off and murder you!'

But Mortimer gained his full height and waved to attract attention. He felt as naked as a bad dream, but a bell had struck in his mind that told him his chance had come to lay his hands on the entire range. They despised him for his bookishness. If they could respect him for his manhood the whole story might change. Their hostility was breaking out in the cries with which he was recognized. 'It's the doctor! – It's the dirt doctor!' they shouted. 'Eat him up, tenderfoot! Give him the dirt he wants, Wilson!'

'I'll try to help you entertain,' called Mortimer to Wilson, and hurried back to the dressing tent near the dance floor. He had a glimpse, on the way, of the puzzled face of Lou Miller and of John Miller fairly expanding with expectant pleasure. In the tent he rigged himself in togs that fitted well enough. Blackie sat slumped in a chair at one side, gradually recovering, his eyes still empty and a red drool running from a corner of his mouth.

'How'd it go, Blackie?' asked Parkman.

'I was doin' fine,' said Blackie. 'And then a barn door slammed on my face.'

Lefty Parkman took his champion down through the crowd, and poured savage advice at him every step of the way. 'Keep your left hand up,' he cautioned. 'Don't mind if he raises some bumps with his left. It's his right that rings all the bells. Don't give him a clean shot with it. Keep jabbing. Work in close, and hammer the body. And if you get a chance try the old one-two. Keep the one-two in your head like a song.... And God help you, Chief!'

The strained, anxious faces of the CCC men were the last pictures that Mortimer saw as he squared off with Wilson after the bell. Then a beautiful straight left flashed in his eyes. He ducked under it and dug both hands into the soft of Wilson's body. At least, it should have been the soft, but it was like punching rolls of India rubber.

They came out of the clinch with the crowd suddenly roaring applause for the dirt doctor, but Mortimer knew he had not hurt the big fellow. He had stomach muscles like a double row of clenched fists. And he was smiling as he came in again behind the beautiful, reaching straight left. Mortimer remembered, with a sudden relief, that the rounds were only two minutes long. But merely to endure was not enough. He wanted to wipe Frederick Wilson out of the Miller mind.

He side-stepped the straight left and used his own. It landed neatly, but high on the face. As Wilson shifted in, Mortimer nailed him with the one-two in which Lefty Parkman had drilled him so hard during those remorseless Sundays at the ranch. It stopped Wilson like a wall, but the right hand had not found the button. Mortimer jumped in with a long, straight left to follow his advantage, and the wave of uproar behind him washed him forward. For there is an invincible sympathy with the underdog, in the West, and even the dirt doctor got their cheers as he plunged at big Wilson.

What happened then, Mortimer could not exactly tell. He felt his left miss and slither over the shoulder of Wilson. Then a stick of dynamite exploded in his brain.

He had hurt his knees. That was the next thing he knew. And his brain cleared to admit a tremendous noise of shouting people. He was on hands and knees on the floor of the ring, with the referee swaying an arm up and down beside his face, counting: 'five … six … seven …'

Mortimer came to his feet. He saw Wilson stepping toward him like a giant crane, and the ready left hand was like the crane's beak aimed at a frog. He ducked under the two-handed attack. But the glancing weight of it carried him like a tide of water against the ropes. Head and body, alternately, the punches hammered him. He saw the tight-lipped smile of pleasure and effort as Wilson worked. The man loved his job; and a bursting rage gave Mortimer strength to fight out into the open.

His head was fairly clear, now. He gave as good as he was taking. He noticed that the gloves were

soft and big. They might raise lumps, but only a
flush hit was apt to break the skin. He threw
another long left. And again he felt his arm glance
harmlessly over the shoulder of Wilson. Again a
blow struck him from nowhere and exploded a
bomb of darkness in his brain. Something rapped
sharply against the back of his head.

That was the canvas of the ring. He had been
knocked flat.

He seemed to be swimming out of a river of
blackness with a current that shot him down-
stream towards disaster. Fiercely he struggled ...
and found himself turning on one side, while the
swaying arm of the referee seemed to sound the
seconds as upon a gong: 'six ... seven ... eight ...'

He got to his knees and saw through a
dun-colored fog John Miller waving his arms in
exultation; but Lou Miller's face was turned away.

That was why Mortimer got to his feet as the
tenth count began. He ducked under the big arms
of Wilson and held on. Then the bell rang the end
of that round, and the savagely gripping hands of
Lefty Parkman were dragging him to his corner.

The whole group of his eight men were piled
around him, Erickson weeping with rage, while he
and Pudge Major and Dink Waller swung towels
to raise a breeze; Chip Ellis and George Masters
were massaging his legs, while Bud McGee
rubbed the loose of his stomach muscles to restore
their normal tension, and Baldy Inman held the

water bottle. But Lefty Parkman, clutching him with one arm, whispered or groaned instructions at his ear.

'Lefty, what's he hitting me with?' begged Mortimer.

'Listen, dummy!' said Parkman. 'When you try the straight left he doesn't try to block it. He lets it come and sidesteps. He lets it go over his shoulder, and then he comes in with a right uppercut and nails you.... You got no chance! He's killing you. Lemme say that you've broken your arm! He'll kill you, Chief; and if he does Jan Erickson is going to murder him, and there'll be hell all over the lot! ... Lemme throw in the towel, and you can quit and ...'

'If you throw in the. towel ...' said Mortimer through his teeth – but then the gong sounded and he stepped out, feeling as though he were wading against a stiff current of water.

Wilson came right in at him, fiddling with a confident left to make way for a right-hander that would finish the bout; and as the ears of Mortimer cleared he could hear the crowd stamping and shouting, 'Sock him, Doc! ... Break a hole in him! ... Plow him up! ... Hi, Doctor Dirt!'

Wilson dismissed this cheering for the underdog with a twitching grin and lowered his right to invite a left lead.

The wisdom of Lefty Parkman's observations remained in the brain of Mortimer as he saw the opening. It was only a long feint that he used. Instantly the device which Parkman had explained was apparent. Without attempting to block the punch, Wilson side-stepped to slip the blow and, dropping his right, stepped in for a lifting uppercut, his eyes pinched to a glint of white as he concentrated on the knockout wallop.

That was what Mortimer had hoped. The feint he held for an instant until his body almost swayed forward off balance. Then he used the one-two which Lefty had made him master. The right went to the chin no harder, say, than the tapping hammer of the master blacksmith. It gave the distance, the direction for the sledgehammer stroke of the left that followed, and through the soft, thick padding of the glove Mortimer felt his knuckles lodge against the bone of the jaw. He had hit with his full power and Wilson had stepped straight into the blow.

It buckled Wilson's knees. He covered up, instinctively, lurching forward to clinch, and over his shoulder Mortimer saw John Miller with his hands dangling limply, unable to applaud this startling change of fortune. But Lou Miller was on her feet, bent forward.

He saw this double picture. Then he lifted two blows to Wilson's head and sent him swaying back on his heels. There was the whole length of the body open to the next blow, and strained taut, as though a hand had stretched a throat for the butcher's knife. Mortimer plunged his right straight into that defenseless target and doubled it up like a jackknife.

He stepped back as Wilson fell on his knees, embracing his tormented body with one arm. The other hand gestured to the referee.

'Foul!' said the lips of Wilson.

'Get up and fight,' ordered the referee, as he began his count. He was a tough fellow, this referee. He had done some fighting in his youth in Chicago and eastward. Now some of an unforgotten vocabulary flowed from his lips. First, with a wide gesture, he invited the scorn of the crowd and got a howling rejoinder. Then, as he counted, he dropped rare words between the numbers, as: '...three, you yellow skunk ... four, for a four-flusher ... five, a coyote is St. Patrick beside you ... six, for a ring-tailed rat ...'

Wilson struggled to one knee, making faces that indicated dreadful agony; and Mortimer saw John Miller shake both fists in the air and then turn his back in disgust. The interest of Mortimer in the fight ended at that moment. He hardly cared when the referee counted out Wilson the next moment. But, as he climbed through the ropes, the hands of his eight men reached up to clutch him with dangerous hands of congratulation.

Afterward, Lefty Parkman rejoiced in the dressing tent. 'You got it just the way I wanted,' he said. 'You plastered the sucker just as he

41

stepped in. Oh, baby, if you chuck this ranching, I'll make a light heavyweight champ out of you inside three years. Nothing but bacon three times a day, and eggs all day Sunday! … Say, Chief, will you throw in with me and make a try at it?'

Mortimer smiled vaguely at him. He had something of far greater importance to think about than a ring career, for, as he remembered the enthusiastic voices that had applauded him as he left the ring, it seemed to him that he might have broken through the solid hedge of hostility which had hemmed him in for two years on the range. There remained one great step to take. If he could win over the girl, it would be the greatest evening of his life, and he had determined to play his cards like a crooked gambler if that were necessary to his winning.

'Start drifting around,' he told Lefty. 'Circulate a little and find out how John Miller took the fading of big Wilson. I'll see you later at the barbecue.'

In his anxiety about further consequences he hardly knew what food he tasted when he found a place at one of the long tables in the barbecue glade, but he was keenly aware of favorable and critical eyes which kept studying him, and it was plain that while he had won over a large number of the hostile, his work was not nearly ended. Then Lefty Parkman leaned at his shoulder and murmured, 'Miller is sour. He must have had a whole roll on that Wilson. When you dropped Wilson, Miller said he wished you'd never showed your face on the range.'

That was serious enough; the grave face with which Lou Miller passed him a little later was even more to the point. She was drifting about among the tables to see that everyone had his choice, and when she passed Mortimer all recognition was dead in her eye. But when he turned his head to look after her, she made a slight gesture toward the trees. He waited only a moment before he left the table and went after her. Her pale figure led him through swaying lantern light that set the tree trunks wavering, and on through silver drippings of moonlight until she reached the edge of the woods.

When he came up, she said quietly, 'You must leave at once. Some of the men here hate you, Harry. And my father won't believe that you beat Fred Wilson fairly. He thinks there must have been a foul blow, as Fred claims.'

The hope of winning over John Miller vanished completely. But there remained the girl, and if she were to be placed in immediate charge of the ranch she would be gain enough.

'I can't leave,' he said.

She came closer to him and laid a hand on his arm. The moonlight that slid through a gap in the leaves overhead made silver of her hair, her throat, and her hand. 'You don't understand me,'

43

she said. 'When I say that you ought to go now, I mean that there's really danger for you here.'

'Is your father going to do me in?' he asked.

'He knows nothing about it,' she answered, 'but I know there are a hundred men here who feel sure Father would be glad if you were run off the range. You have to go – now. I'll stay with you until you're off the place.'

He was silent.

'Will you listen to me?' she repeated. 'Harry, I know what you want. You want to open up the entire range to the new ideas. Maybe you're right about them, but none of us can believe it. Do what a wise man ought to do. Give up. Sell out. Try your luck in some other place where your brains will tell. You've poured in two years on this range. You can waste twenty more and never get forward.'

'That's good man-talk,' he said. 'But Lou, do you ever talk like a woman?'

She laughed a little and stepped back from him. 'Well, what's to come now?' she asked.

'Some silly sentimentality,' said Mortimer.

'Between you and me?' she asked, still laughing.

He drew a slow, deep breath, for he had made up his mind that she was no more than a unit of the enemy to be beaten down or won over, as he could, but there seemed in her now such a free courage and frankness, and the moon touched her beauty with such a reverent hand that his heart was touched and he despised the thing he was about to attempt. That weakness lasted only a moment. He went on along the way which he had laid out for himself.

He said, 'Has it ever seemed a little strange to you that I've given up two years of my life to soil conservation in a country where I'm damned before I start, and where I have to share profits and work under the thumb of a drunk like Charlie Hancock?'

'That doesn't sound like sentimentality,' answered the girl. 'It sounds the truth. No, I've never been able to understand you. I've thought you were a sort of metal monster.'

'But you've noticed me carrying on? And till recently you've seen me hounding your father to get his support?'

'Of course I've noticed,' she said.

'Well, can you think of anything except plain foolishness that would keep me at the work here?' he demanded.

'I'm trying to think,' she answered.

'I'll help you,' he said. 'Remember two years ago? You were out here from school. Easter vacation. I was standing in front of the Hancock place. You rode Hampton – zip over the edge of the hill and down the hollow, and then zooming away out of sight beside the ruins of the old windmills. And wings got hold of my heart and lifted me after you.'

He took another breath after the lie. The girl

was still as stone. The moonlight seemed to have frozen her and the airy lightness of her dress. She said nothing.

'What about the announcement of that engagement?' he asked harshly.

'There won't be any announcement. It's ended,' she replied. 'Harry, what are you trying to tell me? You've hardly looked twice at me in two years.'

'I was being the romantic jackass,' he said. 'The stranger with the great vision and the strong hands. I was going to change the whole range, and then offer you my work in one hand and my heart in the other, like some of the driveling fools in the old books.... I *have* been a fool, Lou, but don't laugh at me if you can help it.'

'I won't laugh,' she said.

He went on: 'I thought that if I ruled out everything but the work, I'd get my reward. Instead of that I have the people laughing at me. And I suppose I dreamed that you were receiving radio messages, so to speak, from the fool across the valley who loved you.'

'Love? Love?' said the girl.

'Before I get out of the country like a beaten dog, I had to tell you the truth,' he lied. And yet as he looked at her he wondered if the lie were altogether perfect. 'I don't expect you to do anything except laugh in my face.'

A thudding of hoofbeats and a creaking of

leather came through the trees behind them. She made a gesture, not to him, but to the ground, the world, the air around them.

'I can't laugh,' she said. 'I believe it all.... My heart's going crazy, and I'm dizzy. It's the moonlight, isn't it? It's the crazy moonlight. You're not snapping your fingers and making me fall in love like this, are you?'

From the trees the riders came out softly, the hoofbeats deadened by the leaf mold. There were a thronging dozen of them, with sombreros pulled low and bandannas drawn up and over their mouths to make efficient masks.

One of them sang out, 'Stand back from him, you!' And as the girl sprang away, startled, something whistled in the air over Mortimer's head. The snaky shadow of the rope dropped across his vision, and then he was grappled by the noose, which cunningly pinned his arms against his sides.

TWO

Sam Pearson, the foreman of the huge Miller ranch, was on the saddle end of the rope with a hundred and ninety pounds of seasoned muscle and nearly forty years of range wisdom. He did not have direct orders from Miller, but the indirect suggestions were more than enough for Pearson. He felt, personally, that it was an affront to the entire Miller legend to have this hostile interloper on the ranch at the barbecue; and there was a virtuous thrill in his hand as he settled that noose around Mortimer's arms.

Sam's mount, which was his best cutting horse, spun like a top and took Mortimer in tow at a mild canter over the flat and then down the slope of the Chappany valley. The screaming protests of Lou Miller shrilled and died out far to the rear, quite drowned by the uproar of Pearson's cowpunchers. They all had plenty of liquor under their belts;

they all felt they were striking a good stroke for the best cause in the world; and the result was that their high spirits unleashed like a pack of wolves. Like wolves they howled as they dashed back and forth around Pearson and his captive. And, as their delight grew, more than one quirt snapped in an expert hand to warm the seat of Mortimer's pants.

The Easterner ran well, Pearson had to admit; he kept up a good sprint, which prevented him from falling on his face and being dragged, until they came over the edge of the level and dropped onto the slant ground, with the five Chappany lakes glimmering silver-bright in the hollow beneath them.

At that point Pearson's rope went slack, and he saw Mortimer spin head over heels like a huge ball of tumbleweed. It was so deliciously funny to Sam Pearson that he reeled in the saddle with hearty laughter. He was still howling with joy and the shrill cowboy yells were sticking needles in his ears when a very odd thing happened, for the whirling, topsy-turvy body of Mortimer regained footing and balance for an instant, while running with legs made doubly long by the pitch of the slope, and, like a great black, deformed cat he flung himself onto Monte McLean, who rode close to his side.

There was plenty of silver-clear moonlight to show Monte defending himself from that savage and unexpected attack. Monte was a good, two-handed fighter and he whanged the Easterner over the head and shoulders, not with the lash, but with the loaded butt of his quirt. However, in an instant Mortimer had swarmed up the side of the horse and wrapped Monte in his arms.

This was highly embarrassing to Pearson. If he yanked Mortimer off that mustang, he would bring Monte down to the ground with him. If he did not yank Mortimer out of the saddle, the Easterner would probably throttle Monte and get away. There was another thing that caused Pearson to groan and that was the realization that he had kept the tenderfoot on such a loose rope that he had been able to work his arms and hands up through the biting grip of the noose. He was held now like an organ-grinder's monkey, around the small of the waist.

Other trouble came on the run toward Sam Pearson. A cry came ringing to him, and he saw a girl on a horse stretched in a dead gallop come tilting over the upper edge of the slope. That would be Lou Miller. She was a good girl and as Western as they come. But there is a sharp limit to the feminine sense of humor, and it was as likely as not that the girl thought this was a lynching party instead of a mere bit of Western justice and range discipline. The idea was, in brief, to start Mortimer running toward the horizon and encourage him to keep on until he was out of sight.

Sam Pearson simply did not know what to do, and therefore he did the most instinctive thing, which was to give a good tug on the rope. To his horror, he saw both Monte and Mortimer slew sidewise from the saddle and spill to the ground.

They kept on rolling for a dozen yards, and then they lay still, one stretched beside the other. Big Sam Pearson got his horse to the place and dived for the spot where Monte lay. He picked the fallen cowpuncher up. The loose of the body spilled across his arm as he shouted, 'Monte! Hey, Monte! A little spill like that didn't do nothing to you, did it? Hey, Monte, can't you hear me?'

The other cowpunchers came piling up on their horses, bringing a fog-white rolling of dust that poured over Monte. And he, presently rousing with a groan, brought a cheer from them. They set him up on his feet and felt him from head to foot for broken bones. They patted his back to start him breathing.

'Put him into a saddle,' said Sam Pearson. 'Old Monte'll be himself when he feels the stirrups under his feet.'

So they put Monte into a saddle and steadied him there with many hands. In fact, he reached out at once with a vaguely fumbling hand for the reins and then mumbled, 'He kind of got hold of me like a wildcat, and he wouldn't loosen up.'

Here the wild voice of Louise Miller cried close by, 'Sam Pearson! You murderer, Sam, you've killed him! You've killed him!'

The foreman, still with a hand on Monte, turned and saw the girl on her knees beside the prostrate body of Mortimer. But at that moment the Easterner groaned heavily, and sat up. And Pearson took that as a signal to go.

'Let's get out of here on the jump, boys,' he said. 'Maybe we scratched up more hell'n we reckoned on.'

He hit the saddle as he spoke, and in the center of the cavalcade struck out at a gallop for the ranch house, with the wavering figure of Monte held erect by two friendly riders. For Pearson wanted to get in his report of strange happenings to an employer who had never yet been hard on him....

Mortimer, sitting up with his head bowed by shock and the nausea of deep pain and bruises, saw the world very dimly for a moment. Next he felt an increasing sharp pain from a rent in his scalp near the crown of the head, where the braided handle of Monte's quirt had glanced in striking; and finally he was aware of a warm, small trickle of blood that ran down the side of his face and dripped off his chin.

'Come back! Sam! Sam! Come back!' shouted a girl's voice. Then two hands took him by the cheeks and tilted back his head. 'They've killed him!' whispered Lou Miller. 'The cowards! The cowards! They've killed Harry Mortimer!'

He could not see her very clearly because the dazzle of the moon was above her head, and to his bleared eyes her face was a darkness of almost featureless shadow. But the moon flowed like water over one bare shoulder, where the chiffon had been torn away, during her headlong riding. These pictures he saw clearly enough, though he could not put them together and make connected sense of them.

As for what had happened immediately before, he could not make head nor tail of it, and it seemed to him that he was still telling the girl that he loved her now, even now, though his brain reeled and the nausea kept his stomach working.

That was why he said, 'If I were dying, I'd want to say a last thing to you, Lou.... I love you.'

'Harry, are you dying? Are you dying, darling?' cried the girl.

She took the weight of his head and shoulders across her lap and in her arms. There was still dust in the air, but there was a smell of sweet, soapy cleanness about her.

'I'm all right,' he told her. Then the theme recurred to him, and he drove himself on to the words: 'I love you.... D'you laugh at me when I tell you that? ... I love you!'

'And I love you, Harry.... D'you hear? Can you understand?' she answered.

The words registered one by one in his mind but they had no connected meaning. They were like a useless hand in poker.

'Tell me where you're hurt,' said the girl. 'Tell me where the worst pain is, Harry.'

He closed his eyes. He felt that he had lost in his great effort. He was not finished. He would still try to make her love him, because, beyond her, opened the gates of a new future which he could bring to the range; beyond her lay unending miles of the pleasant grasslands and the futures of ten thousand happy men. He felt that he was like a general who needed to carry by assault only one small redoubt and then the great fight would be won.

That assault would have to be made in the future. Now, with closed eyes, he could only mutter, 'You smell like a clean bath … you smell like a clean wind.'

She slipped from beneath his weight. He heard cloth suddenly torn into strips. The sound went through his brain and found sore places and tortured them. Then the blood was being wiped from his face and the long bandage was wound about his head, firmly. But it gave no pain. Wherever she touched him the pain disappeared. Then she had his head and shoulders in her lap again, and one hand supported his head.

'Wherever you touch me – it's queer – the pain goes,' said Mortimer.

'Because I love you!' said the girl.

He regarded the words with a blank stare and found no meaning in them. 'Are you laughing at me?' he said.

'I'm only loving you,' said the girl. 'Don't speak. Lie still. Only tell where the pain is.'

'God put a gift in your hands. They take the pain away,' said Mortimer. 'What color are your eyes?'

'Kind of a gray, blue-green…. I don't know what color they are,' she said. 'Don't talk, Harry. Lie still.'

One instant of clarity came to him. He got to his feet with a sudden, immense effort and stood swaying. 'My men are back there in trouble!' he groaned. 'Leave me here. Go back and stop the fight if you can. I'll come along on foot and help out.'

'There'll be no more trouble. That Sam Pearson, like a coward, has made trouble enough for one night. He won't lift his hand again. But can you get into the saddle? I'll help … get into the saddle … lift your left foot.'

He had his grip on the horn of the saddle and stood for a time with his head dropped against the sharp cantle, while the whirling, nauseating darkness spun through his brain. The orders came to him again, insistently. He raised his left foot. A hand guided it into the stirrup.

'Now one big heave, and you'll be in the saddle. Come on, and up you go.'

He felt an ineffectual force tugging and lifting at him; his muscles automatically responded and he found himself slumped in the saddle, his head hanging far down. There was no strength in the back of his neck. He wanted to vomit. But there was that uncompleted battle which had to be fought.

'Are you gone?' said Mortimer. 'I love you!'

Then a blowing darkness overcame his brain again. He managed to keep his hands locked on the pommel; and the nausea covered his body with cold runnels of sweat. A voice entered his mind from far ahead, sometimes speaking clearly, and sometimes as dim and far as though it were blowing away on a wind. Whenever he heard it, new strength came into him, and hope with it.

It told him to endure. It said that they had reached the bridge. In fact, he heard the hoofbeats of the horse strike hollow beneath him. He saw, dimly, the silver of water under the moon. The voice said they were nearing the Hancock place, if only he could hold on a little. But he knew that he could not hold on. A sense like that of sure prophecy told him that he was about to die and that he never would reach the haven of the ranch house.

And then, suddenly, the outlines of the house were before him.

He steeled himself to endure the dismounting, to gather strength that would pull his leg over the back of the horse.

Now he was standing beside it, wavering.

He made a vast effort to steer his feet toward the faintly lighted doorway. The girl tried to support him and guide him. Then many heavy footfalls rushed out about him. The voice of Jan Erickson roared out like the furious, huge, wordless bellowing of a bull. The enormous hands and arms of Jan Erickson lifted him, cradled him lightly, took him through the doorway.

'Louise,' he whispered, 'I love you ...'

He could make out the sound of her voice, but not the answering words. Clearer to his mind was the sense of wonderful relief in finding his men back safely, at the Hancock place. He wanted to give thanks for that. He felt stinging tears of gratitude under his eyelids and kept his eyes closed, so that the tears should not be seen.

He could hear Lefty Parkman screech out like a fighting tomcat, 'Look at his face! ... Look at his *face!* Oh, God, look what they've done to him! Look what they gone and done to the chief!'

And there was Pudge Major giving utterance in a strange, weeping whine: 'They dragged him. They took and dragged him. They took and dragged him like a stinking coyote.'

'Get out of my way!' shouted Jan Erickson. 'I'm gunna kill some of 'em!'

The stairs creaked. They were taking him up to his room. The air was much hotter inside the house, and warmer and warmer the higher they carried him. But he began to relax toward sleep.

The girl, running up the stairs behind the men, cried out to them that she wanted to help tend him. One of the brown-faced, big-shouldered fellows turned and looked at her as no man had ever looked at her before.

'Your dirty, sneaking crowd done this to the chief!' he said. 'Why don't you go back where you come from? Why don't you go and crow and laugh about it, like the others are doing? Go back and tell your pa that we're gunna have blood for this. We're gunna wring it out, like water out of the Monday wash! ... Get out!'

Lefty Parkman left the house and sprinted away for a car to drive to Poplar Springs for a doctor; and Louise Miller went down the stairs into the hall.

The angry, muttering voices of the CCC men passed on out of her ken, and the blond giant who was carrying the weight of Mortimer so lightly. She looked helplessly into the parlor, and there saw Charles Hancock lying on his couch dressed in shorts and a jacket of thin Chinese silk, with the materials for his rum punch scattered over the table beside him. He got up when he saw her and waved his hand. He seemed made of differing component parts – prematurely old boy, and decayed scholar, and drunken satirist.

'Come in, Lou,' he said. 'Your boys been having

a little time for themselves beating up Harry Mortimer? ... Come in and have a drink of this punch. You look as though you need it. You look as though you'd been through quite a stampede yourself!'

She became aware for the first time of the torn chiffon and her bare shoulder. The bleared, sneering eyes of Charlie Hancock made her feel naked. But she had to have an excuse for staying in the house until she had a doctor's opinion about Mortimer's condition. The picture of the dragging, tumbling body at the end of the rope kept running like a madness through her memory, and the closing eyes and the battered lips that said he loved her. For love like that, which a man commingles with his dying breath, it seemed to the girl, was a sacred thing which most people never know; and the glory of it possessed her strongly, like wings lifting her heart. Such a knowledge was given to her, she thought, that she had become mature. The girl of that afternoon was a child and a stranger to her in thought and in feeling.

She was so filled with unspeakable tenderness that even that rum-bloated caricature of a man, Charles Hancock, was a figure she could look upon with a gentle sympathy. For he, after all, had been living in the same house with the presence of Harry Mortimer for two long years. Viewed in that light, he became a treasure house from which, perhaps, she could draw a thousand priceless reminiscences about the man she loved. That was why she went to Hancock with a smile and shook his moist, fat hand warmly.

'I will have a drink,' she said. 'I need one.'

'Wang!' shouted Hancock. 'Hot water…. Take this chair, Lou…. And don't look at the rug and the places where the wallpaper is peeling. Our friend Mortimer says that this is a pigpen. He won't live here with me. That connoisseur of superior living prefers to spend most of his time with the gang of brutes in the big shed behind the houses. Sings with 'em; sings for 'em; dances for 'em; does a silly buck and wing just to make 'em laugh; plays cards with 'em; gives up his life to 'em the way a cook serves his steak on a platter…. By the way, did your boys break any of the Mortimer bones?'

His eyes waited with a cruelly cold expectancy. Loathing went into a shudder through the marrow of her bones, but she kept herself smiling, wondering how Mortimer had endured two years of this. She thought of the years of her own life as a vain blowing hither and thither, but at last she had come to a stopping point. Her heart poured out of her toward the injured man who lay above them, where the heavy footfalls trampled back and forth and deep-throated, angry murmuring continued.

'I don't know how badly he's injured,' she said. 'I don't think any bones … if there isn't internal injury ... but God wouldn't let him be seriously hurt by brutes and cowards!'

Hancock looked at her with a glimmering interest rising in his eyes. 'Ah, ha!' he chuckled. 'I see.'

She had her drink, by that time, and she paused in the careful sipping of it. 'You see what, Charlie?' she asked.

He laughed outright, this time. 'I put my money against it. I wouldn't have believed it,' he said.

'What wouldn't you have believed?' asked the girl.

'For my part,' said Hancock, 'I love living, Lou. I love to let the years go by like a stream, because ... do you know why?'

'I don't know,' she answered, watching him anxiously and wondering if he were very drunk.

He took a swallow that emptied his glass, and with automatic hands began brewing another potion. Still his shoulders shook with subdued mirth.

'I don't want to be rude, but ...' said Hancock, and broke into a peal of new laughter.

The girl flushed. 'I can't understand you at all, Charlie,' she said.

'Can't understand me? Tut, tut! I'm one of the simple ones. I'm understood at a glance. I'm clear glass ... I'm not one of the cloudy, mysterious figures like Mortimer.'

'Why is he cloudy and mysterious?' she asked.

'To go in one direction for two years, and wind up on the opposite side of the horizon ... that's a mystery, isn't it?' asked Hancock, with his bursting chuckle.

'Two years in one direction?' she repeated, guessing, and then blushing, and hating herself for the color which, she knew, was pouring up across her face.

Hancock watched her with a surgeon's eye. He shook his head as he murmured, 'I wouldn't believe it. All in a tremor ... and blushing. Mystery? Why, the man's loaded with mystery!'

'Charlie,' she said, 'if I know what you're talking about, I don't like it very well.'

'Oh, we'll change the subject, then, of course,' said Hancock. 'Only thing in the world I'm trained to do is to try to please the ladies. You never guessed that, Lou, did you? You see, I don't succeed very well, but I keep on trying.'

'Trying to please us?' she asked.

'Yes, trying. But I never really succeed. Not like the men of mystery. They don't waste time on gestures. They simply step out – and they bring home the bacon!'

He laughed again, rubbing his hands.

'Are you talking about Harry Mortimer and me?' she asked, taking a deep breath as she forced herself to come to the point.

'Talking about nothing to offend you,' said Hancock. 'Wouldn't do it for the world.... Can't tell you how I admire that Mortimer. Shall I tell you why?'

She melted at once. 'Yes, I want to hear it,' she said.

'Ah, there you are with the shining eyes and the parted lips,' said Hancock. 'And that's the picture he said he would paint, too. And here it is, painted!'

The words lifted her slowly from her chair.

Hancock was laughing too heartily to be aware of her. 'Mystery? He's the deepest man of mystery I've ever known in my life,' he said. 'There's the end of the road for him. No way to get ahead. Blocked on every side in his mission of teaching us all how to use the range and button the grass to the ground permanently. He's blocked; can't get past John Miller.... But if he can't get past John Miller, at least he can get past an easier obstacle. And he does!'

He laughed again, still saying, through his laughter, 'But the rich Lou Miller, the beautiful Lou Miller, the spark of fire, the whistle in the wind, the picture that shines in every man's eyes ...' Here laughter drowned his voice.

'Sit down, Lou!' he said. 'I tell you, I love an efficient man, and that's why I love this Mortimer. If he can't win the men, he'll try the women. Two years in one direction gets him nothing. So he turns around and goes in the opposite direction, and all at once he's home! Wonderful, I call it.

Simply wonderful! And in a single evening! Even if he's beaten up a bit, he comes safely home and brings Beauty beside the Beast. Knew he would, too. Ready to bet on it.'

'To bet on it?' asked the girl, feeling a coldness of face as though a strong wind were blowing against her.

'What did I say?' asked Hancock.

'Nothing,' said the girl.

'Sit down, Lou.'

'No, I have to go home. The barbecue is still running. Hundreds of people there.... Good-by, Charlie!'

'Oh, but you can't go like this. I have a thousand things to tell you about Mortimer.'

'I think I've heard enough,' said the girl. 'I didn't realize that he was such a man of – of mystery. But you're right, Charlie. I suppose you're right.'

She felt the bitter emotion suddenly swelling and choking in her throat, for she was remembering how Mortimer, stunned and mindless after his fall, had clung still to a monotonous refrain, telling her over and over again that he loved her. She knew that he was a fighting man, and he had clung like a bulldog to his appointed task of winning her even when the brain was stunned. The clearest picture before her mind was of the two men talking in this room, with laughter shaking the paunch of Charlie Hancock as he bet with Mortimer that the tenderfoot could not go to the barbecue and put Lou Miller in his pocket. Shame struck her with the edge and coldness of steel. She turned suddenly and went out into the moonlight to where Hampton was waiting....

When Mortimer wakened late that night he heard the snoring of three of the Hancock cowpunchers in an adjoining room. His brain was perfectly clear now, and only when he moved in his bed did he feel the soreness of bruised muscles.

'How you coming, Chief?' asked the voice of Jan Erickson.

He looked up into the face of the huge Swede, who was leaning from his chair, a shadow wrapped in bright moonlight.

'I'm fit and fine,' said Mortimer. 'Go to bed, Jan.'

'I ain't sleepy,' declared Jan Erickson. 'Tell me who done it to you.'

'A few drunken cowpunchers,' said Mortimer.

'Was that big feller Wilson one of them? The feller you licked?'

'No. He wasn't one of them.'

'That's good,' said Erickson, 'because he's taken and run away from the Chappany. He didn't like the side of the range that you showed him, and he run off to Poplar Springs on his way back home. But what was the names of the others?'

'I didn't recognize them,' lied Mortimer.

'It was some of Miller's men, wasn't it?' persisted Jan.

'I don't think so,' answered Mortimer. 'Stop bothering me and go to bed, Jan.'

'How many was there?' asked Erickson, a whine of eagerness in his voice.

'A crowd. I couldn't recognize anyone. It's all over. Forget it.'

Erickson was silent for a moment, and then his whisper reached Mortimer: 'God strike me if I forget it!' ...

A healthy man can sleep off most of his physical troubles. Mortimer was not roused in the morning when the Hancock cowpunchers clumped down the stairs with jingling spurs. He slept on till almost noon, and then wakened from a melancholy dream to find the wind whistling and moaning around the house and the temperature fallen far enough to put a shiver in his body. When he stood up there were only a few stiffnesses in his muscles. The night before, it was apparent, he simply had been punch-drunk.

A bucket of water in a galvanized iron washtub made him a bath. As he sloshed the chill water over his body his memory stepped back into the dimness of the previous evening. Most of it was a whirling murk through which he could remember the nodding head of Hampton, bearing him forward, and the perpetual disgust of nausea, and his own voice saying, 'I love you!' That memory struck him into a sweat of anxious shame until the foggy veil lifted still farther. He could not remember her answer in words, but he could recall the tenderness of her voice and how her arms had held him.

Lightning jagged before Mortimer's eyes and split open his old world to the core. First a sense of guilt ran with his pulses, like the shadowy hand of the referee counting out the seconds of the knockdown. But she never would know, he told himself, if a life of devotion could keep her from the knowledge. He had gone to her ready to lie like a scoundrel, and he had come away with the thought of her filling his mind like a light. Slowly toweling his body dry, he fell into a muse, re-seeing her, body and spirit. That high-headed pride now seemed to him no more than the jaunty soul which is born of the free range. That fierce loyalty which kept her true to her father in every act and word would keep her true to a husband in the same way. She never could turn again, he told himself. And he saw his life extending like a smooth highway to the verge of the horizon. With her hand to open the door to him and give him authority, he would have the entire range, very soon, using those methods which would give the grasslands eternal life. He had been almost hating the stupid prejudices and the blindness of the ranchers; now his heart opened with understanding of them all.

He dressed with stumbling hands, and noted the purple bruised places and where the skin had rubbed away in spots, but there was nothing worth a child's notice except a dark, swollen place that half covered his right eye and extended back across the temple. He could shrug his shoulders at such injuries, if only the scalp wound were not serious. When he had shaved, he went out to the barracks shed to let Shorty examine the cut.

Shorty took off the bandage, washed the torn scalp, and wound a fresh bandage in place. 'Healing up like nobody's business,' he said. 'Sit down and leave me throw a steak and a coupla handfuls of onions into you, and you'll be as fine as a fiddle again.'

So Mortimer sat down to eat, and was at his second cup of coffee before he remembered the time of day. It was half an hour past noon and yet his CCC gang had not showed up for food.

'Shorty, where the devil are the boys?' he asked. 'What's happened? You're not cooking lunch for them?'

'Well, the fact is that they sashayed off on a kind of a little trip,' said Shorty.

Mortimer stared at him. 'They left the ranch without talking to me?' he demanded.

'They thought you'd be laid up today,' said Shorty. 'And so they kind of went and played hooky on you, Chief.'

'Shorty, where did they go?' asked Mortimer, remembering vividly how Jan Erickson had leaned over his bed during the night and had tried to drag from him the identity of his assailants.

'How would I know where they'd go?' asked Shorty.

Mortimer turned his back on the cook, for he knew that he would get no trustworthy information from him. He tried to think back into the mind of his gang – not into their individual brains but into the mob-consciousness which every group possesses, and the first thing that loomed before him was their savage, deep, unquestioning devotion to him.

With a sick rush of apprehension, he wondered if they might have gone across the valley straight to the Miller place to exact vengeance for the fall of their chief. But Lefty Parkman and Pudge Major were far too levelheaded to permit a move as wild as that. If they wanted to make trouble for men of the Miller ranch they would go to Poplar Springs and try to find straggling groups of the cowpunchers from the big outfit.

Mortimer jumped for the corner of the room and picked up a rifle. He put it down again, straightening slowly. When it came to firearms, his CCC lads were helpless, as compared with the straight-shooting men of the range. He, himself, was only a child in that comparison.

He turned and ran empty-handed into the adjoining shed. The big truck was gone, as he had expected, but the one-ton truck remained, and into the seat of this he climbed in haste.

It was fifteen miles to Poplar Springs and he did the distance in twenty minutes. As he drove he took dim note of the day. The melancholy wind which had wakened him still mourned down the valley, but its force along the ground was nothing compared to the velocity of the upper air. What seemed to be fast-traveling clouds, unraveled and spread thin, shot out of the northwest and flattened the arch of the sky, with the sun sometimes golden, sometimes dull and green, through that unusual mist. In the west the mountains had disappeared.

Three from north to south, three from east to west, the streets of Poplar Springs laid out a small checkering of precise little city blocks. Most of its life came from the 'springs,' whose muddy waters were said to have some sort of medicinal value. An old frame hotel spread its shambling wings around the water. A rising part of the town's business, however, came from the aviation company of Chatham, Armstrong & Worth, which had built some hangars and used the huge flat east of the place as a testing ground. Saturday nights were the bright moments for Poplar Springs, when the cowpunchers rode into town or drove rattling automobiles in from the range to patronize the saloons which occupied almost every corner.

Wherever he saw a pedestrian, Mortimer called, 'Seen anything of a six-foot-four Swede with hair as pale as blow-sand?' At last he was directed to Porson's Saloon.

Porson's had been there in Poplar Springs since the earliest cattle days and still used the old swing doors with three bullet holes drilled through the slats of one panel and two through another. If Porson's had filled a notch for each of its dead men, it would have had to crowd fifty-three notches on one gun butt, people said, for bar whisky and old cattle feuds and single-action Colts had drenched its floor with blood more than once. An echo of the reputation of the place was ominous in Mortimer's mind as he pushed through the doors.

It was like stepping into a set piece on a stage. The picture he dreaded to find was there in every detail. Jan Erickson, Pudge Major, Lefty Parkman, George Masters, and Dink Waller stood at the end of the bar nearest the door, and bunched at the farther end were eight of the Miller cowpunchers, with Sam Pearson dominating the group. The bartender was old Rip Porson himself, carrying his seventy years like a bald-headed eagle. Unperturbed by the silent thunder in the air, he calmly went about serving drinks.

Mortimer stood a moment inside the door, with his brain whirling as though he had been struck on the base of the skull. The Miller punchers looked at him with a deadly interest. Not one of his own men turned a head toward him, but Lefty Parkman said in a low voice, 'The chief!'

'Thank God!' muttered Pudge Major. But Dink Waller growled, 'He oughta be home! This is our job.'

'It's time for a round on the house, boys,' said Rip Porson. 'And I wanta tell you something: The first man that goes for iron while he's drinkin' on the house, he gets a slug out of my own gun.... Here's to you, one and all!'

He had put out the bottles of rye and, as the round was filled, silently, he lifted his own glass in a steady red claw.

The two factions continued to stare with fascinated attention at each other, eye holding desperately to eye as though the least shift in concentration would cause disaster. They raised their glasses as Rip Porson proposed his toast: 'Here's to the fight and to them that shoot straight; and damn the man that breaks the mirror.'

In continued silence the men of the Miller place and Mortimer's CCC gang drank.

Then Mortimer walked to the bar. He chose a place directly between the two hostile forces, standing exactly in the field of fire, if guns were once drawn. 'I'll have a beer,' he said.

Rip Porson dropped his hands on the edge of the bar and regarded Mortimer with bright, red-stained eyes. 'You're the one that the trouble's all about, ain't you?' he asked. 'You're Harry Mortimer, ain't you?'

'I am,' said Mortimer. 'And there's going to be no more trouble.'

'Beer is what the man's having,' said Porson, slowly filling a glass. A smile, or the ghost of a smile, glimmered in his old eyes.

'Set them up, Porson,' said the low, deep voice of Jan Erickson.

'Set 'em up over here, too,' commanded Sam Pearson.

The bartender pushed the whisky bottles into place again. Every moment he was growing more cheerful.

Mortimer faced his own men. 'Lefty!' he said, picking out the most dominant spirit from among them.

Lefty Parkman gave not the slightest sign that he had heard the voice which spoke to him. He had picked out a single face among the cowpunchers and was staring at his man with a concentrated hatred. Odds made no difference to Lefty, even odds of eight to six when all the eight were heeled with guns and hardly two of the CCC men could have any weapons better than fists.

'Lefty!' repeated Mortimer.

The eyes of Lefty wavered suddenly toward his chief.

'Turn around and walk out the door. We're getting out of here,' said Mortimer, 'and you're leading the way.'

The glance of Lefty slipped definitely away from

the eye of Mortimer and fixed again on its former target. For the first time an order from Mortimer went disregarded.

Among Sam Pearson's men there was a bowlegged cowpuncher named Danny Shay, barrel-chested, bull-browed, and as solid as the stump of a big tree. The croak of a resonant bullfrog was in the voice of Danny and it was this voice which now said, 'There ain't room enough in here for 'em; we got the air kind of used up, maybe.'

One of the cowpunchers laughed at this weak sally, a brief, half-hysterical outburst of mirth.

Pudge Major lurched from his place at the bar and walked straight toward the Miller men.

'Go back, Pudge!' commanded Mortimer.

Pudge strode on, unheeding. 'You look like an ape when you laugh,' said Pudge. 'When you open your face that wide, I can see the baboon all the way down the red of your dirty throat.'

Mortimer turned and saw Jed Wharton, among the cowpunchers, hit Pudge fairly on the chin with a lifting punch. Major rocked back on his heels and began an involuntary retreat. Big Jed Wharton followed with a driving blow from which Pudge Major cringed away with both hands flung up and a strange little cry of fear that made Mortimer's blood run cold. Poor Major had gone for bigger game than his nature permitted, and the sight of the white feather among his men

75

struck into Mortimer's brain like a hand of shadow.

He saw in the leering, triumphant faces of the cowpunchers the charge that was about to follow. The man next to Sam Pearson was already drawing his Colt. He had no chance to glance behind him at his own followers, but Mortimer could guess that they were as heartsick and daunted as he by the frightened outcry of Pudge. And he remembered the barking voice of an assistant football coach hounding him into scrimmage when he was a freshman at college: 'Low, Mortimer! Tackle low!'

'Tackle low!' yelled Mortimer, and dived at Sam Pearson's knees. While he was still in the air he saw from the corner of his eye Lefty Parkman swarming in to the attack, and the blond head of gigantic Erickson. Then his shoulder banged into Pearson's knees, and the whole world seemed to fall on his back.

It was not the sort of barroom fighting that a Westerner would expect. That headlong plunge and the charge of Erickson jammed the cowpunchers against the wall. Mortimer, in the midst of confusion, caught at stamping feet and struggling legs and pulled down all he could reach.

He put his knee on Pearson's neck and pressed on toward Danny Shay, who had been tripped and had fallen like a great frog, on hands and knees.

There was hardly room for fist work. Mortimer jerked his elbow into the face of Danny and stood up in the room Shay had occupied.

Guns were sounding, by that time. As he straightened in the thundering uproar he saw a contorted face not a yard away and a Colt levelling at him over the shoulder of another man. But an arm and fist like a brass-knuckled walking beam struck from a height, and the gunman disappeared into the heap.

That was Jan Erickson's work.

Other men might dance away from Jan and cut him to gradual bits in the open, but for a close brawl he was peerless, and now his hands were filled with work as they never had been before. As Mortimer struck out, he saw on the far side of the bar old Rip Porson standing regardless of danger from chance bullets, with his eyes half closed as he shook his head in a profound disgust.

Mortimer saw Pudge Major in it, also. As though the first touch of fear had turned into a madness, Pudge Major came in with an endless screech, like a fighting cat. He ran into the clubbed butt of a revolver that knocked him back against the wall. From that wall he rebounded, swinging a chair in his hands. The chair landed with a crash of splintering wood. Big Sam Pearson, who had managed to regain his feet at last, sank under the blow, and suddenly Mortimer saw that the fight was ended. Those whom

Erickson had hit solidly were down, to remain down. Dink Waller patiently, uncomplainingly, was throttling his chosen victim with a full Nelson. Lefty pounded a defenseless victim against the wall. George Masters was in a drunken stagger, trying to come toward the noise of battle; but the fight was ended.

The attack had been so quick and close that most of the guns were not even drawn. Hardly half a dozen bullets had hit ceiling or floor. Not a single shot struck flesh; but the great mirror behind the bar was drilled cleanly through the center and from that hole a hundred cracks jagged outward.

'Take their guns!' shouted Mortimer. 'Let them be, but take their guns! Jan, it's over!'

Some two minutes after Mortimer dived at Pearson's knees he had eight revolvers and several large knives piled on the bar. Two or three of the beaten men were staggering to their feet. Danny Shay nursed his bleeding face in both hands. Sam Pearson sat in a corner with blood streaming down from his gashed head, which hung helplessly over one shoulder, agape with the shock, and agrin with pain.

Jan Erickson, still in a frenzy, strode back and forth, shouting, 'That's what a Mortimer does. He cuts through bums like you the way a knife cuts through cheese.... Why don't he wring your necks? Because he's ashamed to hurt wet-nosed kids like you are!'

'Get out of the place, Jan,' commanded Mortimer. 'All of you get out! There are no broken bones, I think, and thank God for that. Get our men out, Jan!'

He turned back to the bar and said to Porson, 'I'll pay half the cost of that mirror, bartender.'

His voice could not penetrate the hazy trance of Rip Porson, who continued to stare into space and wag his head slowly from side to side, as he repeated, 'Fourteen wearing pants and not one man among 'em … the world has gone to hell … fourteen milk-fed baboons!' …

There had to be a few rounds of drinks to celebrate the victory. There had to be some patching of cuts. So it was two hours before Mortimer rounded up his crew and had them back at the Hancock place, with the three men who had missed the fight in agonies because they had been out of it.

'Shut up your faces,' said Jan Erickson. 'There wouldn't of *been* no fight if you'd all been there. They wouldn't of dared…. But the sweet spot you missed was the chief taking a dive into them like into a swimming pool; and the waves he throwed up took all the fight out of them.'

Pudge Major sat with his head in his hands when they were in the barracks shed. Mortimer, on one knee beside him patted him on the back.

'I was yella,' groaned Pudge. 'I was a dirty rat. The whole world knows that I'm yella.'

'You needed a sock on the chin before you got your second wind,' declared Mortimer. 'And then you were the best man in the room. Ask the boys. Even Jan wouldn't take you on. Would you, Jan?'

'Him? I'd rather take on a wildcat!' said Jan.

'Jan, d'you mean that, partly?' asked Pudge.

'I mean the whole of it,' said Jan Erickson. 'And when it comes to working with a chair, you're away out by yourself. You're the class of the field.'

Therefore Mortimer left them in this triumphant humor and drove over to the Miller place in the light truck. A Chinese servant opened the door to him but there was no need for him to enter, for John Miller at that moment came down the hall with a jangle of spurs and a quirt in his hand. His daughter was following him. And now he stood tall in the entrance, looking at Mortimer without a word.

'I dare say that you've heard about the trouble in Poplar Springs,' said Mortimer. 'I want to tell you that I didn't send out my men to make trouble; they went off by themselves, and I started after them to bring them back. When I found them, they'd located your people already. I tried to stop the fight, but it got under way in spite of me.'

'Are you through?' asked John Miller, parting his locked jaws with difficulty.

Mortimer said slowly, 'If any reprisals start, it will be from your part, not mine. I've taken my beating and I haven't yipped. But if your fellows come on to make more trouble there'll be murder all over the range. I want to know if you think you can keep your people in hand.'

'Are you finished?' asked Miller.

'I am,' said Mortimer.

'Very well,' said Miller, and walked straight past him.

He turned his bewildered eyes on the girl, as she seemed about to go past him behind her father. His glance stopped her. She was pale; small lines and shadows made her eyes seem older. He had stopped her with his puzzled look, but now as she stood back with a hand against the wall she was looking steadily into his face.

'I wasn't hard, was I?' she asked. 'You only had to whistle and the bird flew right off the tree to your hand. Nothing could be easier than that, could it?'

'What are you saying, Lou?' he asked.

She looked down at his extended hand and then up to the pain in his face before she laughed a little. 'You *are* wonderful, Harry,' she said. 'It's that honest, straightforward simplicity which gets you so far. And then your voice. That does a lot. And the facial expression, too. It's good enough for a close-up. Ah, but Hollywood could make a star of you.... The way it is now, I suppose you hardly make pocket money out of the girls. Or do they run high, sometimes – the bets you place before you go out to make a girl?'

'Hancock ... there was no bet ... Lou ... it was only that I didn't know I'd adore you as I do,' stammered Mortimer.

'You know now, though, don't you?' said the girl. 'You love me all your heart can hold, Harry, don't you?'

He tried to answer her, but felt the words die on his lips.

'And d'you know, Harry,' said the girl, peering at him, 'that I think it was the beginning of a great love? As I went along beside you through the night, I would have given up both hands for you. I would have given my face for you. I would have given my heart. And ... aren't you a rather yellow sort of dog, Harry?'

He saw her go by him with that quick, light, graceful step. Something made him look up as she vanished through the patio gate, and he seemed to find an answer for his question in the swift gray stream that poured across the sky endlessly, as it had been pouring ever since the morning. The sun was small and green behind it.

He got back into the truck and drove blindly toward the ranch. The subconscious mind inside him took note of the gray sweep of mist through the sky and the color of the setting sun behind it. It was not water vapor which could give that color, he knew. It was dust – dust rushing on the higher stratum of the air, headlong. Somewhere the wind had eaten through the skin of the range and was bearing uncounted tons of topsoil into nothingness.

That fact should have meant something to Mortimer, but his conscious mind refused to take heed of it, for it was standing still before the thought of Louise Miller. Then Hancock jumped into his mind and he gripped the wheel so hard that it trembled under his grasp.

He brought the car up short before the entrance of the house. Three or four of Hancock's cowpunchers were lounging in the doorway of the ranch house. He shouldered brusquely through them, and went on into the parlor of the house, where Hancock lay on the couch, as usual, with his rum-punch fixings on the table beside him. He took off his glasses as Mortimer entered, resettled them on his nose, and then smote his paunch a resounding whack.

'Ah, Harry!' he cried. 'You're the one soul in the world that I want to see. I don't mean about battering some of the Miller boys in Poplar Springs. That'll do your reputation on the range some good, though. Tackling guns with bare hands is rather a novelty in this part of the world, of course.... But what's that to me? Do you know what has meaning to me, Harry?'

Mortimer picked up the rum bottle, poured a swallow into a clean glass, and tossed it off. He said quietly, 'What makes a difference to you, Charles?' and his eyes hunted the body of

Hancock as though he were looking for a place to strike home a knife.

But Hancock was unaware of this. A wave of thought had overcome him, and memory dimmed his eyes as he said, 'I'm going to tell you something, my lad. I'm going to tell you about a woman.... Mind you, Harry, it was years ago.... But when I say "a woman", I want you to understand "*the* woman." Rare. Sudden. Something too beautiful to last.... Are you following me?'

'I follow you,' Mortimer said.

The rancher had almost closed his eyes as he consulted the picture from the past.

'I saw her. I adored her. I asked her to marry me. When she accepted me, Harry, the sound of her voice lifted me almost out of my boots. I went away planning my path through the world. And when I was about to take the prize in my hand, Harry – mark this – when I was about to take her to the church, she disappeared. Gone. Vanished absolutely. The way you say this range soil will vanish when the wind hits it just right. What took her away? A little wizened son of a French marquis with no more man in him than there is skin on the heel of my hand. She was gone. Lost to me. Love. Hope. What the hell will you have? She was all that!

'And since that day I've lain here with the rum bottle wondering how the devil I could get back at the whole female race. Can't do anything with them when you lie flat and simply think, because thought, on the whole, is beyond their ken. And therefore I had to wait until you did it for me. D'you see? You show me how women can be handled as easily as they handle men. Love her? *No!* Admire her? *No!* You simply take the woman and put her in your pocket. Who's the girl? Some cheap little chit? No, the best in the land. The proudest. The highest. The top of everything.... I stood here, last night, and saw her eyes melt when your name was mentioned. I saw the whole lovesick story come swooning into her face. And as a result of what? As a result of one evening of work. Why, Harry, when I saw what you had done, I wanted to get down on my knees and beg you for lessons.'

'So you told her everything, didn't you?' asked Mortimer.

Hancock took off a moment for thought. The wind, at the same moment, seemed to descend and grip the ranch house with a firmer hand. The whine of the storm ascended the scale by several notes.

'Told her?' said Hancock. 'I don't think that I told her anything. I couldn't say anything. I could only lie here and laugh. And admire you, Harry, and think how you'd paid off my score. And I want to tell you something, Harry. As I lay here last night I felt a deathless debt – gratitude, and all that. Wonderful feeling, Harry. The first time I've had it in my life. Absolutely extraordinary.'

'I dare say,' muttered Mortimer through his teeth.

'And that's why I'm glad to see you today,' said Hancock. 'Not because you've beaten eight of Miller's best men with your hands, but because you've subdued one woman, opened her heart, put tears in her eyes, made her knees tremble, when you didn't give a hang for her from the first to the last.' He broke into a gigantic peal of laughter which wound up on a gasping and spluttering.

'Close, in here,' said Hancock. 'Cool, but close, and that's strange, isn't it?'

Mortimer could not speak, seeing again the beauty and the pride of the girl who was lost to him.

'Chuck the door open, like a good fellow, will you?' asked Hancock. 'I never had so much trouble breathing. Is the alcohol getting me at last? Well, let it get me. I'll die laughing. I've seen the proud females, the high females, the pure females paid off for me, shot for shot. And I owe that to you, old fellow. Mortimer, I'll love you as long as I last!'

Mortimer went to the door and threw it wide. It seemed to him that ghosts rushed up into the lamplight, into his face. Then it was as though dim horses were galloping past in endless procession, and swifter than horses ever put hoof to the ground. He squinted his eyes into the dimness before he could understand that the swift whirl was a dust storm rushing past him at full

peed; the range itself was melting away before
his eyes.

THREE

A flying arm of dust enveloped Mortimer and set him coughing as he closed the door and turned back into the room.

Hancock was grinning cheerfully. 'There she blows, Harry,' he said. 'There comes the dust storm you've been talking about for two years. Now we'll see if you've buttoned the topsoil down with all your plantings and plowings. Now we'll see if the range *has* been overgrazed, as you say, and what part of it is going to blow away.'

'That dust is blowing from far away,' said Mortimer. 'There isn't enough edge to this wind to tear up the ground badly. It will have to blow.'

The house trembled, as though nudged by an enormous shoulder, and the storm screamed an octave higher. The two men stared at each other; then Mortimer pulled out a bandanna and began to knot it around his throat.

'Get your hand-picked cowpunchers on the job, Charlie,' he suggested.

'It's dark, brother,' said Hancock, 'and the kind of lads I have don't work in the night.'

'All right,' said Mortimer. 'The cattle I save will be my share of the stock, and the dead ones can belong to you.'

He left the room with Hancock shouting loudly, 'Wait a minute, Harry! All for one and one for all …'

When Mortimer stepped into the open the gale was blowing hard enough to set his eyelids trembling. It came at him like a river of darkness. He bumped the corner of the house, turning toward the barracks shed, and then the wind caught him from the side and set him staggering.

The light in the window of the shed was a dull, greenish blur. He had to fumble to find the door, and he pressed his way in, to find a jingling of pots and pans in the kitchen and the CCC men sneezing and cursing in the mist which filtered rapidly through the cracks in the walls of the shed. They stood up and looked silently toward him for an explanation.

He said, 'It's the dust storm, boys. Pulled at my feet like water.… No man has to go out into weather like this, but if any of you volunteer to give a hand …'

Jan Erickson turned his head slowly to survey the group. 'Leave me see the man that *won't* volunteer,' he said ominously.

But not one of them hung back. They were a solid unit, and a speechless content filled Mortimer's heart, till Shorty appeared in the kitchen door, shouting, 'There's gunna be plenty of grit in the flour bin and mud in the coffee, Chief!'

A louder howling of the wind seemed to answer Shorty directly and set the men laughing. They equipped themselves as Mortimer directed, with shirts buttoned close at neck and wrist to keep out the flying sand, and with bandannas ready to pull up over mouth and nose. A big canteen to each should give enough water to wash the mouth clean for a few hours and keep the bandanna wet in case it were necessary to strain the dust out more thoroughly. Four of them would ride with Charlie Hancock's cowpunchers to help handle the cattle, which probably were drifting rapidly before the storm and lodging helpless against the fencelines. The thing to do was to get the weakest of the livestock into the barns and round up the mass of them in the Chappany Valley, where Mortimer's young groves of trees would give some shelter against the whip of the wind and the drifting of the soil. It was true that all this work properly belonged to Hancock's cowpunchers, but under Mortimer's control the CCC men had learned every detail of the ranch work long ago.

They went out with Mortimer now and worked all night.

The wind kept coming like a thousand devils out of the northwest, and into the southeast, at the farthest limit of the Hancock land, Mortimer led a group of the CCC men. They found two hundred steers drifted against a barbed wire fence, with their heads down and the drift sand already piled knee-deep around them. There they would remain until the sand heaped over them in a great dune. It required hard work to turn the herd, shooting guns in their faces, shouting and flogging, but at last it began to move back towards the Chappany Valley.

Streaks and slitherings of moonlight that got through the hurly-burly showed the cattle continually drifting aslant, to turn their faces from the storm. It was like riding into a sandblast. In five minutes a fine silt had forced its way under tight wristbands and down the collars of the punchers, so that a crawling discomfort possessed their bodies. Dust was thick on every tongue, and there was a horrible sense of the lungs filling, so that breathing was more labored, though less air got to the blood.

When they had jammed those steers into the Chappany, letting them drink on the way at the lowest of the two Hancock lakes, they pushed the herd into one of the groves of trees which Mortimer had planted two years before. The slant of the ground gave some protection. The spindling trees by their multitude afforded a fence which seemed to whip and filter the air somewhat cleaner. Even that push against the dusty wind had been almost too much for some of the cattle. A good many of them did not mill at all, but slumped to their knees. The others, wandering, lowing, and bellowing, pooled up around the steers that went down, and presently the entire herd was holding well. But some of those that went down would be dead before morning.

It was not a time to count small losses, however. It was like riding out a storm in an old, cranky, and helpless ship. The cargo hardly mattered. Life was the thing to consider.

Mortimer washed out his nose and throat from his canteen and moistened the bandanna which covered the lower part of his face. He sent his contingent of riders back to find more fence-lodged cattle and aimed his own tough cow pony at a dim twinkle of lanterns high up across the valley, above the three Miller lakes. He could guess what those lights indicated, and the picture of disaster bulked suddenly in his mind greater and blacker than the storm itself.

He took the way straight up the valley, however, and rode the slope toward Miller's thousand acres of plowed ground. Heading into the wind, in this manner, it was impossible to keep the eyes open very long at a time. No matter how narrowly he squinted, the fine silt blew through the lashes and tormented the eyeballs.

He had to pick direction from time to time, checking the pony's efforts to turn its head from the torment; otherwise he kept his eyes fast shut.

There were two square miles of that plowed and hay-covered cropland. He came up on the northern edge of it and found the mustang stepping on hard, smooth ground. When he used his flashlight, he saw that the border acres which edged toward the wind had blown away like a dream. The reddish hardpan, tough as burned bricks, was all that remained!

He dismounted, tried to clear his throat, and found that the choke of the dust storm had penetrated to the bottom of his lungs like thick smoke. Panic stormed up in his brain. He beat the terror down and went on about his observations. There were things to see, here, which should be reported exactly in the notebook that was his source of information to be sent to the government.

It was a dark moment of the storm, for the wind came on with a scream and a steel-edge whistling through the hay, and the moon was shut away almost entirely. It merely showed in the sky vague tumblings and shapeless rollings of dust that seemed to spill more loosely across the heavens than mere clouds ever do; and sometimes it was as though the earth had exploded and the results of the explosion were hanging motionless in the air. But what he wanted to see was far more intimately close at hand.

He went over the bared ground to the rim of the yet standing hay. In places it was rolled back and heaped like matting; sometimes it gathered in cone-shaped masses like shocked hay; but every now and then the wind got its finger tips under the shocks and the rolls and blew them to smithereens with a single breath. On his knees Mortimer turned the flashlight on the edge of the hayland and watched the action of the storm. At that point the life-sustaining humus was about a foot deep to the hardpan. The top portion, which had been loosened by the plow, ran down from four to six inches, and this part gave way rapidly, sifting from around the white roots of the hay until each stalk, at the end, was suddenly jerked away. In the meantime, the scouring blast worked more gradually at the lower, unplowed layer of the soil, which was compacted with the fine, hairlike roots of the range grass. Even this gave way with amazing rapidity.

The hayland was doomed. An army working hand to hand, could not have saved it. As he mounted, the swinging ray of the electric torch showed Mortimer another horseman who sat the saddle not far away, impassive. The long-legged horse kept picking up its feet nervously and making small bucking movements of protest, but the rider held it like a pitching boat in a rough sea. Mortimer, coming nearer, saw the masked face and the sand-reddened eyes of John Miller, who was watching twelve thousand dollars' worth of hay and fifty thousand irreplaceable dollars' worth of topsoil blow to hell. Impassive, by the ragged glimpses of light which the moon offered, the rancher stared at the quick destruction. Mortimer rode to his side and shouted, 'Sorry, Miller!'

John Miller gave him a silent glance, and then resumed his study of the growing ruin before him. Mortimer turned his mustang back into the Chappany Valley.

He passed over a long stretch of the Miller bottom land which had been plowed for onions and potatoes. The deep, black soil was withering away into pock-marks, or dissolving under the breath of the storm. Mortimer groaned as he paused to watch the steady destruction. That heavy loam had formed centuries or hundreds of centuries before among the roots of the forested uplands. Rain had washed it gradually into the rivers. The Chappany floods had spread it over the flat of the valley lands. And this rich impost which nature had spread in ten thousand careful layers was blowing headlong away, forever! It seemed to Mortimer that all America was vanishing from beneath his feet.

He hurried on down the Chappany, looking again and again, anxiously, toward the flickering line of lanterns that shone from the high ground above the Miller lakes. He had warned Miller two years ago, by word and by example, about the danger of those rolling sand dunes, above the bluff. If a great wind came from this quarter, the whole mass of sand might come to life like water and spill over the edge of the bluff to fill the lakes beneath and sponge up the priceless water.

Then the wind came down the Chappany Valley like dark water rushing through a flume, and the lanterns were dimmed.

Out of the sweeping dimness, which sometimes blew his horse sliding, he came back onto the Hancock land and dismounted. With his flashlight he studied half a mile of terrain. On one side, some contour-plowing was commencing to blow a little, but, everywhere else he looked, his trees, his stretches of shrubbery over exposed shoulders, and the tough grasses with wide-spreading roots which he had planted were buttoning the soil to the hardpan, holding the ground like a green overcoat of varying textures.

One shouting burst of triumph filled his throat, but after that the joy slipped away from him and left his heart cold. For somehow his soul had struck roots in the whole countryside. Now hundreds of thousands of good acres all over the range were threatened, and it seemed to Mortimer that children of his body, not the mere hopes of his mind and the planned future, were imperiled.

He turned his horse up the slope, where the

bluff diminished to a reasonable slope. Off to the left the headlights of an automobile came bucking through the dimness. A great truck went by him, roaring, with a load of long timbers.

Mortimer's heart sank, for he knew the meaning of that. He spurred the mustang on behind the lighted path of the truck until he reached the sand dunes immediately above the two long lakes which belonged on the Hancock land and held water for the Hancock cattle.

The sand which came on the whistling wind, up there, cut at the skin and endangered the eyes, but his flashlight showed him no portion of the Hancock dunes wearing under the storm! From the edge of the bluff and back for a hundred yards, he had planted a tough Scotch scrub which had the look of heather, though it never bloomed. For fuel it was useless. No cattle would graze on those bitter, varnished leaves. That shrubbery served no purpose in the world except to shield the ground under it. It grew not more than a foot high, but it spread in such solid masses that wind could not get at its roots.

Behind the shrubbery he had planted fifty rows of tough saplings, close as a fence. They had grown slowly, but the thickened trunks stood up now like solidly built palings against the storm. Beyond them, and stretching as far as the dunes rolled into the back country, Mortimer had covered every inch of the ground with a grass from the Russian steppes, where eight months of the year the earth is frozen, and where for four months this close-growing, stubborn grass covers the soil like a blanket of a fine weave and offers a steady pasturage for wandering herds of small cattle. For two years it had been rooting and spreading, and now it clothed the dunes behind the Hancock lakes with an impermeable vesture. The dunes themselves had been anchored, here, but the flying silt which filled the air was banking up outside the farther lines of his fence of saplings. It was conceivable that if the storm continued for days it might gradually heap the wave of sand so high that the trees would be overwhelmed; but little of the sweeping sand could ever roll over the bluff and drop into the lakes beneath.

Once more the triumph went with a riot through Mortimer's blood; and once more the triumph died suddenly away as he looked at the lanterns that stretched before him along the edge of the bluff.

There were far more lights than he had expected; and, now that he came closer, he found two hundred men laboring in a mist of blow-sand. Orders, yelled from time to time, sang on the wind and vanished suddenly. Here and there men were down on their knees, work forgotten as they tried to cough the dust out of their lungs.

Of course, the Miller ranch could not supply

such a force of working hands as this. The men
were from all the adjacent range. For the first
sweep of the storm had choked a thousand pools
with silt and had begun to damage the water in
many a standing tank. The small ranchers in such
a time of need turned naturally toward John
Miller, but, when they telephoned, the ominous
answer was that the dunes were crawling in slow
waves toward the edge of the bluff above the lakes
which served as reservoirs, during the dry season
not only for Miller's cattle but for the herds of his
neighbors. That news brought men from all of the
vicinity. The trucks of the Miller place carried
timbers to the bluff. And the entire army was
slaving to erect a fence that would halt the slow
drift of the dunes. To fence off the whole length of
the three lakes was impossible, so they selected
the largest of the three, the one just above the
Hancock property line, and here a double
fence-line was being run.

John Miller himself appeared on the scene at
this time and commenced to ride up and down,
giving advice, snapping brief orders. He looked to
Mortimer like a resolute general in the midst of a
battle, but this was a losing fight.

For the whole backland, the whole retiring
sweep of the dunes was rising up in a smother of
blow-sand, heaping loosely spilling masses on the
ridges of the dunes, so that there was a constantly
forward flow as though of incredibly reluctant

waves. And the piling weight of that sand was as heavy as water, also.

The men worked with a sullen, patient endurance, scooping out footholds for the posts, boarding them across, with interstices between the boards, and then supporting the shaky structure against the sweep of wind and the roll of sand with long, angled shorings.

One woman moved up and down the line with a bucket of water and a sponge. As she came near, the workers raised the handkerchiefs which covered nose and mouth. Some of them stood with open mouth and tongue thrust out to receive the quick swabbing with water that enabled them to breathe again. Mortimer saw that it was Louise Miller, masked herself, like a gypsy. He swung down from his horse and laid hold of the bail of the bucket.

'I'll handle this, Lou,' he told her. 'It's too heavy a job for you—'

Weariness had unsteadied her, and the wind staggered her heavily against Mortimer. So, for an instant, she let her weight lean against him. Then she pulled up the bandanna that covered her face.

'It's a great day for you!' she gasped. 'We laughed at you, did we? We wouldn't listen when you talked sense to us? Well, it's the turn for the dirt doctor to laugh while the whole range blows away from under our feet.'

He picked up the sponge from the soupy water of the pail and swabbed off the sand and black muck from her face. He steadied her with one hand against the wind while he did it.

She sneered, 'We're learning our lesson. If the wind leaves us anything, we'll get down on our knees and ask you to teach us how to keep it.'

He passed the sponge over her face again. 'You're talking like a fool, a little, spoiled fool,' he said.

She answered through her teeth: 'Get off our land and stay off. We'd rather let the wind blow us all the way to hell than have you lift a hand to help us.'

She caught up the pail and went on, walking more swiftly, though the sand dripped and blew from about her feet as they lifted from the soft ground.

John Miller came up, fighting his horse into the wind, when a kneeling, coughing figure jumped up suddenly from the ground and gripped the reins of Miller's horse under the bit. With his other hand he gestured wildly toward Mortimer.

'You wouldn't listen to him!' screamed the rancher. 'You *knew!* You laughed at him. You knew *every*thing! He was only a fool tenderfoot. And God gave all the sense to the Millers! ... But look at the Hancock place; look at the safe water; and then look at *you!* Damn you for a fake and a fool! I hope you rot!' He dropped to the ground again, and began trying once more to cough the dust from his lungs.

Miller drove his horse up to Mortimer. 'You've got three men working with us here,' he said. 'Take them away. We don't need their hands. We don't need your brains. Get off the Miller land!'

Mortimer turned without a word of protest, letting his horse drift before the wind. He found Lefty Parkman and gave him the order to leave the work, together with the other two. They trooped back toward the Hancock place with their chief, and, as they went, Mortimer took grim notice of how the first sand fence was already sagging under the irresistible weight of accumulating silt. But the whole storm and the fate of the entire range had become a smaller thing to him since his last glimpse of Lou Miller. The pain of it lingered under his heart like the cold of a sword. It was not the blow-sand that kept him from drawing breath, but the fine, poisonous dust of grief.

Then the thought of Hancock and how the fat drunkard had betrayed him blinded his eyes with anger. He drove the snorting mustang ahead of his men and rushed to the ranch house. The thickest smother of the storm was coiling around him as he broke in through the doorway to the hall.

Then, as he turned from the hall toward the entrance to the parlor, he heard Hancock singing cheerfully to himself, and saw the man stretched as usual on the couch with the rum punch beside him.

'Hi, Harry!' called Charlie Hancock. 'How's the little sand-blow? Been a hero again, old boy? Charmed any more girls off the tree?'

It seemed to Mortimer, as he blinked his sore eyes, that he was looking through an infinite distance of more than space and time toward his ranching partner. The rage that had been building in him sank away to a dumb disgust. Then the telephone at the end of the room began to purr.

'For you,' said Hancock. 'This thing has been ringing all night. The world seems to want Harry Mortimer, after forgetting him all these years.'

Over the wire a strident, nasal voice said, 'Mortimer? This is Luke Waterson over in Patchen Valley.... The wind's blowing hell out of things, over here.... Barn's gone down, slam! Forty head inside it. Mortimer, I don't care about barns and cattle, but the ground's whipping away from under our feet. You're an expert about that. You claim you can keep the ground buttoned down tight. For God's sake tell us what to do. We'll all pitch in and wear our hands to the bone if you'll tell me how to start ...'

Mortimer said, 'Waterson, it makes my heart ache to hear you. God knows that I'd help you if I could. But the only way to anchor the topsoil is to use time as well as thought and ...'

'You mean that you won't tell me the answer?' shouted Waterson.

'There's no answer I can give when ...' began Mortimer. But he heard the receiver slammed up at the other end.

As he turned away from the phone, it rang again with a long clamor.

'This is Tom Knight. Down at Pokerville,' said another voice. 'Mortimer, I've always been one of the few that believed you knew your business. And now the devil is to pay down here. Sand and silt in all three of our tanks. No water. But that's nothing. I've got three hundred acres in winter wheat and, by God, it's blowing into the sky! Mortimer, what can I do to hold the soil? It's going through my fingers like water through a sieve ...'

'I can't tell you, Mr. Knight,' called Mortimer. 'You need two years of careful planting, and less crowding on the cattle range ...'

'Two years? Hell, man, I'm talking about hours, not years! In twenty-four hours there won't be enough grass on my lands to feed a frog! Can you give me the answer?'

'Not even God could help your land till the wind stops blowing, Mr Knight ...'

'Damn you and your books and your theories, then!' roared Knight. And his receiver crashed on the hook.

The instrument was hardly in place when the bell rang again.

'Take it, Charlie, will you?' asked Mortimer weakly.

'I'll take it. *I'll* tell 'em,' said Hancock.

He strode to the telephone and presently was shouting into the mouthpiece, '… and even if he were here I wouldn't let him waste time on you. For two years he's been trying to show you the way out. You knew too much to listen. Stay where you are and choke with dust, or else come up here and see how the Hancock acres are sticking fast to the hardpan!' He laughed as he hung up.

'That's the way to talk to 'em,' he said. 'You're in the saddle now. You've been ridiculed and ostracised for two years. Now let 'em taste the spur. Ram it into 'em and give the rowels a twist.... I wish I had 'em where *you* have 'em. They've sneered at drunken Charlie Hancock all these years. I'd make 'em dizzy if I had the chance, now. I'd tell 'em how to …'

Mortimer escaped from the tirade. He was still weak, as though after a great shock. Sometimes he found himself wondering at the hollowness in his heart, and at the pain, which was like homesickness and fear of battle combined. But then he remembered the girl and the strain of her lips as she denounced him.

He went out into the howl and darkness of the storm for sheer relief.

For forty-eight hours he worked without closing his eyes. Even Jan Erickson broke down before that and lay on the floor of the barracks shed on his back, uttering a snoring sound in his throat though his eyes were wide open, and a black drool ran from the corner of his mouth. Pudge Major developed a sort of asthma. His throat and his entire face swelled. He lay on his bed propped up into the only position in which he could breathe.

Mortimer gave the Chinaman twenty dollars to spend every spare moment at Pudge's bedside; his own place had to be outside, for greater events were happening every hour.

In the middle of the second day of that unrelenting wind, the last defense on top of the bluff gave way and the sand began to flood down into the third of Miller's lakes. The first two had choked up within twenty-four hours of the start of the blow. The backed-up heights of the flowing sand quickly overwhelmed the third. In the thick, horrible dusk cattle were seen, mad with thirst, thrusting their muzzles deep into the wet ooze, stifling, dying in the muck.

That was when John Miller came up to the Hancock house. It happened, at this moment, that Mortimer had dropped into the barracks shed to see the progress of poor Pudge Major and had found him slightly improved. While he was there Wang appeared, coming from the house with incredible speed.

He gave the word that the great man of the range was in the ranch house, and Mortimer went instantly into the parlor of the main building. He found Hancock with his face more swollen and rum-reddened than ever, and in the same half-dressed condition, while Miller, with ten years added to his age, sat with a steaming glass of punch in his hand. He stood up when Mortimer entered.

'He wants help,' said Hancock. His savage exultation at this surrender of his old enemy made him clip the words short. 'I have the vote on this ranch,' he added. 'I have the two-thirds interest behind me, but I want your opinion, Mortimer. Shall we let the Miller cattle water in our lakes? Shall we charge 'em a dollar a head, or is it *safe* to let them use up our reserve supply at any price?'

Mortimer watched the rancher take these humiliating blows with an unmoved face.

'It is true,' said Miller, 'that I am on my knees. I'm begging for water, Mr. Mortimer. Shall I have it?'

'You want it for your own cattle and you want it for those of your friends?' said Mortimer.

'Too many. Can't do it,' said Hancock, shaking his head.

'I would be ashamed to get water for my own cattle and not for the herds of my neighbors,' said Miller. 'Some of us have lived on the range like brothers for several generations.'

'I'm not of that brotherhood, Miller,' snapped

Hancock. He added, 'Can't water the cows of every man under the sky. Can't and won't. There isn't enough in my lakes.'

'I put six feet on each of our dams last year,' said Mortimer.

'Perhaps you did,' said Hancock, 'but still there's not enough to …'

'There's enough water there for the whole community,' said Mortimer. 'We've backed up three times as much …'

'If they get water, they'll pay for it,' said Hancock. 'Business, Miller. Business is the word between us. Do you remember five years ago when I wanted to run a road across that southeastern corner of your place?'

'That was my foreman's work,' said Miller. 'I was not on the place when he refused you.'

'Why didn't you change his mind for him when you got back, then?' demanded Hancock.

'You didn't ask a second time,' said the old rancher.

'Ah, you thought I'd come and crawl to you, did you?' asked Hancock. 'But I'm not that sort. It doesn't run in the Hancock blood to come crawling…. And now I'll tell you what I'll do. I'll let your cows come to my water; but they'll pay a dollar a head for each day spent beside the lakes. Understand? A dollar a head.'

Miller said nothing. His lips pinched hard together.

'This drought may last two weeks, a month,'

said Mortimer, 'before the water holes are cleaned out and before trenches catch the seepage from the choked lakes. The people around here won't pay thirty dollars to water their cows for a month.'

'They won't pay? They will, though,' said Hancock. 'They *won't* pay? I want to see them get one drop of water without handing me cash for it!'

Miller took a deep breath and replaced his untasted glass on the table.

'I think you know what this means, Hancock,' he said. 'There are some impatient men waiting at my house, now. When I tell them what you have to say, I think they're apt to come and get the water they need, in spite of you.'

'My dear Miller,' said Hancock, 'I occasionally have a glass, as perhaps you and the rotten gossips know, but my hand is still steady.' He held out his glass. The liquid stood as steady as a painted color inside it. 'I've lost touch with the rest of the world, but my rifle remains my very good friend,' said Hancock. 'When you and your friends come over, you can have what you wish: water or blood, or both. But for the water you'll pay.'

Miller looked carefully at his host for a moment. Then he turned and left the room in silence.

When he was gone, Hancock threw up a fist and shook it at the ceiling. 'Did you hear me, Harry?' he demanded. 'Did I tell it to him? Did I pour it down his throat? ... Oh, God, I've waited fifteen years to show the range that I'm a man, and now that they're beginning to find it out, they'll keep on finding. Harry, hell is going to pop, and at last I'll be in the middle of it. Not a rum-stew, but a man-sized hell of my own making!'

Argument would have been, of all follies, the most complete. Mortimer sat in a corner of the room with a glass of straight rum and felt it burning the rawness of his throat as he watched Hancock pull on riding clothes. A heavy cartridge belt slanted around his hips, with a big automatic weighting it down on one side. He put on a sombrero and pulled a chin band down to keep it firmly in place. Then he picked up his repeating rifle, and laughed.

A siren began to sound above the house at the same time. It would bring back to the ranch house those fighting cow hands of whom Hancock was so proud and who owed their existence out of jail to his generosity and careless fondness for their bad records in the past. The sound of that siren, cutting through the whirl of the wind, would tell the true story to John Miller as he journeyed back to his ranch. And Mortimer could foretell the great cleaning of guns and gathering of ammunition which would reply to it.

He heard Hancock saying, 'Harry, in a sense it's all owing to you. I've had mental indigestion most of my life because a girl smacked me down. Except for you there'd be choked lakes for Hancock as well as for Miller. But, as it is, I have the bone that the dog will jump for, and I'm going to hold it high! Are you with me?'

'Quit it, Charlie, will you?' said Mortimer. 'You think you're showing yourself a man. You're not. You're being a baby in a tantrum.'

'Before this baby gets through squalling,' said Hancock, 'a lot of big, strong men on this range are going to wish that I never was born. Before I'm through ...'

A hand knocked; the front door pushed open, and a slight figure that staggered into the hallway in a whirl of dust now looked into the living-room with the face of Lou Miller. With her eyes wind-bleared and her hat dragged to the side, and weariness making her walk with a shambling step, she should have looked like nothing worth a second glance; instead, she seemed to Mortimer to be shaped and God-given specially to fill his heart. Her eyes found him and forgot him in the first instant. She said to Hancock, 'My father came to talk business, I know. But he didn't get far, did he?'

'Not one step, Lou,' said Hancock.

'Father came to talk business,' she said. 'But I've come to beg.'

'You?' said Hancock. 'You're Miller's daughter. You can't beg.'

'On my knees, if it will do any good,' said the girl.

'Did *he* send you here?' asked Hancock, with malicious curiosity.

'He doesn't know that I'm here. But if you'll give us a chance I'll let the whole world know the kindness that's in you, Charlie,' she told him.

'Ah, quit all that,' said Hancock.

'Charlie, will you listen to me?' she pleaded.

He began to walk up and down and she followed him, trying to stop him with her gestures.

'They've always smacked me down. By God! If they get anything out of me now, they'll have to fight for it,' he said.

'It can't come to that. God won't let it come to that. Not on this range,' said the girl. She began to cry, and struck herself across the mouth to keep back the sobbing. 'And don't think about the humans. Let's admit that we're a rotten lot, all of us. But think of the poor beasts, Charlie! They're wedged against the fences. The sand is drifting them down. I shone a flashlight across ten thousand pairs of eyes that were dying. Charlie, are you listening to me?'

She pulled softly at his arm, but Hancock was staring up at the ceiling.

'You know something?' he said. 'Back there when I was alive – back there before I turned into rum-bloat and poison ivy, if you'd lifted a finger you wouldn't have had to ask. I would have given you my blood – look – like this – like soup. But the way it is now, I'm finished. I'm going to get one thing out of tonight, and that's a chance to die in a scrap.'

'Don't say that!' she cried out. She stood up on tiptoe, trying to look him in the eye and make him answer her, mind to mind. But he kept his eyes on the ceiling.

He said, 'It's no good. Not if you were Sheba and Cleopatra. I'm cooked. I'm finished. But when they bury me they're going to know that I was a man. Lou, get out. I won't talk any more.'

'I've *got* to talk,' said the girl. 'If you go ahead, there'll be murder in the Chappany.'

'Get out or I'll smack you down,' said Hancock, looking at the ceiling.

It had been an agony to Mortimer. He took the girl by the arm and made her go into the hall with him. 'You can't go home just yet,' he said. 'You're as weak and full of wobbles as a new calf. You can't head off into this wind.'

She leaned against him for a moment, silently gathering strength, and then pushed herself away. She had not met his eyes once; she did not meet them now as she went to the outer door. Mortimer put his hand on its knob.

'Look here,' he said, 'I'm not a coyote or a hydrophobia skunk. You came up and let Hancock talk to you the other day. But what he told you isn't the whole truth. Will you let me speak?'

'I'll go now,' she answered.

'I haven't a right to let you go out and be choked

in the dust,' said Mortimer.

'I'd rather be choked there than here,' she told him. 'Let me go.'

'Sickens you, doesn't it?' asked Mortimer, trying to find something in her face.

'I'll tell you one thing,' she said, staring straight before her. 'There wasn't any hatred in the Chappany Valley till you came. There was love!' Her voice broke. 'We all loved one another. We were happy—'

He said nothing. She made a gesture to indicate that the breaking of her voice meant nothing. Then she added, with a sudden savagery, 'You're from the outside – all of you. Why didn't you stay out? Why don't you go away?'

He felt the words from his heart to his forehead, where a cold pain settled. Then he pulled the door open and took her outside. Her horse had crowded against the house, head down. He helped her into the saddle and saw horse and girl reel as she swung off into the wind. A moment later the darkness ate them up.

He turned and went back into the house.

'Will you listen to me?' asked Mortimer.

'I'll hear no arguments,' said Hancock. 'Now that I'm started I want what lies ahead. You can't turn me, brother!'

Mortimer stood up and tightened his belt a notch. The fatigue which had been growing as a weight in his brain gradually melted away and a cold, clear river of forethought flowed through him. 'I think you mean business, Charlie,' he said.

'I mean it with my whole heart,' said Hancock.

'Do you think your father would approve of this? Would old Jim Hancock refuse water to the cows of his neighbors?' asked Mortimer.

'Old Jim Hancock is an old fool,' said Charlie. 'And he's fifteen miles away in Poplar Springs. Who's going to get to him to ask how he votes on the business? The roads are wind-worn into badlands or else they're drifted belly-deep in silt and sand. Nobody will get to him for a fortnight. And the dance will be over before that.'

'Do you know what it will mean?' asked Mortimer.

'I suppose it means *that*, to begin with,' said Hancock.

He raised a finger for silence, and Mortimer heard it coming down the wind, a long-drawn-out, organlike moaning, or as though all the stops of the organ had been opened, from the shrillest treble to the deepest bass. That was the lowing of the thirst-stricken cattle which milled beyond the fences of the Hancock place, held from their search for water.

Hancock smiled as he listened. 'There it is,' he said. 'The mob's on the stage. They're calling to Oedipus. They want the king. They're waiting for the main actor!' He laughed.

Mortimer struck him across the face with the

flat of his hand. He intended it more as a gesture than a blow, but he hit with more force than he had intended, and Hancock staggered.

'Don't reach for that gun,' said Mortimer.

'No,' said Hancock calmly. 'I know that you could break my back for me.'

'I had to say something to you. Words weren't any good,' remarked Mortimer.

'Ah, you think the ship is about to sink, do you?' asked Hancock, with an ugly twist of his loose mouth. 'You think it's time for the rats to leave. Is that it?'

Mortimer said, 'I came out here on the range to do something that the range didn't want. All I managed to accomplish was to put a prize in your hand that's worth a fight.... Are you hearing me, Hancock?'

'With an extreme and curious interest,' said Charles Hancock.

'I'm not an expert shot,' said Mortimer.

'You're very good if you take time and put your mind on it,' admitted Hancock. 'The making of a real expert.'

'Well, Charlie,' said Mortimer, 'if you kill a man attempting to get his cattle to your water, I'll manage to come to you afterward. You may put the first three bullets into me, Charlie, but I'll kill you as surely as there's wind in the sky.'

They eyed each other with a profound and steady interest.

'Is that all?' asked Hancock.

Mortimer went out of the house and into the barracks shed. He said to Shorty, 'You stay here with Pudge Major. As the rest of the boys come in, send them after me to the Miller place.'

'Send them *where*?' shouted Shorty.

'To the Miller place,' said Mortimer, and went to the barn.

Mortimer did not take a horse from the group of saddle stock which had been tethered in the barn. Instead, he selected a ten-year-old Missouri mule, Chico, with a potbelly that meant as much to his endurance as the fat hump means to the camel, with a lean, scrawny neck, with a head as old as Methuselah's, filled with wicked wisdom, and with four flawless legs and four hoofs of impenetrable iron.

Then Mortimer started the voyage across the Chappany Valley toward the Miller house.

The sky closed with darkness above him when he was halfway across the valley, and he had to put up his bandanna over nose and mouth, as before, to make breathing possible in that continuous smother. The wisdom of Chico, recognizing a trail, enabled the rider to keep his eyes shut most of the way. He opened them to squint, from time to time, at the drifted silt in the valley floor and the bare patches of good grass on the Hancock land, where he had planted the holding coverage to protect the soil.

Here and there, across the Hancock range, acres had given way and blown off like a thought; but the great mass of the soil had held firmly, because for two years he had been covering the weak spots, with a religious zeal. Wherever he had worked, the victory went to him, but it was small consolation. There would be blood on the land before long, he was sure. And in some strange measure that was also his work. But always, as he rode, the sense of irretrievable loss accompanied him, and that hollowness grew in his heart, and that endless defeat. He had acted out with care one great lie in his entire life, and though in the end he had found that it was not acting, but the very truth of his soul, he knew that the girl would never forgive him.

When he got to the Miller place he found automobiles and trucks parked everywhere, with sand drifted body-high around many of them. The patio entrance was three feet deep in drift, and when he reached the interior and tethered Chico to one of the old iron rings that surrounded the court, he stood for a moment and listened to the wind, to the mourning of the cattle down the Chappany, and to the nearer sound of angry voices inside the big house. After that, he entered the place. The uproar came from the big library. He went straight to it and stood winking the grit from his eyes and looking from the threshold over the crowd.

There were fifty men in the room, and none of them were mere cowpunchers. These were the assembled heads of the ranches of the surrounding district, and they meant swift, bitter business. Hancock, if he used guns, would not live long enough for Mortimer to get at him. These armed men would attend to him quickly, and forever.

The whole noise of the argument rolled away into silence as Mortimer showed himself.

John Miller came halfway across the room toward him with quick steps. He said, 'Mr. Mortimer, no man has ever been ordered to leave my house before, but in your case ...'

Mortimer put up a weary hand. 'I'm tired of your pride,' he said. 'I've come over here to see if I can stop murder. Will you listen to me?'

Miller said nothing. He was reaching into his mind for some adequate answer when a gray-headed man said, 'Let's be open about it, Miller. He's younger than we are. He's a tenderfoot. But I've been over some of the Hancock land, and I've seen it holding like a rock. Who made it hold? This fellow did. Give him a dash of credit, and for God's sake let's hear what he has to say. Maybe we have to begin ranching with the A B Cs again; maybe he's to be our teacher.'

Mortimer said, 'Gentlemen, a dollar a head is what Hancock will ask for every head of cattle that waters on our place. That's a good deal of money, and I don't suppose you'll stand for it. If I throw in my third of that dollar, it cuts the price down to sixty-seven cents. I wonder if that will make a sufficient difference to you. Will you do business with Hancock on that basis?'

They were silent as they listened to this proposal. Then John Miller said, 'I understand you donate your third of the spoils?'

'I donate it,' said Mortimer, and yawned. He was very tired.

Miller said, 'Suppose we call this emergency an act of God and refuse to pay a penny for the surplus which our neighbors may happen to have of what means life to all of us?'

'In that case,' said Mortimer wearily, 'I suppose I'm with you. I've sent for my men to follow me over here. I've told Hancock that if he shoots to kill I'll go for his throat.'

He got another silence for that speech. Someone said loudly, 'I thought you said that you knew this fellow, Miller?'

Miller answered in a harsh, strained voice, 'I seem to be a fool, Ollie. It's perfectly apparent that I don't know *any*thing.'

'If you try to rush cattle down to the lakes,' said Mortimer, 'you'll find Charlie Hancock and his men waiting for you, and every puncher on his place shoots straight. There are plenty of you to wipe them out, but there'll be a dozen men dead in the Chappany Valley before the business ends. Another dozen hours won't kill that many cattle out of all the herds that are waiting for water. Let me have that time to get through to Jim Hancock in Poplar Springs.'

John Miller came up to him with a bewildered face. 'You can't get through, Mortimer,' he argued. 'The trail's drifted across knee-deep with sand in a lot of places. I don't think a horse could live through fifteen miles of the dust storm, anyway.'

'A mule could, however,' said Mortimer.

'Suppose you managed by luck to get to Poplar Springs,' said Miller, 'you couldn't get a thing from old Jim Hancock. He hates me and the rest of the ranchers of this district. He doesn't give a hang for anything except a newspaper and a daily game of checkers. I know him like a book, and that's the truth. He'd laugh in your face. He'd rub his hands and warm them at the idea of a war in the Chappany Valley. Mortimer, will you believe me? Very gallant, this intention of yours, but entirely useless. You can't get to Poplar Springs, and, if you do, your trip will be useless.'

Mortimer said, 'Look at these men. They're a sour lot. They mean business. If you can't hold them for a few hours, they'll go down to rush Charlie Hancock's rifles. And dead men piled on one another will be all that I've gained from two years of work.... If I get to Jim Hancock I'll bring him back with me.'

'I can't let you go,' said Miller solemnly.

'I'll have to look at the tethering of my mule,'

said Mortimer. 'Then I'll come back and talk it over with you.'

A maid with a frightened face entered the room and said, 'Mr. Miller, I've been looking everywhere for Miss Louise. She's not in the house, sir. She's not anywhere.'

'Not in the house?' shouted Miller. 'Are you crazy? You mean she's out in this storm? ... Go up into the garret. She'll be there with some of her old gadgets. That's her playground, and she's nine tenths baby, still.'

Of that, Mortimer heard only a whisper that died behind him; he was too full of his own plans and problems. He went back into the patio, untied Chico, and rode out through the patio entrance. The dust-blast half blinded him, instantly, but he turned the mule across the sweep of the wind and headed Chico toward Poplar Springs.

FOUR

Mortimer got three miles of comparatively easy breathing to begin his journey. He saw the whole face of the countryside, sand-buried or sand-swept, and the trail recognizable from time to time, dots and dashes of it in the midst of obliteration.

He had passed the abandoned Carter place, with the sand heaped against the windward walls like shadows of brightness rather than dark, before the storm came at him again like a herd of sky-high elephants, throwing up their trunks and trampling the earth to black smoke. It sounded like a herd of elephants all trumpeting together. He thought he had seen the worst of the business before this, but that black boiling up of trouble was as thick as pitch.

He put his head down and endured, endlessly, while Chico, through that choking smother, found the dots and dashes of the disappearing trail with a faultless instinct. It seemed to Mortimer that the land was like a living body, now bleeding to death. The work of innumerable dead centuries was rushing about him like a nightmare.

Then Chico stumbled on something soft and shied. Mortimer turned the shaft of his pocket torch down through the murk and saw the body of a horse on the ground. It was Hampton. He knew it by the unforgettable streak of white, like a light on the forehead.

He dismounted. Sand was heaped along the back of the dead horse, half burying the body, but the tail blew out with an imitation of life along the wind. Sand filled the dead eyes. The left foreleg was broken below the knee. There was a round bullet hole above the temple that had brought quick death to the thoroughbred. What he guessed back there at Miller's house was true. Lou had headed for town, perhaps in hope of bringing back men of the law to restore peace to the Chappany Valley. She had stripped saddle and girth from Hampton. That meant she was somewhere not far away at this time, with the storm overwhelming her. The saddle would give her a bit of shelter and a shield behind which she could breathe.

He narrowed his eyes to the thinnest slit and held up his hands to turn the immediate edge of the wind, but the rolling darkness showed him only its own face as he rode the mule in circles around the dead body of Hampton. The electric torch was like a lance-shaft, a brittle thing that elongated or broke off short according to the density of the waves of storm that swept upon him. Turning into the wind was like going up a steep hill. Turning away from it was like lurching down a slope.

After a second or third circle he gave up hope, and yet he kept on looking for a sign of her. His eyes saw only splinterings and watery breakings of the torchlight now; they were so filled with fine silt. Then a ghost stepped into the patch of the ray, and it was the girl.

The wind whipped her hair forward into a ragged fluttering of light about her face, and she came on with one hand held out, feeling her way. She thought Mortimer was Sam Pearson and she stumbled on toward the light, crying out, 'Sam! God bless you, dear old Sam! I knew you were my last chance. But I thought ... never could find ...'

The wind blew her words to tattered phrases. It had reddened her eyes like weeping. 'Hampton – beautiful – gone –' she was saying.

The wind thrust her into his arms. She let herself go. There was no strength in all of her except the hands to hold on. He turned and made a windbreak for her. The storm lifted his bandanna from the back of his neck with deliberate malice. The flying sand pricked his skin with a million needle points. Sometimes the drift came bucketing at him out of scoop shovels with a force that staggered him on his planted feet. He had to hold up the girl, too. She was a good weight. He thought of a loose sack with a hundred and twenty-five pounds of Kansas wheat in it. That was why she had a right to despise him, because there was no poet in him. He ought to be thinking of two souls who clung to each other in this wild deluge, this ending of the world. She said, 'I would have gone crazy with fear. But I kept on tying to the thought of you, Sam.'

He had to tell her at once that he was not Sam Pearson, but he could not tell her. He was a thief stealing this moment out of her life, a guilty but inexpressible happiness. The flashlight showed the dust leaping past them, giving a face to the scream of the wind.

She said, 'Father, if he guessed where I was, would simply go plunging out and be lost. But I thought of you, Sam, making up your mind slowly, coming slowly. I knew you wouldn't want to waste all the time you've put in teaching me things. And I knew you'd find me ... God bless you ... God bless you ...'

'Don't say it,' said Mortimer.

His voice put the strength back into her. As her body stiffened, he knew that it was the strength of shock and horror. He turned the light so that it struck upon their faces. No, it was not horror and

128

disgust that he saw, but a profound wonder. The wind kept whipping her hair out like a ragged moment of light in the darkness of the storm. She still held to him.

'*You* came for me?' she asked.

He wanted to bring her back closer into his arms. He wanted to tell her that it wasn't hard to find her; he could have found her in the steam of hell because there was an instinct that would always show him the way. But he couldn't say that. He had to be honest, like a damned fool.

'*You* came for me?' she had asked.

'Partly for you,' said Mortimer.

All at once she was a thousand leagues away from him though she had merely taken one step back.

'Take Chico. He'll pull us through,' said Mortimer, and helped her strongly up into the saddle.

He should have said something else. He should have made some gallant protestation, he knew. Now she was despising him more than ever, as a gross, stupid, grotesque fool; or as a brute who saved her life not for love or pity, but from a sheer grinding sense of duty. He felt that he had lost his chance and that it would never come to him again.

Chico was the captain of the voyage, for through the whirl his instinct clung to the trail; Mortimer clung to a stirrup leather and floundered on, hoping to God that his knees would not give way.

When the sand and flying silt he breathed had choked the wise old mule, he halted, with his head down. Then Mortimer would swab out the nostrils and wash out the mouth of Chico. Sometimes, as he worked, the light from the pocket torch showed him the wind-bleared face of the girl, like a body adrift in the sea. Death could not have taken her farther from him, he knew. Yet she seemed more desirable than ever.

It was not always thick darkness. Sometimes the sky cleared a little, as long rents tore through the whirling explosions of dust, and then by daylight they saw the immensity of the clouds that rolled through the upper heavens and dragged their skirts along the ground.

They had gone on for hours when Mortimer, floundering through a darker bit of twilight, jostled heavily against Chico. The girl halted the mule and stood on the ground offering the reins and the saddle to Mortimer. He was staggering with weariness, but this proffer seemed to him an insulting challenge to his manhood. For answer, he picked her up and pitched her, like a child, high into the saddle. A sweep of the flashlight showed her face saying angry words which the wind blotted out.

Then they went forward again, with the anger clean gone from him. He could see now, in retrospect, that it had been merely a most gallant gesture on her part, but he had been as drunk with fatigue as he was heartsick now.

An age of desperate struggle followed, with his knees turning to water under his weight; and then something cried above him in the wind. It was the girl, pointing. He was able to see, though blurred and dimly, the outlines of Poplar Springs immediately before them!

A moment later they were in the town, they were approaching a light, a door was opening, they were entering a heavenly peace, with the hands of the storm removed and the voice of the storm increasing far away.

He lay on his back on the floor, coughing up black mud and choking on it. A young lad swabbed off his face, and said, 'Your eyes are terrible. I never seen such eyes. Don't it hurt terrible even to wink? Can you see anything?'

'Get that mule into shelter and water him, will you?' said Mortimer.

'He's fixed up already,' answered the lad.

Mortimer groaned and stretched out his arms crosswise. The great fatigue was flowing with a shudder out of his body; the hard floor soaked it up. He closed his eyes. Afterward there were a thousand things to do. This was the rest between rounds and then the hardest part of the fight was to come.

He heard a woman's voice cry out from another room, 'They're from the Chappany! They've come clear down the Chappany! This is Louise Miller!'

Someone jumped across the room toward

Mortimer. He opened his burning eyes and saw a man with a cropped gray head leaning over him and shaking a finger in his face. 'You didn't come down the Chappany!' he shouted. 'Did you come down the Chappany through all that hell?'

'We came down the Chappany,' said Mortimer.

'Bud, I'll take care of him. You run get Mr. Sloan and Pop Enderby and Jiggs Dawson and tell 'em they're going to hear what's happening in the Chappany. If it's blowin' away, Poplar Springs is gunna dry up and fade out. We don't live on nothing much but the Chappany trade.'

Mr. Sloan, the banker, and Enderby, the big cattleman, and Dawson, of the General Store, were only three among thirty when Mortimer sat up to face the crowd that poured into the house. They looked at big Mortimer in a painful silence, those thirty men who were packed across one end of the room. The front door kept opening and people stamped in from the storm, and hushed their footfalls when they saw what was in progress. Now and then the voice of the storm receded and Mortimer could hear the painful, excited breathing of those people in the hall.

Nobody talked except Oliver Sloan, the banker, and he was the only one of the visitors who sat down. He was a huge, wide man with a weight of sagging flesh that seemed to be exhausting his vital forces. In that silence he asked the questions and Mortimer answered.

'How's it look in general?'

'Bad,' said Mortimer.

'Hear from the Starrett place?'

'Yes. It's a sand-heap.'

'Over by Benson's Ford?'

'Don't you get any telephone messages?' asked Mortimer.

'All our lines are down. Hear from over by Benson's Ford?'

'I heard yesterday. The only thing that's left over there is hardpan.'

Half a dozen men drew in long breaths, drinking up that bad news. In Poplar Springs lived retired ranchers from all over the range.

'What about McIntyre's?' asked Sloan.

'The sand is fence-high,' said Mortimer.

'The Hancock place ... that's your own place, isn't it?'

'The soil is holding there. It's only going in spots,' said Mortimer.

'That's your work,' said the banker wearily. 'You said that you'd button down the topsoil; and you've done it?'

'I've done it,' said Mortimer. He broke out: 'I wish to God I could have helped the whole range. I wish I could have taught them. It's a poor happiness to me to save my own land and see the rest go up in smoke.'

No one said anything until the banker spoke again. He paid no attention to Mortimer's last protestation. 'Jenkins' place?' he asked.

'Those hills sheltered that land pretty well,' said Mortimer, 'but the sand is spilling over the edge of the hills and gradually covering the good soil.'

'See Crawford's?'

'Fence-high with drift.'

'The Grand ranch?' asked Sloan. He looked up with desperate eyes at Mortimer.

'I'm sorry,' answered Mortimer slowly.

'It's gone, is it?' whispered the banker.

'Hardpan,' said Mortimer.

Sloan pushed himself up out of his chair. How many of his mortgages were on mere heaps of blow-sand or hardpan acres, no one could tell; but from the ruin in his face the crowd pushed back to either side and let him out into the hall.

Mortimer called after him, 'But there's two thirds of the Chappany still holding. The worst of it there is that the water holes are silted up; even Miller's lakes are gone; and Charles Hancock won't let the cows come to his water. Cattle out there by the thousands are going to die. Is there any way of persuading Jim Hancock to give his son orders to let those cattle in to water?'

'Persuade him?' shouted Sloan. 'By God! I'll wring the orders out of his withered old neck with my own hands! Persuade him! We'll take the hide off his back, and see if that will persuade him!'

The whole mob poured out from the house;

among the rest, Mortimer had one glimpse of the
pale face of Lou Miller, and then she was lost in
the crowd. They moved into the street. They
flowed against the rush of the dust storm into the
General Merchandise Store of Poplar Springs.

To Mortimer's watery eyes the whole store was
like a scene under the sea. A score of men lounged
around the stove, retaining the winter habit in the
midst of the hot weather. There was constant
coughing, for the fine dust which was adrift in the
air constantly irritated the throats of the men. In
a corner two very old men leaned over a checker
game, one with a fine flow of white hair and beard,
and the other as bald and red as a turkey gobbler,
with a hanging double fold of loose red skin
beneath the chin. He gripped with his toothless
gums a clay pipe, polished and brown-black with
interminable years of use. He was Jim Hancock.
In his two years on the ranch, Mortimer had seen
him only once before.

'You talk to him first,' said Sloan.

Mortimer walked toward the players. Someone
near the stove muttered, 'See the eyes of *that* one?
Looks like those eyes had been sandpapered.'

'What will you say to him?' whispered the girl at
the side of Mortimer.

He gave no answer but, stepping to the table,
said, 'Sorry to interrupt you, Mr. Hancock, but ...'

'If you're sorry for it, don't do it,' said Jim
Hancock.

Ben Chalmers, the time-tried opponent of old Hancock, lifted his eyes and his hand from the checkerboard. He stared briefly at the interloper, and dragged his hand slowly down through his beard as he returned his attention to the game.

'Do you remember me, Mr. Hancock?' persisted Mortimer.

'I never heard of nobody I less remembered,' said Hancock, without looking up.

'I'm Mortimer, from your place on the Chappany,' said he.

'Then why don't you stay there?' asked Hancock.

'Miller's lakes are choked with sand.'

'I wish Miller was laying choked in one of 'em,' said Hancock.

'The water holes all over our part of the range are silted up, and so are most of the tanks. There's a water famine. Cows are going to die by thousands unless they can get water,' explained Mortimer.

'Cows have died by the thousands many a time before this,' replied Hancock.

'Thousands and thousands of cattle are milling around the fence between the Miller place and your two lakes,' said Mortimer.

'Let 'em mill and be damned,' answered Hancock.

'More than cattle will be damned,' stated Mortimer.

Hancock jerked up his head at last. 'D'you see me playing a game of checkers, or don't you? Is a man gunna have a little peace in the world, or has he gotta be hounded into his grave by fools like you?'

'The men who own the cattle ... they won't stand by and see them die of thirst. They'll cut the wire of the fences and let them through. It means gun fighting,' said Mortimer.

'Let 'em cut, then,' said Hancock. 'What do I care?'

'Charlie is out with his cowpunchers and rifles to keep those cows back,' the voice of Louise Miller said. 'He intends to shoot.'

Mortimer turned to her. She had sifted through to the front of the crowd.

'I hope he don't miss, then,' said Jim Hancock. 'Charlie always was a boy that wasn't worth nothing except when it comes to a fight. But, when it comes to a pinch, he's the out-fightingest son-of-a-gun that I ever seen. Now shut up, Lou, and don't bother me no more.'

Mortimer cried out, 'If the fight starts, there are two hundred armed men to take care of Charlie and his boys. They'll wash over them. A dozen men may die, but Charlie's sure to be one of them!'

'I hope he is,' answered Jim Hancock. 'It'll save a lot of rum for decent people if Charlie dies now.'

Mortimer moved suddenly with a gesture of surrender. Sloan, the banker, stepped in beside him, and remarked, 'I'll try my hand.... Jim, there's been damned near enough grazing land wiped off the range to ruin Poplar Springs; and if the cattle die this town'll ruin mighty fast. There's nobody but you can give the cows a second chance, without there's a war. Are you going to sit there and let everything go to hell?'

In place of an answer in words, old Jim Hancock reached back to his hip, produced a long-barreled, single-action forty-five, and laid it on his lap. Then he returned to his contemplation of his next move, merely saying, 'Sorry there's been all this damn' palavering, Ben.'

'I don't care what you're sorry about,' said Ben. 'You're spoilin' the game with all this fool talk.'

Another man from the crowd began to shout at old Jim Hancock with a loud voice, but Mortimer had seen enough. He felt sick and weak and utterly defeated. He jerked the door open and went across the street, leaning his body aslant into the thrust of the wind, to Porson's saloon. In the vacant lot beside it the tarpaulin cover which housed a caterpillar tractor flapped and strained like clumsy wings trying to take flight in the wind.

In the saloon he found only two dusty cowpunchers who stood at one end of the bar. Old Rip Porson, himself, leaned in an attitude of profoundly gloomy thought in front of his cracked mirror. He put out the bottle and tall glass for Mortimer's Scotch and soda.

'Ain't I seen you before?' asked Rip.

'Once or twice,' agreed Mortimer.

'You wasn't connected with mirror-busting, a while back, was you?' asked Porson. His angry, birdlike eyes stared into Mortimer's face. 'Because,' said Porson, 'there was thirteen high-power skunks in here, along with one man.'

'That's him, Rip,' said one of the cowpunchers. 'I reckon that's Mortimer, that done the kicking, and the others were them that were kicked.'

'Are you him?' said Rip Porson, sighing. 'I was kind of half hoping that I'd have a chance to open up and speak the mind that's in me to one of them low-down hounds. There used to be *men* on this range, but now there ain't nothing but legs and loud talk, and no hands at all,' said Rip Porson, tipping two fingers of whisky into a glass and tossing it off. 'Now we gotta import strangers like you. So here's to you, and drink her down.'

He sloshed more whisky into the glass and tossed it off. Instead of taking a chaser, he opened his mouth and took one long, panting breath.

Somewhere through the storm came the lowing of a cow, as though she mourned for her calf, and Mortimer's eye wandered as he thought of the milling thousands of foredoomed cattle up the Chappany. A bowl of fresh mint sprigs that stood behind the bar caught his eye, with its suggestion of that green and tender spring which would not come again to such a great portion of the range.

He thought, also, of that stubborn old Jim Hancock, all leather, without blood or heart.

'Can you mix the sort of julep that really talks to a man's insides?' asked Mortimer.

'Me? Can I mix a julep?' asked Rip Porson. 'I don't give a damn what time of year it is, the fellow that drinks my mint julep knows it's Christmas.'

'Build me a pair of them, then,' said Mortimer. 'Build them long and build them strong.' And he laughed a little, feebly, as he spoke. A moment later he was carrying the high, frosted glasses into the General Merchandise Store. For, when he remembered how the whisky in the barroom had relaxed his own troubles, it came to him, very dimly, that perhaps even the iron-hard nature of Jim Hancock might be altered a little.

As he went in, Sloan was going out, with a gray, weary face. He looked at Mortimer with unseeing eyes and passed on; but the remainder of the crowd was packed thick around the checker game where old Jim Hancock, with the revolver on his lap, still struggled through the silent fight against Ben Chalmers. Each had five crowned pieces. Mortimer put down the drinks at the right hand of each player and stepped back.

'It's no good,' said a sour-faced man. 'You can't soften up that old codger. There ain't any kindness left in him.'

The hand of Ben Chalmers left its position

140

beneath his chin, extended, wavered for a moment in the air, seized on a piece, and moved it. Continuing in the same slow, abstracted manner, the hand touched the glass, raised it, and tipped the drink at his lips. Jim Hancock, stirred by the same hypnotic influence, lifted his glass at the same time. Hancock put down his drink with jarring haste.

'Rye!' he exclaimed, making a spitting face. 'Rye!'

'I disrecollect,' said Ben Chalmers slowly, 'but seems like I *have* heard about folks ignorant enough to make a mint julep with Bourbon.'

'Ignorant?' queried Jim Hancock.

'Ignorant,' said Chalmers.

'There's only one state in the Union where a mint julep is made proper,' declared Jim Hancock. 'And that's Kentucky.'

'The Union be hanged,' said Ben Chalmers, 'but the only state is Virginia.'

'Kentucky,' said Jim Hancock.

'Virginia,' said Chalmers.

'Have I been wastin' my time all these years with an ornery old fool that don't know good whisky from bad?' demanded Hancock.

'You come from too far west to know good whisky from bad,' said Chalmers. 'When I think of a man of your years that ain't come to an understanding of a right whisky ...'

'East of Louisville, a right whisky ain't made,'

said Hancock. 'I'm drinkin' to Kentucky and the bluegrass, and to the devil with points east and north ...' He took a long drink of the mint julep and made another face.

'In points east of Kentucky,' said Ben Chalmers, 'this here country got its start. When Washington and the immortal Jefferson was doing their stuff, Kentucky was left to the wild turkeys and the Indians.'

'The breed run out in Virginia,' said Jim Hancock. 'They still got some pretty women, but the men went to Kentucky about a hundred years ago.'

'An outrage and a lie!' said Ben Chalmers.

He pushed himself back with such violence that the table rocked to and fro. The kings on the checkerboard lost their crowns and shuffled out of place as Ben Chalmers rose.

'A Virginia gentleman,' said Ben Chalmers, 'wouldn't go to Kentucky except to spit!'

'Who said Virginians were gentle and who said that they were men?' asked Jim Hancock, rubbing his chin with his fist.

Ben Chalmers uttered an inarticulate cry, fled to the door and through it, into the twilight of the storm outside.

'It *is* a great state, that Kentucky,' suggested Mortimer.

'Son,' said Jim Hancock, 'maybe you ain't quite the damn' fool that I been making you out.

Kentucky is the only state in the country where they breed men and hosses right.'

'They breed horses and men with plenty of bone and blood and nerve,' suggested Mortimer.

'They do,' said Hancock.

'Which is why nobody can understand why you're afraid to go back up the Chappany and keep Charlie from killing a dozen men or so and winding up with a rope around his neck,' continued Mortimer.

'Afraid? Who said afraid?' demanded Hancock, jumping up from the table.

'Shake hands on it, then, and we'll go together as soon as the storm gives us a chance,' invited Mortimer.

'Damn the storm! Why should we wait for the storm to give us a chance?' asked Hancock.

Beyond the window, dimly through the rush and whirl of the dust, Mortimer saw the tarpaulin which covered the caterpillar tractor flapping in the wind like a bird awkwardly tied to the ground. Nothing in the world could move like that caterpillar, through all weathers, over all terrain.

'Who owns that caterpillar?' he asked, pointing.

'It's mine,' said the manager of the General Store.

'Let me rent it to go up the Chappany,' said Mortimer.

'Rent it? I'll give it to you!' cried the manager. 'And, by God, there's nothing else that will take you where you want to go!'

The big machine was ready for use, with a full tank of gas; and the engine started at a touch. Mortimer tried the controls, rear, left, and centre, and the machine answered readily to the levers. Old Jim Hancock, thoroughly equipped with goggles, huddled himself into as small a space as possible on the floorboards. They started without ceremony. A great outbreak of shouting from the crowd seemed to Mortimer only a farewell cheer. He waved his hand in answer and shoved the tractor against the full sweep of the wind. He had full canteens of water and old Jim Hancock on board, and that was all he asked for, except the entire ten miles an hour that the caterpillar could make. That ten miles, added to the cutting edge of the wind, blew the dust right through the wet bandanna that masked him, nose and mouth; it blew the fine dust down to the bottom of his lungs.

Well, there is dust pneumonia also. He thought of that as the machine hit a five-foot sand drift and went through it part climbing, part awallow, with a flag of dust blowing and snapping behind it.

They entered the wide mouth of the Chappany Valley as the tractor put its nose into the soft of a bog, a water hole entirely clogged by drifted silt. Mortimer was backing out of this when a masked figure came up beside him, staggering, with outreaching hands.

144

He knew who it was. He knew instinctively, with a great stroke of the heart. He stopped the caterpillar clear of the bog, pulled Lou Miller into the machine, and put her on the floor. She must have ridden on the bucking, pitching tail of the tractor all the way from Poplar Springs, with the choking torrents of its own dust added to the blind onpouring of the storm. She was almost stifled, now, as he pulled down her bandanna and flashed his torch into a face begrimed and mud-caked to the eyes. Half a canteen squirted over her rinsed her white again, but she still lay gasping. He put his lips to her ears and called, 'Your lungs ... are they burning up? Can you get your breath?'

'I'm all right. Go on!' she answered.

'I'm turning back to Poplar Springs,' he answered.

She caught his arm with both hands and shook it. 'If you turn back, I'll throw myself out of the tractor,' she cried to him desperately. 'Go on! Go on! Think of what's happening up the Chappany!'

'Ay, go on! Go on!' yelled old Jim Hancock with a sudden enthusiasm.

Mortimer went on. The wind-beaten lights of the machine showed him a ten-foot sand drift, curving at the top like a wave about to break. He put on full speed and crashed through it. Sand flowed like heavy water over the entire tractor. He was blinded utterly, but the vibration of the racing caterpillar bucketed out the cargo of sand swiftly, like water. If the fine dust did not get to the bearings, and if the motor was not choked, they might get through.

Another sand wave heaved vaguely before him. He headed at full speed for it, straightening the nose of the caterpillar like the head of a spear for a target....

Far up the Chappany the murk of the day's end had joined the shadow of the storm, and with the coming of the thicker darkness John Miller prepared for the final action. While there was even a flicker of daylight to give the rifles of Charlie Hancock opportunity to aim he would not let his men move forward, but now the night had thickened the air of the valley to soup.

A floundering horse with a rider bent forward along its neck came by, the rider yelling, 'Miller! Hi, Miller!'

'Here!' shouted Miller, and the rider turned in toward him.

He leaned out to grip the pommel of Miller's saddle, and coughed and choked for a moment, head down, before he could speak. Miller took him by the shoulders and shouted at his ear, 'Shorty, was she at the Grimes place? Did you find her at Hogan's? Is there any word?'

'Gone!' gasped Shorty. 'Dave Weller come in and says she ain't at Parker's neither. There ain't no word.'

'The storm has her,' said Miller.

He pulled up his bandanna and spat down-wind. But he could breathe no better after that.

'There's twenty-one years of my life gone,' said John Miller. 'And God be kind to her ...' He gave the word to attack, then. The men were eager for action.

They had waited long enough, they felt, and the great, mournful song of the thirsty cattle was maddening to their ears. The whole throng of ranchers and cow hands poured into the Chappany.

They came with enthusiasm and a determination to rush Charlie Hancock and his men off the face of the earth, but when they put their eyes on the actual field of battle, some of their enthusiasm left them. Near the edge of the Hancock lake a flat-topped mesa jumped up a hundred feet above the valley floor. To climb the boulders and flat walls of the mesa was hard work, even in full daylight without the burden of a gun; to clamber up the height through these streaks of dark and light, with a rifle to manage and good marksmen taking aim from above, looked very bad work, indeed. If the storm had offered complete darkness, they could have fumbled through the safe darkness and grappled with Hancock and his men, but now the sky was half the time covered and half the time lighted through rents and explosive openings. Those gleams were sufficiently frequent to give Hancock's riflemen an excellent chance to command the approaches to their rock.

Miller sent some of his people to climb the bluff above the lake, but when they reached the high land they were able to make out only glimpses of the men among the rocks; and the distance was too great for any sort of accurate shooting. Some of the ranchers wanted to cut the fences and let the cattle go trooping down to water, anyway, but it was readily pointed out to them that Hancock would enjoy nothing more than a chance to practice marksmanship on dumb cattle before he started on human targets.

It was a clumsy impasse. The storm kept bringing them the dolorous chorus of the cattle. They knew the cows were dying momently, going down from weakness and trampled by the milling herd. That was why Miller's crowd wanted blood and wanted it badly, but no one wanted to lead the rush against that impregnable rock.

There was a big rancher named Tucker Weed among Miller's following, a fellow with a voice as loud as that of a champion hog-caller from Missouri. It was he who raised a sound as shrilling as a bugle call and drew the attention of everyone to a pair of lights that staggered up the valley into the breath of the storm.

'What is it?' yelled Tucker Weed. 'It ain't an automobile. No automobile could head into this smother. What is it? It ain't the old red-eyed devil come looking for us, is it?'

John Miller saw the lights disappear, then reflect dimly on the whirl of the storm as the light pointed straight at the sky.

'It's something that knows a fence when it finds one,' said Miller. 'It's hit a fence with a sand drift backed against it.... What can it be?'

The two lights swerved down again, pointed at the earth, and then wavered out into the level of the valley, approaching the huge, melancholy sea-sound of the bellowing cattle. It ran straight for only a moment, however, and then swerved to the left and headed for the rock of Charlie Hancock....

The mourning chorus of the cattle behind the Miller fences had been with them for miles, but now, in a greater burst of light, as the black of the sky opened in a wide central vent, they could see the living acres that milled beyond the fences.

Old Jim Hancock stood up to see, and Mortimer steadied him by gripping his coat at the small of the back.

'Why, damn my old heart and eyes!' said Jim Hancock. 'Why didn't you tell me there was so many thirsty cows up here on the Chappany?'

It made no difference that he *had* been told. They had a demonstration of another sort a moment later when half a dozen young steers, finding some low place in the fence or, more likely, climbing over dead bodies that gave them a take-off to jump the wire, came clear of the fences and rushed at a gallop toward the water of the lake. The leader, after half a dozen strides, bucked into the air, landed on his nose, and lay still. Another and another dropped. From the top of the rock beside Hancock Lake little sparks of light showed where the rifles were playing. The half-dozen steers lay dead long, long before they brought their thirsty muzzles near the water.

'There he is!' shouted Jim Hancock. 'There's that doggone boy of mine, up there and raising hell. Good shooting, Charlie! Good shooting, old feller! ... But, by God, I'm gunna make you wish you'd never seen a gun!'

A sweep of horsemen poured suddenly about him out of the night. As he saw the masked faces and the guns, Mortimer brought the caterpillar to a halt. The cowpunchers were thick around them in an instant, and a voice was yelling, 'It's the dirt doctor and old poison-face Jim Hancock himself ... and there's Lou Miller, as much alive as you and me ...'

There was Miller, himself, at the side of the machine; and now Lou was in his arms, while Jim Hancock piped, 'Clear away from us. Leave me get at that Charlie fool of mine. I'm gunna teach him what comes of spoiling good beef when he ain't hungry.'

Someone reached in and smote the shoulder of

Mortimer; someone shouted, 'Great work, old-timer!' And then the crowd was drawn back and he shoved the caterpillar on toward the rock through a moment of darkness that swallowed the entire picture instantly. The headlights sometimes showed the way a hundred feet ahead; sometimes the brilliant cone choked off a stride away and they were charging blindly into the smoke and smother of the wind; then the zenith split open and light rushed back over the Chappany. They were under the great rock. They were not fifty paces from the rising wall, when a whole volley of bullets struck them. The headlights went out. One of the endless tracks stopped. The caterpiller began to turn clumsily.

Mortimer caught at old Hancock and with him dropped to the floor of the tractor as he shut off the engine. 'Are you hurt, Jim?' he asked.

'Hell, no!' said Hancock. 'But I guess they've shot a leg off this old horse of ours.'

The plunging rain of bullets still rang about them until that open funnel of brilliant sky above them misted over and then closed suddenly with a river of black.

'Will you go on with me, Jim?' shouted Mortimer. 'Will you try to climb up to them with me and talk to Charlie?'

'Don't be a damn' young fool,' said Jim Hancock. 'I'll go alone. Why should you let 'em get at you with their guns?'

151

But Mortimer went with him. He hooked his arm around the hard, withered body of the old man and fairly dragged him through the blind current of the storm until they found the loom of the rock, and then, suddenly, the wall itself. They paused there a moment, gasping, coughing as though they had just escaped from the smoke of a burning house. Then they started up. The big boulders at the foot of the wall offered stepping-stones to begin with, but above them came almost a sheer rise. They had to wait for the next break in the windy darkness of the sky before they could continue, taking advantage of a fissure here and a projection there. Mortimer, keeping just below, helped the old fellow strongly up while Hancock muttered, 'I'll fix him ... beef butcher! ... damn' fool! ...'

They were well up the rock when guns crackled above them rapidly, like pitchpine burning. A bullet streaked a white scar across the rock in front of Mortimer's face; another raked him through the back muscles with an exquisite stroke of agony; then a fist-stroke and knife-thrust combined lanced him in the side. He had a good handhold on a projecting spur of rock, so he managed to keep his place; and when old Hancock dropped, suddenly, he managed to catch him by the coat and hold him swinging out over empty space, though that effort cost him nearly the last of his strength.

A mercy of the wind closed up the gap in the sky, at that moment; and in the darkness the gunfire ended.

Old Jim, agile as a dried-up tomcat, went clawing up the rock, screeching, 'Charlie! Charlie! You double-jointed jackass! Put down them guns or I'll ...'

Mortimer followed the inspired fury of the old fellow, but his strength was running out of him. The light came back a moment later and made him shrink as though it had been the flash of a knife. And then he saw Jim Hancock standing on the lip of the rock above him, shaking one fist above his head. Men loomed beside him. The soft bulk of Charlie Hancock appeared. And Mortimer drew himself up to the flat top of the mesa. When he got there, he had to lie out flat. The pain left his side and burned only in his brain.

He could hear Jim Hancock shouting, 'Get down there! I hope they drill you full of lead when you come to 'em, begging, with your hands up. Get down there and tell 'em to open the fences up and let the cows through! Save your damned face if you can – tell 'em it was a joke! Your ma died for you, and, damn you, you been nothing but a long, cold winter to me all your life. Get out of my sight!' ...

There seemed to be light still in the sky, but a darkness crawled out of Mortimer's brain and covered his eyes.

After a time he saw that he was lying near a fire that burned behind a screen of boulders at the top of the mesa. A withered forearm with a bandage around it appeared in his line of sight. A hand lifted his head.

'Take a shot of this,' said Jim Hancock, holding a whisky flask at his lips.

He got down a good, long swallow of the stuff. It burned some of the torment away.

Jim Hancock said, 'You take the rest.... If you die, I'm gunna have 'em hanged, every damn' one of 'em ... and we won't wait for the law, neither.'

'No,' said a big voice. 'We won't wait for no law!'

That was Jan Erickson. And there were others of the gang watching their chief with grimly set faces.

'Yes, sir,' said Jim Hancock, 'if you pass out, we're gunna string 'em up, and I'll help pull on the ropes. So you rest nice and easy.'

It was an odd way of giving comfort. Mortimer tried to laugh a bit, but fingers of pain seemed to tear him half apart.

'I'm gunna lift up your head and leave you have a look at what's happening,' said Hancock.

Accordingly, slowly and carefully he lifted Mortimer's head and shoulders until he could look over the sloping top of the mesa and down into the valley of the Chappany at Hancock Lake. The waters of it seemed to have living shores until his eyes cleared a little and he could see the cattle ten and twenty deep as they drank up life and new strength.

'That's pretty good,' said Mortimer. 'I'm glad I saw that,' he said.

'Don't talk,' said Hancock. 'They've got you drilled right through the lungs, and talking is sure poison for you.'

The darkness, like living shadows in the corners of a room, began to crawl out over the eyes of Mortimer. If he were shot through the lungs, he had to die and he was sure that he was dying at that moment. 'I've got to talk,' he said.

'Shut your mouth!' commanded Hancock.

Mortimer forced out the words slowly: 'Tell Lou Miller it was never a joke. I loved her. Tell her I loved her, but I don't blame her for the way she felt....'

He seemed to be walking, then, through infinite darkness, opening doors, feeling his way down blank walls, finding more doors, opening them, and something was whistling to him far away. He opened his eyes. It was the scream of the storm that he had been hearing, but far withdrawn again into the heart of the sky.

He looked down at the big arch of his chest and the great bandage which was being unwrapped by slender hands, unlike the hands one finds on a cattle range. His lips were saying, 'Somebody promise to tell Lou Miller ...'

Someone leaned over him, saying, 'I know —

darling!'

Now, by an effort of peering into distance, he made out her face. She was much older. She was so drawn and white and old that, to any ordinary eye, half of her beauty was surely gone; but his eye alone, which knew how to see her, found her far more beautiful than ever.

His breast lay bare as a voice said, 'Don't let him talk.'

'Make him stop talking, Lou,' said Miller's voice out of the darkness.

She touched the lips of Mortimer, and he kissed her hand. If there were only a few moments left, words were no good, after all. Touching her and looking at her was all that mattered.

The crisp voice of command said, 'He's lost blood. He's lost buckets of blood, but I don't think … give me that probe.'

A finger of consummate pain entered his breast, his side, glided back.

'Certainly not!' said that voice of authority. 'The man has ribs like the ribs of a ship. And the bullet glanced around them.'

The darkness covered Mortimer's eyes with a sudden hand, but through the shadow he could hear the sudden, joyful outcry of the girl, fading out of his consciousness rapidly, but lodging somewhere in his heart the promise of life and of happiness.

THE CROSS BRAND

One

Jack Bristol removed his feet from the table-edge and sat up. It was a tribute of attention which any other man in Arizona would have paid, willingly, to Sheriff Harry Ganton; but what filled the eye of Jack Bristol was not the sheriff's person but the sheriff's horse.

The sight of the brown mare plucked a string in his heart of hearts and filled him with a melancholy of yearning. Such a horse as that could not be bought or bred. She was one of those rare sports which are produced by chance. A grayhound had more speed; a mountain sheep was more nimble climbing the rocks; but brown Susan could imitate both. She was put together with a mathematical nicety, like Jack Bristol's gun, of which she often made him think. But above and beyond physical prowess, it was Susan's personality which delighted Jack. Her starred forehead, her quick-stirring little ears, her great, bright, gentle eyes, and a wise way she had of cocking her head to one side; in short, she fitted nicely into the heart of Jack Bristol and he groaned to think that another man must always ride her.

She came to a stop just in front of the house. The big sheriff dismounted. As he stood beside her, his six feet and odd inches of height, his two hundred pounds of bone and muscle, made her seem hardly more than a pony – in fact she was a scant fifteen three, Jack knew – yet she had carried Ganton prodigious distances between sunrise and dark.

She was the foundation upon which his reputation had been raised. Two years before Susan was a tender three year old and Harry Ganton was a newly elected and youthful sheriff. In the past twenty-four months Susan had demonstrated that robbers who committed crimes in the district which Ganton protected were fools if they depended for safety upon the speed of their horses. Brown Susan ran them down with consummate ease, and once she brought Harry Ganton within range he was a known fighter.

The sheriff stepped out of sight and appeared again at the door of the house; Jack Bristol greeted him with a wave of the hand and went to the window where Susan had come to whinny to him with bright eyes of expectancy. He began to slit apples into narrow sectors. She took them daintily from his fingers. The sheriff, in the meantime, took a chair which he could tilt back against the wall.

'Too bad you don't own Sue,' he said. 'You and her get on uncommon well, Jack.'

The head of Jack Bristol jerked around.

'Maybe she's for sale?' he asked. But he sighed and shook his head without waiting for the answer.

'Suppose she were?' said he sheriff. 'Would you have the price to spare?'

'I'd find the price,' said Jack. He held a glistening bit of apple away, while she reached greedily and vainly for it. 'I'd find the price.'

'How?' insisted Ganton.

Jack Bristol turned to the other with a peculiarly characteristic air of disdain, as though he were one for whom probabilities had no interest. He was a handsome fellow with lean, clear-cut features and a blue eye which was almost black; and he had a bold and confident glance which now dwelt upon the sheriff with unbearable steadiness. He seemed to have many words on the tip of his tongue, but he only said, 'There are ways!'

At this the sheriff shrugged his shoulders. They were of one age, just at thirty; but Jack Bristol looked five years younger and the sheriff seemed in excess of his real age by the same margin. Burdens honorably assumed and patiently borne, fierce labor, honest methods, had marked him with a gray about the forehead and lined his face to sternness or to weariness. But the skin of Jack Bristol was as smooth as the skin of a child. His eye was as clear. The fingers which poised the fragment of apple above the velvet nose of Susan were as tapered as the fingers of a woman. Labor had never misshaped that hand or calloused it. The sheriff marked these things with a touch of bitterness. They had gone to the same school at the same time. He had fought his way through the studies. Jack Bristol, never opening a book, the hours of his bright leisure never encroached upon, had always led the class. Now, so many years later, it mattered not that Ganton could savagely assure himself of his success and Jack's failure. The instant he came into the presence of the latter, he felt his crushing inferiority.

'There are ways, eh?' echoed Ganton. 'But how, Jack? The cards?'

This time Jack Bristol turned his back squarely upon the mare, though one hand, behind him, continued to pat her.

'What the devil do you mean by that?' he asked.

'I mean that everybody in town knows how you've kept your head up,' answered the sheriff. 'We know that you're a fat one with the cards!'

'A crooked gambler, eh?'

'I haven't said that. I think you'd be honest at it.'

'Thank you.'

'Simply because you're too proud to admit that another man might have better luck than you.'

'What the devil ails you, Ganton? What do you mean by coming here with this sort of talk? What have I and my ways to do with you? Have you turned sky-pilot, maybe? Going to try for two jobs at once?'

The sheriff flushed.

'I'll tell you why I've come. I've always kept out of your way —'

'Because you had nothing on me!'

'Maybe. I say, I've never bothered you until you mixed up with my business. Then I had to let you know that I was around.'

'In your business?'

'Last week you went to Hemingworth to the dance in the schoolhouse, didn't you?'

Jack Bristol was again half turned away, paying far more attention to the feeding of the mare than to the words of the sheriff. But Ganton persisted in his questions in spite of this insulting demeanor.

'I suppose I did,' nodded Jack. 'I've forgotten.'

'Forgotten! That's the place where you met Maude Purcell and danced half the dances with her and made her town talk next day and ever since.'

'Maude Purcell? I remember that name.'

'I guess you do!'

'She's a girl with pale eyes and freckles across her nose. Kind of cross-eyed, too, isn't she?'

He spoke carelessly, busy with the feeding of Susan. But from the corner of his eye he saw the sheriff writhe and it gave him a malicious pleasure.

'I can't let you talk like that,' burst out the sheriff. 'Jack, you didn't know or else not even you would of dared to talk like this, but me and Maude are engaged to get married!'

'You are?' said Jack. First he gave the last of the apple to the mare. Then he took out a handkerchief and began to wipe his fingers. Last of all, he turned to the sheriff. 'Of course,' he said, 'in that case I'm mighty sorry, Harry. Wouldn't have hurt your feelings for the world!'

The sheriff, very red of face, watched him narrowly, and sighed. He had a perfect conviction that Jack Bristol knew all about his relations with pretty Maude Purcell. He was reasonably sure that it was on this very account that Jack had flirted so outrageously with Maude on that evening. But Bristol was no man to force into a corner; it would not do to anger him unless that were a last resource.

'What I mean,' said the sheriff, 'is this: Maude and me *were* engaged. But – the other day we busted it off!'

Jack started. He flashed at the sheriff a glance of real concern, but the latter was looking down in anguish to the floor and when he raised his head again, Jack had succeeded in smoothing his expression to indifference.

'She gave me over,' said the sheriff again. He

mopped his forehead. 'And the reason she done it was because – because of the way you talked to her that night at the dance! That's why I've come here to talk to you, Jack!'

Jack Bristol looked back into his mind in dismay. Maude Purcell, on that night, with her yellow hair and blue dress and gay smile, had been the prettiest girl on the dance floor. Also, she gained piquancy through Jack's knowledge that she was the bride-to-be of the sheriff. He and Harry Ganton were old enemies. They were the bywords of the town. He was the example of riotous living and idleness held up to the youth of the community. Harry Ganton was the example of what a young man may accomplish by industry and frugal living. It had been a shrewd temptation to win the girl away from thoughts of her lover for a single evening. But to lead to this result certainly had never been in his mind.

'And the first thing I got to ask,' said the sheriff, 'is this: what sort of intentions have you got toward Maude?'

Jack Bristol had been on the verge of stepping across the room, shaking the hand of Harry with an apology for his conduct, and promising his best assistance in smoothing out the tangle. But the stern voice of the sheriff threw him back into another mood at once. He could never be driven with whips where he might be led by the slightest crooking of a finger. In fact, the humor of Jack was generally that of a spoiled boy.

'Are you her father?' asked Jack. 'Where's your right to ask me what my intentions are?'

'I got the right of a man whose happiness is tied up in what you may do!' exclaimed poor Ganton, turning pale with emotion.

'Well, Harry, I haven't made up my mind!'

'Then, gimme a chance to help you make it up!'

'Go as far as you like.'

'In the first place, are you the sort that makes a marrying man?'

'How d'you mean by that?'

'Ain't a man, if he's going to marry, got to be the sort that will provide a home for his wife and enough for her and their kids to live on?'

'You think I couldn't do that?'

'You could do it plumb easy. That ain't the thing. Would you do it? Wouldn't you get tired of the house and everything in it? Wouldn't you want a change? Ain't that the way you've been all the rest of your life?'

'Maybe it is.'

'It's a sure enough fact. Look around here at this house. Why, I can remember on the day your father died, this was the best house in Red Bend. We all used to look up to it. It was the sort of a house that we all wanted to build and live in some day if we ever got to be that rich. And look at the house now! Look where the rain has leaked in through the roof that you ain't ever repaired; see where it's streaked and stained the walls! Look where the wallpaper is beginning to peel off and where it's faded. The flooring is all in waves in your big dining-room. You've sold all the good furniture. You've got only a bunch of junk left. The roof of your big barn is busted and sagging in. Your cows have been sold down to just a few dozen. You only got a couple of hosses. You've loaded your ranch up to the ears with mortgages. And now I ask you, Jack, to stand back and look at things fair and square, including yourself. After you've had a good look, tell me if you're the kind that makes a family happy. Are you?'

Against his will, Jack Bristol had been forced to follow the eager words of the sheriff. The unhappy picture was painted in vivid strokes, and out of his memory was drawn the coloring for it. All the prosperity of his youth floated past him like a tantalizing vision. Behind it was the face of his father, that too-indulgent man.

It is when we feel our guilt too keenly that we are most apt to anger. Also, no doubt the sheriff had paid more attention to truth than to tact.

'Ganton,' said Jack. 'I'm glad to know what you think of me. But it don't follow that that's what I think of myself. As for the girl, if she got tired of you I'm sorry for you, but maybe she figures it shows she has sense. We all have a right to our opinions, eh?'

The sheriff changed color again. But he kept himself strongly under control.

'You're hot-headed now, Jack. But I know that you ain't as hard as all that. You ain't going to keep up your game with Maude just for the sake of putting me in the fire, eh?'

'What game?' said Jack. 'Suppose that Maude and I should decide to step off together? What then? Why shouldn't we marry?'

'Why?' echoed the sheriff, looking wildly about him. 'Jack, you don't mean it!'

'Is there any law on your side to stop us?' asked the other cruelly.

'There is,' said the sheriff, and he rose from his chair.

'Name it, partner!'

'It's this.'

The sheriff tapped the gun hanging at his side.

'I'll put an end to you first, Bristol. I've seen you spoil everything you've touched. I ain't going to see you spoil her face – not while I'm wearing a gun!'

Jack Bristol gasped, as one immensely surprised. Anger followed more slowly. 'You damned blockhead!' he fumbled for words. 'Stop me with a gun – me?'

His right hand trembled down to his own weapon and came away again. He whipped out Bull Durham and brown papers and rolled himself a smoke which he lighted and walked hurriedly up and down the room, a wisp of smoke following him and banking up into a little cloud when he turned.

'Get out, Harry!' he implored the sheriff. 'Get out before something happens. I know you're a good fighter. Everybody around these parts thinks that you can't be beat. But you know and I know that I'm faster and straighter with a gun. I dunno what's got into your crazy head. Are you hunting for a way to die?'

'It don't make no difference,' said the sheriff. 'I've come here to make you promise that you'd give up Maude. If I couldn't persuade you to do it, I was going to make you. And that goes! I'd rather see you dead and me hanging for the murder than to have Maude's life ruined. What are both of our lives compared with hers?'

'Harry, go home and think it over,' said Jack Bristol. 'You ain't talking sense. You know you can't budge me. You ain't man enough. You never were!'

'Answer me one way or the other, Jack. Will you give her up? You know that even if you had her you couldn't be true to her. You ain't made that way. All your life the girls have talked soft to you. You've had your way paved with smiles. They don't mean nothing to you. Maude would be getting the first wrinkles before long. And then you'd be through with her. I know how it'd be. You'd leave her. You've never stuck to the same girl for a whole summer. Ain't that a fact? So I ask you – will you give her up?'

'I'll see you damned first!'

'Then God help one of us!'

He pitched himself to one side while a swift flexion of hand and wrist brought out the Colt. It began spitting fire and ploughing the floor with lead. The first bullet split a board at the feet of Jack Bristol. The second, as the gun was raised, was sure to drive into the body of Jack himself. But before that second shot a forty-five calibre slug struck the sheriff in the breast and knocked him against the wall.

He recoiled, gasping, fired from a wobbling hand a bullet that tore upward through the roof, and then dropped upon his face.

Two

That impact forced up on either side of the body a puff of dust, which was deep on the floor. Before the little clouds settled, Jack Bristol was beside the prostrate man and had jerked him over to his back. There was a deep gash across his forehead where he had struck the floor. Blood was hot and thick on the breast of his coat. Jack kneeled, fumbled for the pulse, felt none, and sprang up again to flee for his life.

Down the street men were calling. He heard them with wonderful clearness.

'Hey, Billy, come in! There's hell popping up at –'

'I'm coming. Where's Jordan? Hey, Pop, we've got to get –'

'Run, boys. There's enough of us!'

But still they clamored as they swept slowly up the street. No, they were not moving slowly. They were only slow by comparison with the leaping speed with which the brain of Jack Bristol was considering possibilities.

Should he stay to demand his trial as a man fighting in self-defense? No, that would never do; he could hear beforehand the roar of angry mirth with which Red Bend would hear of this plea from

15

Jack Bristol, gambler from time to time, spendthrift on all occasions while the money lasted, and gunfighter extraordinary. No, he must never dream of standing his ground. His first difficulty would be to find a fast horse. His gray gelding was fast enough to escape most pursuit, but the gray was in a distant pasture. But why should be worry about getting a fast horse when brown Susan herself stood just outside his window? And why not be hunted for horse-stealing as well as murder?

He was out of the window as that thought half formed. Susan drew back, but only a step. He whipped into the saddle with half a dozen men plunging toward him, the leaders not fifty yards away, with the liquid dust spurting up around their feet. He had known those men all his life. But now they went at him like town-dogs at a wolf, yelling, 'He's got Harry – he's dropped the sheriff – shoot the hound!'

Jack Bristol sent Sue into a racing gallop with a single word. In an instant he had twitched her around the corner of the house with a flight of bullets singing behind her. She took a high fence flying. She sprinted across a cleared space beyond. She winged her way across a second fence and was hopelessly out of range for effective revolver shooting before the pursuers reached the corner of the house. So they tumbled into the house, instead of continuing, and there they found the sheriff, dripping with blood, in the act of rising from the floor.

'Leave Jack alone!' were his first words. 'I'm not killed. I brung this on myself. He glanced a chunk of lead along my ribs, and I deserved it! Get Doc Chisholm, boys!'

'But Jack has grabbed Susan!'

Here the sheriff groaned, but almost at once he controlled himself and answered, 'Then let him take her till he finds out that he ain't wanted here. All I hope to God is that he don't turn desperado because he thinks that he's done one killing already.'

Of course Jack Bristol could not know it, but that was the reason there was no pursuit. He himself attributed it to the known speed of brown Susan. The good citizens of Red Bend knew enough about her not to expect to run her down in a straight chase; only by maneuver and adroit laying of traps could they expect to capture the man who bestrode her. Such was the reason to which Jack Bristol attributed the failure of any pursuit, though, as a matter of fact, Sheriff Ganton was sending out hasty messages in all directions striving to head off the fugitive and let him know that the law had no claim against him. It was all the easier for the sheriff to send those messages because, that night, Maude Purcell sat by his bed to nurse him. The more brilliant and dashing figure of Jack Bristol might have turned her head for the instant, but when she heard of the wounding of Harry Ganton all doubt was dissolved. A voice spoke out of her heart and drove her to the sheriff's side.

But that night Jack Bristol squatted beside the thin and wavering smoke of his camp-fire and peered from his hilltop into the desert horizon with the feeling that the hostility of the world encompassed him with full as perfect and unbroken a circle. And in truth it was not altogether an unpleasant sensation. It was a test of strength, and he had plenty of that. He stretched his arms and felt the long muscles give with a quiver. Yes, he had plenty of strength. He felt, also, that for the first time he was playing the rôle for which he was intended. He was no producer. He was simply a consumer. He was framed by nature to take, not to make. He was equipped with an eye which saw more surely, a hand which struck more quickly, a soul without dread of others. And all his life he had felt that law was a burden not made for him to carry.

Now the band was snapped and as a first fruit of his labor – behold brown Susan! He turned with a word. The mare came to him like a dog. She regarded him with glistening, affectionate eyes until a cloud of smoke filled her nostrils. She snorted the smoke out and retreated. But still, from the little distance, she regarded him with pricking ears. He had known her since she was a foal. He had loved her from the first as a miracle of horseflesh. Harry Ganton, consenting to his plea, had allowed him to break the filly in her third year. And now, in her fifth, what wonder was it that she obeyed him almost by instinct. The sheriff had been like an interloper upon her back. Here was her true master! And was it not worth while to be guilty of a theft when stealing brought such a reward as this?

In a sort of ecstasy, Jack Bristol sprang up and began pacing up and down. They would never catch him, now that he had brown Susan. No doubt they were laying their traps, even now. But their traps would never catch him. Other men, weaker men, after they committed their crimes, were sure to circle back to their home towns sooner or later. But he would prove the exception. There were no ties of a sufficient strength to make him return.

No, he would lay a course straight to the north and strike a thousand miles into the mountains.

He lived up to the letter of that resolution. For the three following days he pressed on at great speed to outstrip the first rush of the pursuit. At the end of that time he struck a more steady and easy gait and every stage of the journey brought him further and further on the journey north. During the first week, if he had gone into any town, he would probably have found news which would have made him return on his tracks. But he avoided all towns, and soon he was in a strange land to which the following messages of honest Harry Ganton never extended.

So the day at last came, far, far north in the Rockies, when he decided that he must have come into a new land where no one could have heard of him. Brown Susan had just topped a great height. From the shoulder of the mountain they saw a host of smaller peaks marching away in ridge on ridge to the farther north, all as sharp as waves which a storm has whipped up to points. Heavy forest filled the hollows and the lower stretches. It thinned as it climbed, until it came to the desert at timberline.

From that point of vantage, it seemed an eternity of mountains. They seemed to roll out in all directions to the end of the world. It was sunset time. The summits were bright; the lowlands were already black. And Jack Bristol, born and bred to the open of the flat desert, shuddered a little before he allowed Susan to lurch onto the downslope.

All strange country is apt to be terrible. This prospect chilled the man from the desert to the very heart. But he reassured himself. He had lived on the country through a thousand mile trip. He had not spent a cent. On one occasion he had slipped into an outlying ranch-house and stolen an ample supply of ammunition. Otherwise he had not needed the assistance of men. Neither had brown Susan. She had the lines of an Arab; but she had the incredible durability of a mustang. Now she was a trifle gaunt of belly, her forward ribs were showing, but her head was as high, her eye as bright, her tail as arched as when she began the long journey. If horse and rider could survive what they had survived, there was surely nothing to concern them even in a forest wilderness. Where there were living trees other things must live also.

But when they reached the bottom of the slope, Susan going with goat-footed agility among the rocks, and the damp, thick shadow of premature night closed above their heads, Jack Bristol cursed softly, and it seemed to him that half of the high spirit went out of the mare at the same instant. She went timorously on. A great roaring grew out at them from the right. It turned into the distinguishable dashing of a waterfall. And this, in turn, struck out a thousand varying echoes from cliffs and steep hillsides, so that noises continually played around them. Next, they entered a blackness of a great forest. They made their way, not by light, but by distinguishing shadows among shadows. And the penetrating dampness was like an accumulating weight upon the spirit of Jack Bristol.

The way at length began to pitch up again. The trees grew more sparse. And presently, opening into a pleasant clearing, he found himself face to face with a little cabin. It was made of logs, but it was quite pretentious in size. Rather than use up any of the arable land in the level space below it, and on account of which, no doubt, it had been built, the cabin stood among the rocks of the farther slope, leaning back to keep from a fall. Altogether, it seemed to Jack Bristol the most beautiful dwelling he had ever looked upon.

A horse neighed from a small pasture near the house. Susan quivered on the verge of replying, but a sharp slap on the flank made her shake her head and change her mind with a soft little grunt. In the meantime, from his place of secure shadow, Jack watched the smoke rise straight above the stove-pipe until it reached a region of greater light. The smoke column, for mysterious reasons, was an assurance that kindly people inhabited the house. To be sure, it would be better to go on, but when the wind carried a faint scent of frying bacon to the nostrils of Bristol, he gave way.

He crossed the clearing. Without dismounting, he leaned from the saddle and tapped at the door. It was opened by a bald-headed man with a Roman nose and a great mass of dirty-gray beard. His sleeves were rolled up over hairy forearms. In one hand he carried a great butcher knife, greasy and steaming.

'Howdy,' said Jack Bristol. 'Have you got room for an extra man tonight?'

'Howdy, stranger,' said the man of the log cabin. He paused while he surveyed Jack keenly. 'I reckon I might.'

Three

When he came in, carrying his bridle and the saddle heavy with his pack, he found that the interior of the cabin was less in keeping with its exterior and more in keeping with the appearance of the big man of the bald head. For there was a great deal of dirt and confusion and darkness. The cabin had been laid out and built upon a most pretentious scale as though there had been any quantity of muscle and ax-power available at the time of its construction. Besides this big central room, there was another room at each end of the house, though apparently these apartments were now of use merely as junk rooms.

It was plain, at a glance, that a number of men, and only men, lived here. No woman could have endured such confusion for an instant. Guns, harness, old clothes in varying stages of dirt and decay, rusted spurs, broken knives, homemade furniture, shattered by ill usage, littered the floor or hung from pegs along the wall. Every corner was a junk heap. The useable space on the floor was an elipse framed with refuse. No one who lived in this adobe had ever thought of throwing things away. What was broken lay where it fell until it was kicked from under foot and landed crashing against the wall.

Jack went into the room at the western end of the house and cleared a space to lay down his blankets. Then he returned to the host who was in the act of dropping more wood into the stove. As he did so, the red flame leaped, and by that light he saw the mountaineer more clearly. The skin of his face glistened as though coated with a continual perspiration, in all the places where the beard did not grow. But the beard came up high on the cheeks and was only trimmed, one could see, where it threatened to get in the way by becoming too long. To ward against that, it was chopped off square a few inches below the chin. And it thrust straight out in a wiry tangle.

The outthrust of the beard completed the regularity of the facial angle. The slope carried up from the beard along the hooked nose, and from the nose along a narrow, sharply slanted forehead. In the middle of that forehead was a peculiar scar in the form of a roughly made cross. Jack had not seen it at first, but when the fire leaped, the scar glistened white and was plainly visible.

Altogether he was an ugly fellow, and his ugliness was summed up in a pair of eyes which, considering the great length of the face and the great bulk of the body, were amazingly small. When Jack came closer, he noted a peculiar freak about those eyes. The beard was chiefly gray and dirt in color. But once it must have been a rich red. And the eyelashes, which were of remarkable length, were still of the original deep red, unfaded to their very tips. So that when he squinted it was almost as though he were looking out of reddish eyes.

He was squinting now, as he looked across at Jack Bristol.

'A hoss like that one you ride — a man must be pretty interested in traveling fast to want a hoss like that,' observed the mountaineer.

'Maybe.' said Jack, and as he spoke he went to the back door of the house, opened it, and whistled. At once brown Susan whinneyed in answer. During their three weeks on the road they had grown wonderfully intimate, wonderfully in accord.

The man of the cabin marked this interchange of calls with a gaping interest.

'Might be a circus hoss, to be as smart as that!' he suggested.

'Might be,' answered Jack Bristol.

His reluctance to talk brought a scowl from the other. The big man shifted his weight from one foot to the other, widening the distance between his feet, and hitched his trousers higher. They were secured with a heavy canvas belt, drawn extremely tight. For, in spite of his fifty odd years of age, the man of the cabin was as gaunt-waisted as a youth. He was almost as agile, also, in his movements around the cabin, stepping with the gliding ease of a young athlete. Jack Bristol watched him with a growing aversion. He could not talk to such a great beast of a man, but since he was about to accept the hospitality of the fellow he was ill at ease.

Supper, however, was now ready. They ate boiled potatoes, half seared bacon, stale corn pone, and coffee which was an impenetrable and inky black. And while they ate, on either side of the rough-hewn plank laid on sawbucks which served as a table, they spoke not a word. Jack Bristol rallied himself once or twice to speak, but on each occasion his voice failed him – for when he lifted his glance he never failed to be startled and awed by the red-tinted eyes of the man of the mountains.

Afterward, Jack retired to the pasture, saw that all was well with the mare, and then came in to his blankets. He had barely turned himself in them when he was soundly asleep.

That sleep was broken up by a crashing fall. He sat up and found that the door to his sleeping room was dimly outlined with light, but after the noise there was no sound. A sudden fear gripped Jack Bristol. He realized, in fact, that all his nerves were on edge, for in his sleep he had dreamed of the man of the bald head and the red-fringed eyes, and the dream had been a horror. He stole to the door, and lying down flat on his side, he found that he was able to look into the larger room, and there he saw not one, but two men. The one was his host of earlier in the evening. The other was a younger man, who was also less bulky. The lower half of his face was shrouded, like that of the elder man, with dense beard, save that in his case the beard was of jetty black. They sat now with their heads raised, in the attitude of people listening. The stranger was in the act of finishing a meal. His right hand still surrounded his tin coffee cup. His left hand shoved back his plate.

Presently he shrugged his shoulders, leaned, picked up from the floor another tin plate, whose fall had apparently caused the racket. They conversed for a moment, now, in murmuring voices, not a syllable of which reached the understanding of Jack Bristol. But he had seen and heard enough to alarm him seriously. The fall of a plate would not have been enough to freeze them into such attitudes as he had discovered them in if their minds had been innocently employed. And neither would it be necessary for them to lower their voices so much now. Certainly it was not mere consideration for the sleeping guest which controlled them.

The younger man was now talking eagerly, with many gestures, while the other listened with a scowl so black that the shining scar on his forehead quite disappeared. He shook his head violently from time to time, but the younger still insisted and finally seemed to beat down the resistance of him of the bald head. He half rose. He swept his right hand through a curving, horizontal line in the air, then, with both hands he gestured down. And it came sharply home to Jack Bristol that they were talking about a horse. They were talking about a horse and therefore they must be talking about Susan. For who could speak of any other when brown Susan was near?

The conclusion they reached was now patent. They started up from the table of one accord. Once the elder man was persuaded, he was completely of the youngster's mind. He caught up from the table a long revolver which had been lying there while they talked. The youth produced two weapons of the same sort, and side by side they strode softly down the room and straight toward the door behind which Jack Bristol lay. But the revolvers were not the chief center of his interest. That upon which his gaze fastened was the forehead of the youth which, when the latter turned toward the door, displayed upon it a great glistening scar in the shape of a cross!

For a moment Jack could not stir. Even noticed at random upon the face of one man, that scar had been a grisly and forbidding thing, but seen on another it was increased a thousand fold in interest. It became a horror. It was a human brand, and certainly there was a grim story behind it. What was of first importance to Jack was that men who were forced to bear this grisly mark of identification in their foreheads would be capable of any sort of action.

He himself rose to his feet, stepped back to his blankets, found his cartridge belt, and drew forth the long revolver which hung in a holster attached to it. So armed, he stole on to the window, but when he came closer to it he saw that he could not attempt to leave in that manner. It was so narrow that he was almost sure to be wedged in it. And if he were he would be at the mercy of the others.

Before he could make a more careful examination, the door to the main room opened and the two entered, the younger man walking first with both of his weapons raised and his shadow lunging before him. He leaned over the blankets, then straightened with a gasp.

'Dad, he's gone!'

The instant he lowered his guns, as he spoke, Jack Bristol sprang forward. He had no will to fight them both in those cramped quarters. Either, by himself, would have been more than enough to engage a hardy man. Together, they made tremendous odds. As he leaped in, Jack aimed and drew the trigger. But instead of an explosion and a bullet driven into the body of Black-beard, there was only a loud click and a hollow jar of the hammer descending upon an empty chamber. His gun had been emptied before the attack was undertaken.

Black-beard whirled with a short cry, both guns blazing, and Jack sprang to the side. A bullet stung his side – a mere clipping of the skin. Before him loomed the two-gun man with weapons leveled and not two yards between them. Jack dropped to his knees as the guns roared in unison. The flash had been in his very eyes; the scent of powder was choking and stinging in his throat. Half-blinded, he dived in toward the legs of the other. His shoulders struck beneath the knees. Down upon him toppled the mountaineer with a yell of alarm.

They whirled into a tangle of clutching, striking hands and twining legs. In the background, Jack saw the bald-headed man stepping swiftly about, striving to get in a blow or a shot, but never able to secure a chance without endangering his son. Strong fingers caught at Jack's throat. He beat the hand away, the finger tips tearing into the flesh like hot irons. And as they whirled again he caught at the flash of the revolver which Black-beard still held, jerked it down, and strove to tear it away. The gun exploded, Black-beard sank in a limp heap, and Jack Bristol stood up with an effective weapon in his hand.

He stood up with the roar of the father ringing in his ears and a storm of bullets pouring toward him. He raised the gun to answer that outburst of fire and lead, but he was struck on the head a blow that knocked the flash of the mountaineer's exploding Colt into a thousand sparks. He toppled back into a sea of fire that did not burn.

Four

He wakened with a grip of rope stinging his wrists. There was a bandage around his head. His face and neck and shirt were still wet from the water with which his wound had been washed. Above him were the stars. He was seated upon the damp ground, his shoulders resting against the log wall of the cabin.

His brain noted these changes in swift succession. Then a shadow crept over him. It was the shadow of a man swinging up and down across the shadow of a lantern as he dug with a spade in the dirt. The silhouette grew more living as his senses returned. All at once he recognized the face and the bulky body of the father. He stood in a hole which was already almost hip deep, and it was sinking rapidly. At the edge of the growing heap of dirt which the laboring spadesman threw out, lay a limp form, with the pale glimmer of the forehead turned up to the sky and the lower part of the face lost in the black shadow of a beard.

And Jack knew that he was watching the burial of the son by the father. He himself had been dragged out there for what end? To be buried alive with the dead body of the boy? There was no brutality, he felt, which was past the capacity of the man of the bald head. The care with which his head had been bandaged might augur a more terrible torment for which he was being saved.

He moved his legs. The feet, he found, were tied together as fast as the hands, and he was utterly helpless.

In the meantime, the hole sank with astonishing rapidity to the midsection, the shoulders, and the head of the digger. Finally there was only the grinding of the spade against stones, now and then, and the briefly seen shadow of the spade as it swung up above the mound of dirt for an instant. Then the big man climbed out and stood mopping his forehead and neck with a handkerchief. He was breathing heavily, and when he put away the handkerchief, he turned, leaning upon the spade, and peered into the depths of the hole he had just finished digging.

'That ain't bad,' he said at length. 'That ain't bad work – not for me getting old. Hello!'

Jack had neither stirred nor spoken, but with this exclamation, the mountaineer wheeled about and strode up to his captive. Propping his hands against his knees, he leaned over and stared into the face of Jack.

'Wide awake and feeling fine, eh?' he suggested. His cheerfulness made Jack shudder. He returned no answer.

'Wide awake and feeling fine,' repeated the other, as though a proper reply had been made. 'That's as it should be.'

He turned again, lifted the body beside the dirt mound, climbed the heap and disappeared into the shadow beyond. After a little time, he reappeared, and stood for some time at the verge of the grave, buried in thought. The place was so profoundly quiet that Jack could hear the rustling of the leaves blown to him from the far side of the clearing, swishing and crisping together like silk skirts on dancers.

And with every moment the horror increased. The big man came back to him, touched the rope which bound his feet with a knife, and then helped him strongly to his feet. He was led in silence to the edge of the grave. The mountaineer held up the lantern until the light fell upon the pale young bearded face within the shadow, glistening on the cross which marked his forehead.

'What I ask you man to man, stranger,' said the older man, 'is: D'you think when God sees him like that, he'll bear any malice for what he's done? What d'you think?'

The certainty that he had to do with a madman swept over Jack, but while his blood was freezing in the first shock of that conviction, the other went on to quietly answer his own question.

'No, there ain't going to be no malice borne. Look at the chance that he had? It wasn't no chance at all!'

He dropped a heavy hand upon the shoulder of Jack.

'Him down there,' said the mountaineer, 'was the youngster of the lot. His beard came out blacker'n hell. But he ain't no more'n twenty-two. Look how white his face is! The sun didn't have no time to burn him brown. He was the youngster of the four, and he was worth the other three. If it come to walking, running, riding, shooting, there wasn't a one of 'em that could touch him. I seen a time when he wasn't more'n fifteen and the rest of us got nothing but snow off the mountains. Out would go Charlie. No matter what kind of weather. That wouldn't stop him. And he'd come back with a mess of partridge – a meal of something. I seen a time when he was sick. The rest of us done the hunting for a week. We got nothing; nothing to speak of, that is. Charlie gets up from his bunk. He goes out. It was along in the first black of the evening. Two minutes after he started we heard his rifle working. We run out, and right yonder on the far side of the clearing we seen him standing over a bear that he'd just drilled clean. And when we come up we seen that the foam from the bear's mouth was slavered all over Charlie's boots. That's the sort of nerve he had even when he was a kid. He just stood up and kept pumping lead into the bear till the varmint dropped in the nick of time. That's the sort that Charlie was!'

He dragged off his battered hat and looked up.

'If I'd had ten wives instead of one and all of the ten had four sons, there wouldn't of been another Charlie! And he was enough to of got back at the rest of 'em for me! He'd of made 'em get down and crawl in the end – damn them, damn them to hell!'

He uttered the last words with a quiet savagery. His voice did not rise, but his whole big body shook with his rage.

'Well,' he said finally, 'that's finished! I take my luck the way I find it. Charlie's gone. I'll find some other way of getting back at 'em!'

He turned upon Jack a baleful glance.

'Get back over yonder,' he said. 'Don't try no running away. You got your hands tied behind you, and that way you couldn't run fast enough to keep away from me. And if I caught you, I'd make you think that hell was a church party compared to what I'd do to you!'

He spoke these violent words in a voice of no more than conversational loudness but they were more convincing to Jack than if they had been shouted at his ear. He obeyed the order and stood quietly while the other shoved and scooped the great mound of soft dirt into the grave. When it was ended he stepped to the side of the clearing, stooped and then returned staggering under the weight of an immense rock which, when dropped upon the mound, sank half its diameter into the soft earth. The father kept up the labor until he had covered the grave of his son with a great heap of boulders. At length he stepped back, filled a pipe, and while he lighted it, looked with great complacence upon his work.

'Take it by and large,' he said, 'it would be considerable wolf that could dig down under them rocks, eh?'

He chuckled softly, then turned his back upon that scene and escorted Jack to the house. Here he hung the smoky lantern on a high peg, motioned Jack to a seat on one of the stools which served the place instead of chairs, and, since the night was growing rapidly cold, kindled a brisk fire in the stove. The draught roared up the chimney and set the flimsy stovepipe shaking and softly rattling. The glow of warmth spread. Above it floated the wide drift of the mountaineer's pipe smoke.

'Speaking by and large,' he said, 'a man might say that no good comes out of fine looking hosses. They's only one thing that racing is good for, and that's for the hosses that does the running. Them that own the hosses go to hell. I've seen 'em start.

I've seen 'em finish.'

He delivered this little series of moralities without looking at Jack in a fashion which was peculiarly his own, canting his head and gesturing toward Jack, while he faced quite another point in the compass.

Jack found no reply which he could make. So he waited, and all the while his eager, restless eyes went up and down the strong body and the unhuman face of the other. He was striving to solve a riddle and meeting with no success. The big man now picked up a poker and inserted it into the fire under one of the top covers of the stove.

'You think,' said Jack at last, 'that I'm going to make a fuss about what's happened. But that ain't what's in my mind. Fact is, I'm glad enough to be up and kicking. I'll give you my word that you'll hear no more of me the minute I get my hands free. Or, better still, keep my hands tied, let me get on the back of my hoss, and then turn us loose. How does that strike you?'

The other smoked steadily and gravely throughout Jack Bristol's speech. He regarded his captive with the most profound attention, wrinkling his brows until the scar, as usual, went out of sight.

'I suppose maybe that sounds like the right thing for you to do,' he said at length, 'but I got something else figured out. You wouldn't see the why of it if I was to tell you. But a gent needs patience to get on any place. A gent needs a pile of patience. And I'm a patient man! After they done their trick with me, I come up here with my family. Anybody else would have tried to get back at 'em one by one, right away. But I didn't do that. I waited. I come up here where there was nobody else, and I waited and waited for my boys to grow up. They growed up strong and straight, and every one of 'em was a hard fighter, and a good shot. But I lost the three of 'em by hard luck. And still I had Charlie, that's worth all the other three.

'D'you think that I turned Charlie loose on 'em then? No, partner, I didn't. I kept him here all quiet. He was wise enough and quick enough to of gone down at 'em like a wolf. But I waited and waited. I'd get him bigger and stronger. I'd get him quicker still with a gun. And then I'd give him a list of 'em and turn him loose. That was what I was waiting so patient for. I've waited more'n twenty years for it. And at the end of the twenty years, just when Charlie is about to be sprung on 'em, along you come, all made up of hell-fire and claws. And yonder is my twenty years of hoping and waiting a-lying in the ground.'

At the conclusion of this long speech, during all of which he had failed to meet the eye of Jack for a single instant, he rose from his chair.

'What I been saying,' he said, 'you mostly don't understand right now. But you'll know more about in a year from now.'

Jack Bristol drew a longer breath. Whatever devilry might be stirring through the strange brain of this man, at least he did not intend murder.

'A year from now,' continued the mountaineer, 'you'll be riding your hoss around these hills and then you'll understand everything that I been saying now. And I got patience enough to wait till then.' So saying, he stepped to the side of the room, took down a length of rope, and with it approached his victim.

There was no possible purpose to be gained by resistance. Jack submitted while he was trussed hand and foot, so that he could not move. Even his head was lashed into a rigid position against a stake which was passed down his back. With this done, the other stepped back, regarded Jack for a critical moment, then went to the stove and took from it the poker.

The fire had turned the end of the iron rod into a living thing. It pulsed with heat. Light waves ran up and down it. It snapped sparks to a distance, and it cast a white radiance over the slanting face of the mountaineer.

The first premonition as to his purpose struck through Jack Bristol. Yet he could not believe. It was only when the big man advanced squarely upon him that he cried, 'You infernal devil, if –'

Realization of his helplessness stopped his mouth. He waited. A great hand thrust out and the strong fingers twisted into his hair, which he wore quite long. Looking up, quite fascinated by the horror, it seemed to him that the red-gray beard barely sufficed to cover a grin of pleasant anticipation. Then the white-hot iron was thrust against his forehead.

He closed his eyes. A hot fume and smoke of burning flesh choked him. He felt the burning point pass down his forehead. Then it crossed the first mark with a line to the side.

Five

The longest days are our silent days of inaction. And the weeks which followed were to Jack Bristol a more interminable period than all the life which went before. He was guarded night and day with the most scrupulous care, and when his captor, whose name he had discovered in the interim to be 'Hank' Sherry, left the cabin to go hunting, Jack was chained like a dog in the corner, and hands and feet secured so that he could not stir. For the rest, when Hank was at home he allowed his captive a reasonable liberty.

Twice a day, immediately after the branding of Jack's forehead, the mountaineer had changed the dressing upon the wound, treating it with the utmost care. But as for the reason behind the mutilation, or as for the purpose for which Jack was held in the shack, no information was vouchsafed. On any other subject Hank Sherry was voluble. Though he chiefly dwelt upon the exploits and prowess of Charlie, the last of his sons, yet he was quite willing to talk of other things, such as hunting, or storm and stress of weather there in the mountains, or any of a thousand topics, saving any which tended to expose his past life. And so the long days passed slowly, one into another, until a time came when big Hank Sherry sat opposite him at the supper table, combing his red-gray beard and staring out of his red-fringed eyes.

'Suppose a man wants to get a dog fighting mad, what does he do with him?' asked the mountaineer. He went on to answer his own question, turning his face away from Jack in that way he had, and addressing his speech to a distant corner. 'He takes the dog and ties him up and waits till he gets will to be free. Then he sets him loose. And the hardest job he has is to get himself out of the way of that dog's teeth.'

The glance of Hank reverted for an instant to Jack.

'Suppose I was to turn you loose?'

Jack looked hastily down, but even so the other had seen the sudden and fierce light of exultation.

'What you're thinking,' said Hank, 'is that you'd jump for my throat and work your hands through my beard till you got a grip on the windpipe.'

Still looking to the corner, he slipped his own hand under his beard and seemed to touch his throat tenderly.

'But if I was to say to you first, "Give me your word of honor that if I turn you free you'll not lay a hand on me," what would you say?'

Jack Bristol made no answer. But he watched the big man as a fox watches the chicken beyond the shielding net of wire. Hank laughed softly. There was something about the attitude of the other which seemed to please him immensely.

'Blood,' said he, 'that's what you want. Oh, I can see that! I see a bull terrier go at a Great Dane, once. He slipped in under him and set his teeth in the Dane's throat. There was a lot of threshing around, but in the finish the Dane lay down on his side nice and peaceable and the terrier choked him to death. And if you got at me, it'd be the same story.'

He shook his head, his eyes looking afar upon the remembered battle. He seemed more pleased than ever.

'The fine part of it,' continued Hank, 'is that you're going to be on my side agin the rest of 'em, in the end.'

'On your side?' said Jack Bristol.

'I'm a patient man,' said Hank. 'I'm willing to wait and wait. And now about that promise. Most like you been telling yourself over and over what you're going to do when the time comes that you get loose. You been seeing my eyes get glassy in your dreams. That's why I got to have your promise. You hear?'

Jack paused. If mere words could buy his freedom, would he not be pardoned if he broke his vow when his hands were loosed?

'What promise?' he asked.

'Why, a promise that you'll do me no harm.'

'I'll give you that, then.'

Hank nodded and behind the vast shrubbery of his beard he seemed to be smiling.

'Keep right on thinking,' he said. 'You keep it in your head that if I wanted to play safe I could dig another hole out yonder. I could make it big enough to hold a hoss and a man. And after I put you and your Susan hoss in it, who'd ever guess that you'd been here? Who'd ever ask questions?'

The skin prickled upon Jack's head.

'You can't keep murder under your hat,' he declared. 'It comes out sooner or later.'

'How many has been up to ask about Charlie?' remarked the mountaineer. 'Been some weeks now, and there ain't been a soul by to speak for him, has there?'

Into the silence drifted the cry of a wolf, howling on the verge of mute distance. In some way it showed Jack more plainly than words could have done, how utterly he was in the hands of the other.

'I've given you my word,' he said.

'And you've had a chance to think it over,' said the mountaineer, 'so there you are!'

As he spoke, he took from the table the razor-edge butcher knife. He took no time to untie ropes which he would not need again. One slash set the feet of Jack at liberty. Another cut free the hands which had been tied behind his back. He was loosed from his bonds! His life was set suddenly to music of a higher scale. His strength of body was multiplied. And in the grip of his hands stood the man who had brutally disfigured him for life and then chained him up like a dog. He crouched that infinitesimal bit which tells of tensed muscles ready to leap and strike.

But big Hank Sherry had calmly turned his back, tossed the butcher knife onto the table, and now approached the stove, lifted a lid, and shoved in a stick of wood to replenish the dying fire. As he did this, he was engaged in humming faintly an old tune whose words Jack had never known, but whose music he could never forget thereafter. His own fury to attack was checked and dammed up in him. He could not spring at the man while his back was turned.

The fire was roaring again around the new fuel. Hank replaced the lid and turned – not directly toward Jack, but merely enough so that the latter could see the face of his late captor covered with sudden perspiration. So he walked straight toward the door of the cabin.

'Sherry!' called Jack.

The latter halted, seemed about to turn, and Jack set himself to rush while, in a semi-hysterical fury, he felt possessed of strength enough to tear the big man limb from limb. But after that momentary halt, the mountaineer continued straight on his way and went out into the night. Still, for an instant, Jack stared at the door. Then he rushed out into the night, but he found that the other had melted away among the trees near his house.

'Sherry!' he called at the top of his voice. 'Sherry! Where are you?'

He heard no answer and at length he turned and stamped back into the cabin. As his disappointment subsided, he was beginning to realize the consummate nerve and steadiness which the older man had shown. He had known that the plighted word of his captive meant little or nothing in such an extremity. But he had trusted to the instinctive honor which would keep the man of the desert from attacking while his back was turned.

At least, the mountaineer would return after he had allowed his late captive sufficient time to cool down. To fill that interval there was one thing of importance for Jack to do.

In the corner was the old closet in which Sherry had placed the mirror on the first day. Jack took the ax which leaned against the wall and with one stroke smashed the lock. Then from the interior of the closet he saw the faint glimmer of glass as the lantern played feebly upon it. He snatched the mirror out, held it up, and looked upon the image of his face for the first time since his captivity began.

What he saw was a black and curling beard that covered the lower part of his face. All the skin that the beard did not cover was extraordinarily pale. But whiter by far than the skin of his forehead was a scar which formed a perfect cross, glistening in his flesh. Truly he was branded forever!

With a cry he snatched up the revolver from the holster of the mountaineer hanging against the wall, and with that weapon in his hand, he ran out into the night. In a blind madness he ranged among the trees. Twice he fired into empty shadows which seemed to move.

And so he came back at last to the cabin and saw, by the lantern light, the peaceful figure of the mountaineer with his stool tilted back against the wall while he whittled calmly at a piece of wood and puffed on his pipe. 'Stand up!' thundered Jack.

But Hank Sherry merely removed the pipe from his teeth and shook his head as though in gentle reproof.

'It looks to me,' he said, 'like the end of a day's work. Why should I stand up?'

'Because it's the end of a life and a day all at the same minute,' said Jack. 'Damn you, get up!'

'I've got your word,' replied the other.

'You yaller livered skunk!' cried Jack. 'D'you dare to talk about promises to me? You tried to murder me sleeping. Now you talk about honor?'

'My honor?' echoed the big man, and as always his voice remained singularly small and even. 'I ain't said a word about my honor. What I'm talking about is yours. Lord God, man, I've done pretty near every bad thing in the calendar; and I've busted more'n one promise amongst the rest. But ain't you different? Why, sure you are. If I hadn't knowed you was different, d'you think I'd of trusted to your promise? I knowed that you'd get heated up at first, and that's why I kept my back to you. But after a while I come back because I figured that when I seen you, there'd be no more'n a lot of words and smoke and no fire. And I see that I'm right! You're talking hard, partner, but you ain't got it in you to do what you think you can do!'

Jack dropped onto a nearby stool. The revolver clattered upon the floor. He buried his face in his hands. As the thoughts whirled maddeningly through his brain he realized that Hank Sherry was right, and still that steady voice went on.

'Ten minutes is all you needed. And if you come right down to it, ten minutes is all most folks need. The things we do that send us to hell, and the things we do that send us the other way – why, there's only ten minutes thinking between 'em!'

Six

He waited not even to shave the black beard from his face, but in five minutes his pack was made and he was on the back of brown Susan. From the darkness beside him he heard the mountaineer calling, 'So long! I'll be seeing you later, son!'

Jack returned no answer. The very sound of Sherry's voice roused him to a wild desire for murder. But in another moment Susan was at full gallop across the clearing and the fresh wind was beating into his face, and blowing out of his memory all the horrors of the cabin.

That shuddering sense that he was marked to the end of time kept him cold of heart as the good mare climbed the first long grade toward the west, but, after a time that thought began to grow smaller and smaller in his mind. And finally it was forgotten.

For he was young, and the night was new, and over his shoulder he could look at the pale, thin sickle of a new moon rising, and no matter through what horrors he had passed, the point of importance was that they now lay behind him.

He climbed the top of that long slope. Below him, he saw a valley opening out, long and narrow among the peaks, and brown Susan went down the descent like a racing deer. Before she reached the leveler going below, Jack Bristol was on the verge of singing, and all that had happened fifteen miles behind him among the mountains might as well have been fifteen years ago.

It was a pleasant valley into which he had dropped out of the highlands. It was thick with houses. A narrow river went talking through the midst of it, and it watered a fertile land on either side. For the fields were small, telling of close tillage. The barns were numerous, which told that the yield was rich.

He could not make out much in details, for now a mist of high-blown clouds began to veil even the faint light of the new moon; but he could at least make out the forms of horses and cattle in the pastures. And even in the dark of night he could sense the happy prosperity of that region.

Brown Susan, in the meantime, was frolicking along a road far smoother and better kept than those to which she was accustomed. And she made the best of the fast going. She had a colt's love of sprinting, and now she kept up on the bit, fairly dancing with an eagerness to get away. Once or twice Jack indulged her, but on the whole he kept her back to a steady jog. He had only one great purpose in mind, and that was to put as much distance as possible between himself and the cabin among the mountains. At one long ride he wanted to get out of the district of all who might know Hank Sherry and his branded forehead.

A schoolhouse, aflare with lights for some entertainment or dance, sadly shook his purpose, however. It was many a long week since he had danced, and now the sound of a shrill violin, blowing faintly to him, made Jack Bristol turn Susan to the side and bring her up into the shadow of a dense little grove of trees.

From this point of vantage he could hear every strain of the music, and even the slipping of dancing feet upon the floor was plainly audible. Between dances, too, he saw the couples pour out of the little school and waltz hither and yon over the schoolyard, and then their voices, and even fragments of their talk floated plainly to him. It was all wonderfully enticing to Jack. The deep voices of the men were like a challenge; the sweet voices of the girls were like a call to him. In another time he would have ridden to the hitching racks and tethered his horse and gone in to find a partner, but now he carried on his forehead the brand which held him more effectually than even rope or chain could have done. For the first time there dawned in his brain an understanding of what Sherry might have meant when he said that he would soon see Jack again. For might not the world shun him and drive him back to the one shelter which remained open to him?

That thought had hardly come home to him with a stunning blow when he heard two voices, speaking so close to him that they seemed to blow up out of the ground.

' — so I said, "Let 'er stop, then. Cut me off. I'll get on by myself".'

'Lee, why are you always so antagonistic when you talk with your father?'

'Because he's always so antagonistic when he talks with me.'

'But he has a right to talk severely to his own son.'

'Not about you, Nell. He can damn me all he pleases about other things, but when he begins to talk about you –'

The man paused in a silence of outraged and virtuous indignation. For a moment the girl did not answer.

'Just what does he say?' asked Nell at length.

'In the first place, he strings out a long lingo about what I owe to my family.'

'Don't laugh at that, Lee. It is an old family and it has an honorable record.'

'There'll be nothing in the whole record as fine as my marriage with Nell Carney.'

'You silly boy!' breathed Nell. And her pleasure put a quiver in her voice. 'You'll never listen to reason.'

'After we're married, then I'll listen to tons of reason.'

'But has he anything else against me? Dad's poverty, I suppose.'

'No, that doesn't bother the governor. But he has an idea that I should be making a good fat income before I marry. That's nonsense! Mining engineers don't begin on a salary equal to a millionaire's income. I tell him that, but he refuses to see the light! But once we marry, Nell, we'll –'

'Do you really think that might change him?'

'Think? I know! It couldn't help but change him!'

'Oh, listen!'

The music struck into a swinging waltz.

'Well, what's up?' queried the man.

'Don't you hear? Let's hurry in!'

'That waltz? I danced to that last winter till I was sick of it. No, let's stay here. There's something more important than dancing, I guess!'

She was silent. Then Jack could hear her humming the air lightly. Her escort, in the meantime, lighted a match and applied it to a "tailor-made" cigarette. The flare showed Jack Bristol, first of all, a big, well-made, handsome youth in his middle twenties, nattily dressed, with his hair sleek back on his head. Then, as the cigarette caught the flame and he opened his cupped hands, the smoker allowed the light to reach to the girl opposite him. It was only for a flash before the match streaked downward to the ground and was tramped out. But in the first flash Bristol saw enough.

From that instant what they said on the far side of the tree was not simply casual chatter. Every word she uttered was of vital importance that tugged Jack forward in his saddle and held him breathless to the end, as though she were disposing of his destiny as well as her own.

'Now, to get down to business,' said the man of the tailor-made cigarette, 'I'll tell you what I really think – that when you marry me the old man will rave like the devil for a few days, and after that he'll forgive us and take us home!'

'Take us home?' echoed the girl a little sharply. 'But I don't want to be taken home. I don't want to sit about in that big house of your father's and have your family circle about in the offing freezing me with glances and half-smiles!'

'They'll never do that, dear. Ten minutes of you in that house will thaw out the whole crew. They'll forget themselves and fall in love with you in a flock. I know them, Nell!'

'But after all, don't you want to start a home of your own, Lee?'

'That used to be the idea,' said the man, 'but times have changed. This is the twentieth century and homes don't start without plenty of coin mixed in with the foundation concrete. Don't be out of date, my dear!'

'You say that in a rather patronizing way,' protested the girl with a touch of acid in her tone that pleased Jack immensely.

'I don't mean it in that way,' answered the other at once. 'But the point, Nell, is that we have use for the old man even if he has no use for us!' He laughed at his joke. Jack noticed that he laughed alone. 'A man can't get along on a beggarly beginner's salary,' went on Lee. 'Not when he's been raised as I've been raised. It won't do. A man can't bring up his son to million dollar tastes and then dodge him, all at once, and tell him to start for himself. And the old man wouldn't dream of doing that – not if I'd marry where he wants me to marry. Don't you see how the whole nasty mess turns out? First he gives me the tastes of an English lord, and when those tastes are fixed in my blood he has me in his power. He can dictate my course of action. If I displease him, no matter where or when, he can simply hold over my head the threat of cutting off my allowance –'

'Lee! You don't mean to say that you still get an allowance from him!'

'Why not, dear? Why not? Anything disgraceful in that? Good gad, they pay mining engineers nothing to speak of but experience for the first few years. And a man can't keep up his bridge, to say nothing of his poker, when his salary is chiefly experience.'

He laughed again at this jest, and again he

laughed alone. Once more Jack was greatly pleased.

'The thing for us to do,' declared Lee at length, 'is to step out and get married and tell the old man about it later. That's what I've fixed up for tonight.'

'Lee! I didn't tell you –'

'I didn't have time to ask you first. I knew you'd agree.'

'But I don't agree!'

'You will when I explain. You see, it was devilish hard for me to break away this evening. It has taken three days of lies for me to lay all the plans. And even now, if I go back, I'll have to face a battery of questions. So I decided that we'd make the fullest possible use of our time and that will be to ride down the road and let the minister –'

'Lee, what on earth are you talking about?'

There was a breath of silence, then, 'Nell, have I taken too much for granted? Haven't you really meant what you said to me? Or was it as I've often suspected – simply that when they carried me into your house all smashed up by the fall from that fool of a horse, you set your teeth and decided that you'd save my life simply because it was so nearly gone; and when my life was saved you thought that you were in love with me simply because you'd been with me so long! Is that it?'

Jack Bristol liked the stranger better than before. He had spoken slowly, seriously, humbly.

'No,' said the girl. 'It isn't that. I really do care for you, Lee. But a marriage like that –'

'What's wrong with it? You're as hot-headed as they come. I know you don't object to the rush of it, Nell!'

'No, not a bit. Not if it was serious and honest.

But it isn't. It's all a bluff with which we're trying to force your father's hand. Isn't that so?'

'A bluff? No, it's a great big game, Nell!'

'That's a polite name for it!'

'Will you do one thing?'

'Of course.'

'Then get your horse and ride down the road. I'll meet you there in ten minutes beyond the cemetery. We can have it out on the road. If you don't agree – well, it will have to stand that way. If you do agree, then we'll be on the way to the minister's house. Is that fair, Nell?'

'I suppose so, but –'

'You've given your word!' cried Lee eagerly.

'Very well, then,' said the girl without enthusiasm. 'I'll be there!'

Seven

Jack watched them go. He waited until they were well out of sight toward the schoolhouse and the tangle of horses in front of the building. Then he drew back brown Susan and surveyed the road.

He had no right to come any further into the business than his involuntary eavesdropping had, in the first place, brought him. But he had no full control over what he did that evening.

The long imprisonment in the Sherry cabin among the upper mountains had served to store up an immense energy in him. Now it was striving for an outlet, and the first opportunity which he saw was to work with might and main to prevent the meeting of the young mining engineer and the girl.

What he should do after that did not enter his head. The first and important task was to see that the two did not meet again.

Now he saw the girl go scurrying down the road on a fast-stepping galloper. She disappeared around a distant bend, and after a considerable interval, another figure on horseback followed, a big man on a big horse. Unquestionably it must be the man named Lee.

Jack let him go back. Then he loosed brown Susan in pursuit. She had traveled hard and far already this night, but the brief rest under the trees had been sufficient to breathe her. Once more she was full of running, and she showed her delight on being turned loose by sprinting down the road at a dizzy pace that brought her in striking distance of the other within the first half mile. Indeed, so swift was her approach that though the velvet dust on the road muffled her hoofbeats, the big man turned in his saddle to watch his pursuer.

'Hello!' called Jack Bristol.

And as he waved his hand in the dark, the other drew rein and waved in return. Jack swept up on him like a thunderbolt. It was hardly fair, but he had been lately deeply schooled in unfair tactics.

'What's up?' called the other.

'A fight, damn you!' said Jack, and as the mare shot alongside, he leaned, wound his arms around the waist of Lee, and dragged him out of the saddle while Susan went by.

As for the gray which Lee had been riding, no sooner did it feel the weight lifting from reins and saddle than it flirted heels high in the air and then bolted down a by-path and across country.

'Hell and fire!' shouted the dismounted man. 'Is this a joke or a hold-up? You infernal hound, I'll break you in two!'

He had twisted around as he spoke. In vain Jack strove to free himself from his burden. In another instant they both toppled heavily to the ground while brown Susan danced a few paces away and stood watching them, deeply bewildered, with one ear pricked and one ear back. Surely it was strange to see men act as these were acting.

Taken by surprise in the first onset, the mining engineer needed only an instant to rouse himself, and then he proved a man's task to handle. For he had some twenty odd pounds of advantage in weight, and all that advantage was in trained muscle. Besides, he was a skilled boxer and wrestler. Jack could tell that in an instant, for as they fell he found himself caught in a bone-crushing grip that threatened to smash in his ribs. He freed himself from that hold by clipping his fist across the back of Lee's head. With an oath the latter disentangled himself and sprang to his feet.

Up himself with the speed of a cat, Jack was in time to duck under a straight-shooting left. And then he began to fight!

He began to fight with a silent song somewhere behind his lips. He began to fight as he had not fought since he was a child. For in latter years in moments of crises it had been gunplay, always, and never fists. But a good lesson once learned can never be entirely forgotten. The old rhythm of dancing feet and darting hands returned to him almost at once. And he put into the fury of his attack all of the unspent wrath which had been heaping up in him since Hank Sherry caught and made him a prisoner.

Big Lee, trained athlete and courageous man that he was, fought back heartily, but Jack split upon him as rain splits upon a roof-rim. It was in vain that Lee stopped one rush with a thudding blow which landed squarely on Jack's chest. It was in vain that he knocked the smaller man flying with a second pile-driver which snapped flush upon the point of his chin. For Jack rebounded from the earth and dove in again for more. His left hand was a shadow with a weight of a sledgehammer flying in it; his right hand was a thrust of flameless fire.

Before the one, big Lee staggered; and when the right crashed home he went down on his face, wrapped in a heavy sleep.

Jack Bristol, singing through his teeth, dropped to his knees and pressed an ear to the back of the fallen man. The beat of the heart was slow but steady. And Jack sprang up again, leaped into the saddle upon Susan, and sent her off down the road again at a rattling pace.

In his heart, too, there was a sense of great and satisfactory accomplishment. The waters of wrath which had been piling up in him for the many days had now burst the dam and were expended. In his heart, there was only a great goodwill toward all the world.

He put a mile and a half behind him. Then, to the left, he saw the pale glimmer of the white headstones in the graveyard, seen indistinctly through the night and among the trunks of the trees which overgrew the cemetery. He rounded the curve beyond it, and there was the girl, her horse only faintly perceptible where it stood beneath a thin screen of young poplars.

But Jack reined Susan to a stop nearby.

'Lady,' he called, 'I'm bringing you a message.'

She rode out to meet him.

'A message?' she echoed him. 'From whom? And who are you?'

'From Lee.'

'And?' she urged.

'He can't come.'

'Ah!'

'There was an accident.'

'Of what nature?' asked the girl.

'He met a man, and —'

'Well?'

'And there was trouble.'

'About what? Good heavens, what are you trying to say? Has Lee been hurt? I heard no gun!' cried the girl, and the dread and pain in her voice went through and through Jack. 'One of those brutal bullies – some gun-fighter who hated him for his good English and his clothes. Oh, tell me everything – no – I can find out what has happened when – take your hand off my reins!'

For as she started to spur past him, Jack caught at the reins and stopped her.

'There's no such hurry,' said he. 'He ain't hurt bad. There was no gunplay.'

'But you said there was trouble –'

'There was. It was all with the hands, though, that trouble.'

'They mobbed him, then!' cried the girl in angry scorn. 'Oh, the cowards.'

'Maybe you'd call it a mob,' said Jack, and he grinned in spite of himself, 'but there was only one man that stopped him.'

'One man!' breathed the girl. 'One man stopped Lee Jarvis? I don't believe it!'

'He'll be coming along in ten or fifteen minutes,' said Jack. 'Then you can ask him. He's got to catch his hoss first, and after that he'll be coming along.'

'But he sent you –? I don't understand. My head is whirling. Will you tell me just what happened?'

'It all started,' said Jack, 'when he scratched a match.'

'Is this a joke?'

'Not for me, lady. I'm plumb serious.'

'Then try to explain, if you please.'

'You're willing to wait here till Lee comes along?'

'Of course; that is, if he hasn't been seriously hurt.'

'It goes back to that match I was talking about,' said Jack. 'When he lighted that match and his cigarette he thought that as the end —'

'Ah,' cried the girl, 'I think I understand! You were under those trees! You were eavesdropping!'

'I was just listening in,' said Jack, 'because I thought it would save you and him from a pile of embarrassment, at first, if I didn't tell you that I was there and that somebody else had heard the secret. It didn't make no difference what I heard because I was on my way West and out of this part of the country, and I'd never see you or hear of you again. You see that?'

'I don't fully understand anything you say.'

'But then he scratched that match,' said Jack, 'and — d'you know what an old man I once knew used to say? That a pretty girl belonged to the whole wide world; every man jack of us had a right to admire 'em! But that's what the match showed me.'

'What in the world is in your mind?' cried the girl, and now her voice was a trifle high and strained.

'Well,' said Jack, 'when I saw your face I knew that it wouldn't work.'

'You knew what?'

'I knew that Jarvis could never put his deal through because you'd never help him, and you'd never help him because it wasn't square!'

He paused. The girl did not reply.

'But at the same time, there was no use letting him try to sweep you off your feet,' went on Jack. 'So, after you'd gone by, I waited until I saw him start up the road, and then I dropped in behind and stopped him. We had a little argument, and he stayed behind, and here I am!'

'Will you let me pass?' asked the girl in a very small voice. 'Will you let me go back?'

'I see,' nodded Jack. 'You're afraid. But, after all, I guess you won't go.'

So saying, he dropped the reins and drew Susan back. She stepped away nimbly and allowed plenty of room to the girl to ride down the road. In fact, she spoke to her horse, but she drew the animal up before it could make a step. One prophecy, at least, had come true!

Eight

Once more they faced each other in a breathing space of silence, and how eloquent, felt Jack Bristol, silence could be.

'Why did you say that?' asked the girl at length.

'That you wouldn't ride away yet?'

'Yes. What made you presume to read my mind like that?'

'Because,' said Jack, 'I'd seen your face by the light of that match.'

'You talk queer nonsense,' said the girl.

'And I knew,' continued Jack, 'that you wouldn't run where there was no danger.'

'I wonder,' said the girl, 'if you are not more dangerous than you seem. But will you continue and tell me everything?'

'Why I stopped him?'

'It makes my blood boil to think that any one man could stop him,' cried the girl.

'It was a lucky right,' said Jack meditatively.

'A what?'

'It landed right on the point of the chin,' said Jack. 'He went to sleep as though someone were rocking a cradle.'

'Ah,' said the girl, 'no matter by what trickery you struck him down –'

She paused.

'To go right back to the beginning,' said Jack, 'I saw that it wouldn't be right for you to meet him. Because it wouldn't be square.'

'Not honest?'

'Not exactly. What Jarvis wants to do is to hold up the old man by marrying you. He figures that his father ain't going to let his son live too poor. So he'll take a chance on marrying you and waiting for old Jarvis to raise the coin. Isn't that the straight of it?'

'It's – but why should I talk about such things with you?'

'Because it's night,' said Jack, 'and it don't do no harm to let a gent that you'll never see again help you think.'

'And I'm never to see you again?' asked the girl, taking up that part of his statement.

'Never,' said Jack. 'I'm gone before morning if there's any luck with me.'

'Who are you?'

'I can't tell you that. If I could be so free with my name I wouldn't be in such a hurry.'

'You've done something wrong,' said the girl eagerly, 'and you're running away from the consequences?'

'I've done something right,' corrected Jack, 'by keeping a girl from dong something wrong.'

'You've chosen to act as my conscience, then?'

'I've done what ten minutes of thinking would have made you do,' said Jack. He quoted old Sherry with gusto. 'I stepped in between you and a jump in the dark, that's all.'

'What makes you so sure?'

'Because if you'd have waited for him here, you'd have gone on with him.'

'Never! That is — not unless I'd made up my mind that he was right.'

'That's what you think you'd have done. But I figure that you couldn't help yourself. Once folks get started — why, it's like trying to dam a river that's running down a steep hill. They climb right over the dam. Nope, you couldn't help yourself, lady. Besides, it's at night. And when folks can't see what's around 'em all chances look good. It's what the night does. Suppose you'd met me like this by daylight. D'you think I'd of had a chance to talk one minute to you? Nope, you'd of rode on down the trail and showed me nothing but a cloud of dust.'

'You're a very queer fellow,' said the girl. 'And I think you're right about part of what you say. How do you explain it? Why am I staying here and listening?'

'Because it's the faces of people that we're afraid of; not their talk. It isn't what they say. It's the ugly faces of 'em while they're saying it. Am I right?'

'I suppose you are,' said the girl slowly. 'And —'

'Listen!' broke in Jack.

Down the road came the rapid and muffled beat of the hoofs of a horse.

'It's Lee Jarvis coming on the jump to get you,' said Jack.

'Oh!' cried the girl.

'We can hide by riding down that alley,' said Jack.

'Hide? Why should I hide?'

'Do I have to fight him again?'

'Fight?'

'Lady,' said Jack, 'it's been a long time since I've had a real, honest-Injun, all-leather fight. If you say the word him and me tangle. But if you figure there's a premium on his face, just ride down that little trail with me and wait under the trees till he's tired of looking for you around here.'

'This outrage –' cried the girl.

'There's no time for talk,' said Jack. 'You can lay to this, lady: I ain't started all the trouble that I've taken tonight to give up at the last minute without a fight. You can tell me what you think of me and my kind later on!'

There was a muffled exclamation from the girl. Then, without a word, she swung the head of her horse to one side and galloped him down the lane. It was but a twisting little bridle path among the trees and instantly they were lost to view from the main road. A hundred yards from their starting place, Jack dropped from the saddle and, standing in front of the girl's horse, held his hand ready to choke off a neigh if Jarvis' horse should be heard in the distance. At the same time he spoke to Susan, and the mare came up and nosed his shoulder inquisitively.

In the meantime, the beat of the hoofs of the Jarvis horse sounded small and dull on the road. The sound stopped. There was silence for a minute or two. Then the hoofbeats were heard retreating.

'And there you are,' said Jack, swinging back into the saddle once more. 'The thing's done and no bones broken.'

Her answer astonished him.

'You and your horse are wonderful chums,' she said. 'It's easy to see that.'

'Susan and I?' said Jack, gaping at the girl through the darkness. 'Of course we are, but, lady, suppose I see you home?'

She began to laugh, and the sound of that

laughter paralyzed Jack. At a stroke, the initiative, which he had maintained from the first, was lost to him.

'I can find my way home alone,' said this strange girl, who seemed to rise all the stronger out of defeat. 'But if you wish to come along, why, I'll be very glad to have you.'

He fell in at her side. They cut straight across country, jumping the fences as they came to each barrier. They went at first in another of the silences which, from time to time, fell between them. But after a time she said, 'Of course, you were wrong about one thing, and that was that I could be swept off my feet by Lee Jarvis.'

'Maybe I was wrong,' said Jack humbly. 'Right now I'd figure that you could handle about anything.'

'That's a way men have,' said the girl. 'After they've done something for a woman –'

She stopped herself short and switched to a new topic.

'A little while ago you said that you were never coming into this part of the country again. I really wish that you'd tell me why.'

'When I started through,' said Jack slowly, 'it was because I wanted to get out to new country. But now there's another main reason.'

'Well?'

'It's one I can't tell you.'

'That's not fair.' said the girl. 'You know I'll never rest until I hear what it is.'

'I couldn't tell you,' said Jack frankly, 'except that I'm never to see you again; but you're the reason, lady. If you were a little bit different, I'd come back through hell-fire to find you again. But if I talked to you long enough you'd do nothing but laugh at my grammar.'

She shook her head.

'I think it would take a most unusual person to laugh at you on any account,' she said. 'And certainly bad grammar is nothing but –'

She came to another abrupt pause, reining in her horse.

'There's my house, d'you see? That's dad's house yonder on top of that little hill.'

'I'll stop here, then.'

'You won't take me to my door?'

'If you want me to,' said Jack sadly, and not another word passed between them until he had reached the horse shed and drawn the saddle from her horse.

'I wonder if Lee Jarvis has come here already to inquire about me?' murmured the girl.

'I figure he won't,' answered Jack. 'He doesn't bother your father much, eh?'

He was walking by her side toward the house, with brown Susan following at his heels. Now the girl stopped short.

'Why did you say that? How did you know that? And who *can* you be?'

'Lady,' said Jack. 'I'm a friend that wishes you luck. Let it go at that.'

She walked on. Before he knew it they stood at the door of the house.

'Good-by,' said Jack, and held out his hand. 'Good-by, and good luck, and no Lee Jarvis in your luck!'

Instead of taking the extended hand, she struck back sharply at the door which flew wide and allowed a bright shaft of light to fall upon Jack. He saw the half-mischievous smile of expectation which had formed upon her lips die. Her eyes, fixed on his face, grew large wih terror, and with a shriek she turned and fled into the house – fled in mortal agony of terror, with her head half turned to watch the horror pursue.

And Jack knew that she had seen the cross on his forehead.

Nine

If there were men about the place that woman's
scream would bring them out with guns in their
hands. Jack Bristol paused to ask no questions. He
flung himself back into the saddle on the mare and
put her over the first fence and then cantered
across the meadow beyond. In the meantime, the
little house behind him, which he had been
watching over his shoulder, fairly boiled with life.
Lights stirred across the windows. Three or four
men ran out, slamming doors and shouting to one
another. A lantern went swinging toward the barn.
Then someone sighted the fugitive. There was no
preliminary warning, no call to him to stop, but a
rifle began crackling at once in the hands of an
expert, for only an expert, shooting at such a
distant and moving target by such a light could
have put his bullets so close to the mark.

A word to Susan sent her on a re-doubled speed
and out of all danger almost at once. But as she
leaped the fence into the open road, Jack heard the
quick rattling of hoofbeats across a wooden
culvert far behind and knew that the armed men of
that household were out upon his trail, and out for
blood.

Not until this moment did he have an

opportunity to think, but he could come to no conclusion. All that he knew was that the girl had seen the gleaming scar on his forehead and after that she had fled with a shriek, as though from a wild beast! But what did that cross represent? Why had it been placed upon the faces of Hank Sherry and his son Charlie? Who had placed it there? A horrible explanation began to form dimly in the back of his brain, but before it became a real conclusion, the remembered shriek of the girl ran back across his mind and blotted out the rest.

In the meantime, they could never catch brown Susan. The run from the upper mountains had, apparently, merely served to loosen her muscles. The pause while the master talked to the girl had completely rested the mare again, and now she was as full of running as ever.

So Jack let her drop back until the pursuers were fairly close. The wind had scoured the sky clean of all clouds, by this time. And in the faint light of the sickle moon he saw the blotchy shapes of the riders bobbing up and down as they spurred in pursuit. Now and again they loosed a scattered volley at him in the chance of striking the man or the horse with a random shot, but all those bullets flew wild, and Jack laughed at their efforts. He would win one small revenge out of this night's work, he decided. He would lead them at his heels until dawn, making them think, every moment, that they were about to run him down. And at the end of that time, he would simply canter away from them as though on the wings of the wind.

Indeed, the horses behind were laboring at full speed, while Susan, keeping up her long, striding gallop, was holding them even without an effort.

Two miles, three miles flew beneath her, and Jack was forced to rein her in as the pace told on the riders behind. He saw a fork in the road before him, now, and was about to take the branch to the left, because it promised to lead out of the valley and into the higher ground beyond, when he saw, by the growing moonlight, a sweep of a dozen horsemen coming far off down that road. With an oath he swung Susan onto the other road.

But how had they been able to spread the alarm? He looked up, and he saw the moonlight running in a cluster of straight, horizontal lines above him. Telephone wires, of course; what a consummate fool he had been! He had thought to play tag with them and they, in the meantime, were throwing a circle of danger around him. While the men rode at his heels, the girl stayed at the telephone spreading the alarm. Jack Bristol looked away at the tall mountains to the left from which he had been shut off, then he loosed the reins and Susan bounded away.

But a wild yelling began the instant he turned onto that right fork. And the yelling was echoed from squarely in front of him. Yes, down the road before him swung a new body of horsemen, small with distance, but riding hard. They had blocked him on every road.

But he turned Susan to the right and sent her sailing over the fence into the open field beyond. What difference did it make to her whether she ran on smooth roads or rough fields? She flew like a swallow, dipping up and down with her long leaps, and crossed the wide field, sailed the next fence, again, and – struck in new-ploughed ground beyond!

Jack, with an exclamation of dismay, felt her flounder into a laboring trot through the muck, and leaning to the side, he peered ahead to make out how far the field extended. The moon-haze was thick before him, but in the little distance he could make out the outlines of a fence. Toward this, then, he pressed on, and glancing back over his shoulder he saw the posses tearing across the field in pursuit and gaining now at a fearful rate.

Well, let them run as they pleased. When they reached the ploughed ground it would stop them more effectually than a wall of stone. Brown Susan, stepping more than fetlock deep, struggled on toward the fence, stepped onto a strip of firmer going just beside it, leaped the obstacle like a cat, and landed on deeper and newer ploughed ground just beyond!

That was the meaning, then, of the triumphant shouting behind him and to the sides. They understood that he had run into a trap from which there was no exit. No, he was helpless, for looking to the side, he saw a group of riders spurring down some undiscovered lane to skirt around and gain the front of him. There, hemmed in on all sides, they would shoot him to death from a safe distance.

Already they were opening fire. The rifle bullets began to sing their short, weird lyrics in his ears. Another moment and gallant Sue would be struck. So Jack sprang to the top of the fence, so that his body would be clearly outlined, and threw up his hands. The firing ceased almost at once. Men began to run across the ploughed area toward him, and Susan, knowing well enough that they had been in flight from just those people, crowded close and whinneyed softly and anxiously to call him away.

They came around him with a rush. They came silently, like wolves that are wild with starvation. And literally they leaped at his throat. Men sprang from either side. He was smashed to the ground. His revolver was torn from him. His arms were bound behind his back. Then he was dragged to his feet again.

He found a crowd of more than thirty angry faces around him, all dimly and ominously outlined in the moonlight. Out of the jargon of many fierce voices speaking at the same time came a call for silence.

'It's Captain Carney,' said some of those nearest. 'Let's hear what he has to say.'

'We'll get a light, first,' said the heavy voice which had been calling for silence. 'We'll get a light and see that Nell wasn't looking at a ghost that didn't exist. Girls are tolerable skittish and they see double when they get excited. But if it should turn out to be what she said, we ain't going to act hasty, boys, are we?'

'We'll talk it over plumb quiet, Cap,' answered the other.

So Captain Carney scratched a match whose first light showed Jack the face of a middle-aged man, a stern face but the face of a just man, withal. Next that light was cupped in the shielding hands of the captain, and when the flame had flared out to the full the hands opened and a yellow burst of light fell on Jack. It brought a shout from the crowd.

'It's him! I seen it clear as day! There's an oak, yonder, and I got a rope that ain't working. Let's finish him right here and now, Cap!'

Men from the rear began crowding in. Hands reached for Jack, but the father of Nell struck those hands away.

'Boys,' he said, 'you ain't here to butcher a

maverick. This here is a man the same as you and me –'

'That's wrong as hell,' thundered someone. 'He's a coyote done up in a man's hide!'

That exclamation brought a growl from the others.

'That's a true word. No use wasting words over him, Cap! Shoot the dog and leave him lie!'

Jack twisted himself away from restraining hands. He pressed close to Carney.

'Captain!' he shouted through the rising clamor, 'for God's sake give me half a chance. I'm not the man you think. Let me have five minutes to prove it!'

Captain Carney dropped a reassuring hand upon his shoulder.

'You're going to have a chance to talk,' he said. 'Don't worry about that. Boys, stand off, will you? Give him a chance to say what he's got to say. Give him five minutes, boys!'

His huge voice cleared a circle. The others pressed back and waited.

'Now speak up, Sherry,' said Captain Carney. 'Boil it down and make your yarn short, and leave out all the lies you can. We know that you're talking for your life and that may make you want to string out the story. But make it short or we'll have to interrupt you, and if we interrupt you there won't be no chance of you speaking again!'

'Boys,' said Jack. 'I'll tell you the straight of things just the way they happened. I was coming over the mountains a few weeks back and I hit on a house in the evening just when it begun to get dark. Seemed nacheral to ask for chuck and a place to sleep here. I done just that and a gent with a hook nose and reddish looking eyes let me in. That night while I was asleep they decided to murder me, but when they tackled me I managed to fight back. I killed Hank Sherry's son, Charlie, with his own gun, but then Hank knocked me out.

'He knocked me stiff, tied me up, and then heated a poker red-hot and burned this cross into my forehead. After that he kept me up there for weeks. It was only this morning that he turned me loose, and when I came down here on my way out of this country the things began to happen that you know about. And that's the truth, so help me God!'

He paused. And there was a heavy silence over the listeners. The vigor of his speech had won him some belief.

'Why he done it,' said Jack, 'why he didn't kill me to get even for the killing of Charlie, I dunno. Maybe you folks can figure it out, for a gent that has this scar on his forehead seems to be worse'n a ghost to the rest of you.'

A muttering assent reached his ears. Susan, who had been kept away by the jostling circle of men now found a way to break through and came up to him, snorting. Captain Carney picked upon that incident.

'Look at that, boys,' he said. 'I guess a gent that has a hoss trained like that ain't all snake. I say, we're going to listen to some more that this gent has to say. You say you ain't Charlie Sherry?'

'I'm not.'

'What might your name be, then?'

'Jack Bristol.'

'And where might you come from, Jack?'

'From down Arizona way.'

'The hell you say! All that ways to up here?'

'That's the straight of it, Carney.'

'How come you to make a trip as long as that? Just started out to see a piece of the country?'

Jack paused to consider.

'Fact is,' he admitted, at length, 'that I got into a scrape down yonder. I had to get out and get out quick, and the best thing for me was to get as far away as I could. So I started north and never stopped until old Hank Sherry got his paws on me!'

'That sounds like queer talk to me,' said Carney, 'but it sounds like the sort of talk that a gent wouldn't make up in a minute. What d'ye say, boys? Ain't there a sound of truth in what he says?'

A dubious, but growing chorus of assent answered him. Then a big man appeared from the background and shouldered his way to the front.

'Boys,' said the voice of Lee Jarvis, 'you've been hearing a good deal of strange talk. If you'll let me ask this fellow a few questions, I'll guarantee that I'll show you his guilt. Will you let me ask them?'

Ten

'It's Lee Jarvis,' said Captain Carney ingratiatingly. 'I guess we can listen to Oliver Jarvis' son, boys? Step up and talk to him, Jarvis.'

'Thank you, Captain,' said the other, and came into the little circle which was now occupied by brown Susan, Jack, and the captain.

'In the first place,' he began, 'I don't mind telling you why I'm interested. This infernal blackguard rode up behind me, held me up, took my wallet, and then struck me in the face with his revolver and knocked me senseless. Then he went on and met Nell Carney and told her that he was a messenger from me.'

'By God!' cried Jack, 'that's the grandfather of all the lies that were ever told!'

'I've got proof to show you,' said Lee Jarvis.

And he calmly lighted a match and held it cupped so that the light would fall upon his face. It showed to Jack the complete story of the work which he had done with his fists and he found that story to be far more extensive than he had imagined. The mouth of Jarvis was puffed and bloody. A purple bruise decorated his chin. There was a red gash under one eye and the other was nearly closed by a discolored swelling. Moreover, his face, his hair, and his clothes were covered with unbrushed dust.

A murmur ran through the crowd at the sight.

'Does it look as though one blow had done all that?' asked Jack of the crowd. 'Tell them the truth, Jarvis – that we stood up and fought a square fight till you went down!'

'You lying rascal,' said the bigger man, though he kept his voice admirably under control. 'You know that I fell head foremost from my saddle and struck on rocks by the road! But we'll put that to one side. What was in his mind about Nell Carney, God alone knows. She's safe at home; how she got there we'll find out later on.'

The quiet and assured manner in which Lee Jarvis uttered his misstatements staggered even Jack, and it was plain that they made a great impression upon the others.

'Now,' went on Lee Jarvis, 'we'll ask you a few simple questions. In the first place, what was the crime on account of which you were forced to run for your life from Arizona?'

'There's nothing I've done there which has anything to do with what I have done here.'

'Answer me yes or no!' exclaimed Jarvis. 'Did you or did you not kill a man in Arizona before you started north?'

The picture of Harry Ganton lying on the floor of his house flashed back upon the mind of Jack.

'I'll not answer that,' he said.

'You're doing yourself a harm,' said Captain Carney sternly. 'If you could have actually established that you were in Arizona, of course it would have proved that you are not Charlie Sherry. You understand that?'

To be hanged for the murder of Sheriff Ganton, or to be lynched by a mob here — what difference was there between those fates? Jack shrugged his shoulders.

'Let's go back,' said Lee Jarvis, 'to the yarn which he has just told.'

He planted himself squarely before Jack, his hand dropped upon his hips.

'When you saw the cross on the forehead of the old man,' he asked, 'of course you°asked what it meant?'

'I did not,' said Jack, 'and I still don't know what it means.'

'Shall I tell him, then?' said Lee Jarvis. 'Shall I let him in on the secret?'

'Go ahead,' said Carney.

'Well, Charlie Sherry,' said Jarvis, 'we understand that you know it well enough, but I'll tell it to you over again. It goes back to a time when your father was living in this valley and when you were a little shaver, you and your three brothers. Hank Sherry was always the black sheep of the community. The Sherry family, as a matter of fact, had always been the black sheep. They'd raised hell in one way or another for a couple of generations. If there was ever a theft, or a horse stealing, or a murder in the community, it was always safe to hunt up the Sherrys, in the first place. Because the crime was, nearly always, traced back to one of them. Finally the crowning horror came. Fire broke out in the house of the minister one night. Everyone in the valley knew the minister. He'd put his shoulder under every man's troubles, at one time or another. He had slaved up and down the length of the valley for thirty years doing good.

He'd married a girl in the valley; he'd raised a family of three children late in life.

'Fire, as I say, broke out in the minister's house. It began with the explosion of a revolver. When neighbors ran out into the street they found the minister shouting, "Stop thief," and pointing down the street and crying that Oscar Sherry had robbed his house. But the crowd could not chase your uncle. They had work closer at hand.

'In his flight, to distract the attention of the minister, the thief had thrown a burning lamp upon the floor of the house. The oil washed the fire across the floor. Instantly the lower part of the house was on fire.

'It was an old house. The fire spread wonderfully fast. When the minister turned to go back into his house, after he had chased the thief out, his way up the stairs was blocked with the flames. And his wife and three children were cut off from help above. I remember that night, and the crowd in the street, and the way the men fought the fire and tried to get through to the family.'

A groan arose from the crowd. They pressed a little closer. There were older men in that assemblage who had actually fought the flames on that night.

'But they couldn't keep the fire down with their bucket lines,' went on Lee Jarvis, 'and finally one of the children began screaming upstairs and the minister couldn't stand it. He ran through the flames and got upstairs. And that was the last of him. A minute later the upper floor caved in. The walls of the house held in a furnace and the minister's family perished in it, five of them died there, Charlie Sherry!'

In the pause Jack heard the heavy breathing of the men who surrounded him.

'Afterward,' went on Lee Jarvis, 'they hunted down the Sherrys, as usual, and they found the plunder from the minister's house in the home of Oscar Sherry.

'That was enough. Oscar Sherry was lynched and hung to the highest tree in the village. He died cursing the rest of the world. And after his death the men of the valley decided that something had to be done to get rid of the curse of the Sherry family. And they decided to send them out of the valley, Hank Sherry and his four sons, and mark them all so that they could never come back without being known. It was a stern thing to do, but five deaths had just been laid to the door of the Sherry family, and there were other murders – a long list of 'em – stretching back over the years. So a band of masked men took your father and the four of you – think back to that night, Charlie! – and they branded a cross on the forehead of each of you and then sent you out of the valley with a warning that if any one of you ever came back again he'd be killed!

'And they did come back. Five years ago a horse thief was caught at Lower Falls. There was a cross branded on his forehead. On him were found the wallet and the watch of a man who had been murdered on the road three days before. The thief and murderer admitted that he was Mike Sherry, the oldest of your brothers.

'Six months later there was a highway robbery. The robber was run down by a posse. He killed Tom Evans before he was captured and when he was caught the posse found a cross on his forehead and he gave his name as Gus Sherry.

'The next was only ten months ago. Jud Sherry
came down into the valley and tackled Hal Sewell.
But Hal was lucky with his gun and dropped the
murderer in his tracks.

'Last of all, here you come, Charlie — the
smoothest liar of the lot. All of your brothers have
shown the same poison in their blood. They've all
been raised, like you, to hate the rest of the world.
And we caught them all in murders, or on the edge
of murders. And we finished every one of them
just as we're going to finish you, Charlie Sherry!
Boys, am I right?'

'Right!' they answered.

One voice opposed.

'Not right enough to suit me,' said Captain
Carney. 'I've got to hear more than that. You've
framed up an ugly story, Jarvis. But where's the
facts?'

'Facts?' said Jarvis fiercely. 'What he did to me is
one fact. Not a doubt in the world that he thought I
was dead and that he left me for that reason.'

'Search him for the wallet,' said the captain.
That will be proof enough.'

Matches were lighted. Busy hands probed the
pockets of Jack's coat, and 'Here!' cried one. 'Here
it is!'

Before the amazed eyes of Jack was exposed a
thin wallet which had been drawn from his pocket.
The leather case was opened. A thin sheaf of bills
was exposed.

'All twenties and bigger,' said Captain Carney.
'Not a bad haul for him, at that.'

'Is that proof enough now?' asked Lee Jarvis.

'Hang him! Send him to hell and be done wih
him!' was the loudly voiced consensus of opinion,

but Captain Carney still held them back with the weight of his single opinion, as a strong and honest man can often do, even with thousands. All around Jack Bristol they swayed and stirred. But Carney was steady as a rock.

'Wait a minute,' he commanded. 'This shows that he robbed you. That's the sort of a thing that Sherry might do. But it ain't proof that he is Sherry.'

'Captain,' exclaimed Lee Jarvis, 'you're arguing flatly on his side. I've proved the robbery. And now you see the scar. It's simply blind obstinacy to doubt any longer!'

He added, 'I'll show you one thing more.'

He lighted another match and held it so that the light gleamed in the eyes of Jack.

'Look at that scar. Does it seem like a new one? It's an old, white scar, Carney!'

'If that wound got good care, it might look like that inside of a few weeks. There's no proof in what you say now, Jarvis.'

'No proof in any one thing I've said, but there's a lot of proof when the entire number are strung together. What speaks up for him?'

'Two things,' said Carney. 'The first is that he keeps silent. That's a good thing. No whining. No begging. No matter what else he may be, he's a man, Jarvis.'

He waited a moment for that point to sink home.

'The second thing is: why did he ride home with Nell? I only had ten seconds to hear her yarn but from what she said I gathered that he talked like a decent fellow. How do you explain that, Jarvis?'

'Leave it to a vote of the crowd,' suggested Jarvis.

The malignance of the man astonished Jack

though the explanation could be found in his desire to get rid of a man who had beaten and shamed him.

'I've got one thing to say,' said Jack at length, before the roar of the crowd had begun calling for the end of him. 'Take a guard and bring me up to face Hank Sherry. If he calls me his son, that'll settle it. Is that fair?'

'A fifteen mile ride through the hills to prove a thing we already know?' stormed Lee Jarvis. 'Why should we do that?'

'Because there's a man's life balanced in this,' answered Carney. 'And that's the thing that we're going to do. I'll ride in the morning. Jarvis, I'll count on having you along. Pat, Steve, Joe, will you ride up with us?'

He carried them before him. The objections of Lee Jarvis were over-ruled. In five minutes the posse which was to ride in the morning was formed, and it was agreed who should guard the prisoner during that night.

Eleven

In the first cold gray of the morning they came to Jack Bristol in the cellar room of the Carney house where he was being guarded. A cup of black coffee and a piece of bread with a couple of slices of bacon on top made the breakfast. And a little later they started up the valley with brown Susan dancing gaily on the way while her rider was held in the noose of a lariat which was twisted around the horn of Carney's saddle.

Jack looked back at the house and he saw, in a window which opened just above the roof of the veranda, the face of Nell Carney watching him depart, with a strained expression of loathing and terror. His hands were lashed together, but he raised them both and lifted his sombrero to her. She disappeared to the side at once and Jack, as he settled the hat back on his head with a grim smile, saw Carney himself eyeing him with a measure of grim interest, but not a word was spoken.

It was plain, however, that whatever Nell had told her father, she had not completely prejudiced him against her escort of the night before, for all during the ride Captain Carney rode near the prisoner. It was at his suggestion that the rope was removed from Jack and attached merely to the neck of Susan. And above all, something in his manner was a steady assurance to Jack that in a pinch there was one man in the posse who would see that some measure of justice was meted out to the captive.

As for the others in the group, riding before and behind Jack, they maintained a resolute silence, so far as the man they guarded was concerned. They avoided even looking at him, as though they feared that if they met his glance they would have to recognize him as a human being worthy of mercy, at least. So grim was their mood that even when they spoke to one another it was in lowered voices.

So they worked their way quickly out of the valley before the morning fires began smoking in the chimneys they passed. They were entering the hills before, looking back, Jack saw a dozen ghostly and wavering fingers of smoke rising. The valley was still half lost in dimness, but the crests above them were already brightening with the sun. The sun itself came gleaming over an eastern mountain as the posse rode into view of the Sherry cabin.

They heard him before they saw him. An ax was swinging lustily somewhere below them, where the roof of the cabin was visible, and with every blow the thin and tempered steel rang loudly. Captain Carney bent his head to one side and listened with a critical air.

'That's a good ax man,' he said. 'He's sinking her up to the wood every wallop, pretty near. That's old Hank Sherry himself, I should say. He was always fast with an ax!'

Jack Bristol, fresh from the land where wood is dug up rather than chopped down, listened to the opinion with wonder. And now they heard a crackling and rustling among the trees near the cabin. Next, with a rush like a great wind, down rushed a huge pine and fell crashing and splintered. The steep hills caught up the echoes and sent them flying off into faint distances. Then the riders came into view of the woodsman. It was Hank Sherry, of course. He leaned upon his ax and, wiping the sweat from his forehead, looked down upon the white stump, glistening with the chisel strokes of the ax and bristling in the center with a tuft of splintered wood.

But at sight of the approaching procession, he tossed the ax far to one side and ran upon them with a cry of agony. He ran straight to Jack, and though one or two of the riders laid hands upon guns, they offered no resistance. The odds were too safe upon their side.

'Charlie!' cried the old villain, taking hold of Jack's imprisoned hands. 'Oh, God A'mighty, I knew it would come out like this! You shouldn't have gone down into the valley. I begged you and I prayed you not to go. I knew they'd get you. There's a curse on us down yonder. And now they've brought you up here to hang you before my eyes –'

He bowed his head into his hands and rested his forehead against the neck of Susan. And the bright-eyed mare turned and sniffed kindly at his shoulder.

As for Jack, he was utterly stunned. Only dimly his mind began to grope toward an understanding of the mountaineer, if indeed Hank Sherry had schemed so elaborately simply to have the slayer of his son hung by the citizens of the valley. And now Lee Jarvis, who had kept carefully in the

background and offered not a single opinion
during the journey, pressed forward. In the
morning light all the bruises of the battle of the
night before showed plainly. One eye was half shut
and the other swollen, giving a strangely sleepy cast
to his expression. That sleepiness was belied by the
timbre of his voice. It was plain to Jack that shame
and rage had worked together in Jarvis until he
was in a murderous passion.

'With all due respect to you, Captain,' he said to
Carney, 'I imagine that this proves what I've been
arguing about. Yonder is a tree with a conveniently
horizontal branch. We have half a dozen ropes with
us. Why not finish the business at once? I suppose
there is no more argument about whether or not
he's the son of Hank Sherry?'

'Carney,' said Jack, 'so help me God, you're
doing a murder if you let this go through. I'm not
Charlie Sherry. He was a bigger man by two inches.
I haven't had a chance to shave. This beard has
grown out and made me look more like him. My
hair and eyes are black like his. What this hound,
Sherry, has been driving at, I don't know. But part
of it seems to me that he wants to get me hung as
his son!'

'Get him hung?' exclaimed Hank Sherry,
stepping back and looking wildly around at the
posse. 'Gents, gimme a chance to buy him. No
matter what he's stolen, I'll try to pay for it. Or if
he's hurt somebody, then take me instead of him.
Gents, he's all that's left to me! You've taken the
other three. You've killed 'em one by one. I don't
say it wasn't justice. I don't accuse none of you. I
don't say it was done without no court approving of
what you done to 'em. But I say, for God's sake,

friends, let me have this last one! Carney, you've got a daughter!'

'Stop this damned noise,' said Carney loudly. 'Jarvis, you're right. Something has been holding me back. I don't know what. There is a queer, straight look about the eyes of this fellow that's not at all like the look of the other Sherrys. But of course it has been proved six times over. This is Charlie Sherry. And he hangs for it. Steve, throw your rope over that branch, will you? We'll get the dirty business ended.'

Steve, a leather-skinned and much wrinkled cowpuncher of middle-age, looked down upon his rope as though he pitied it the horrible duty which it was to perform. Then, with the utmost dexterity he shot the noosed end over the designated branch. Jack Bristol followed that movement with dull eyes. His mind refused to understand. He found himself noting more than the dangling rope the singing of a bird in the higher branches, and the fragrance of the pines, and the brightness of the sun as it fell, brilliant but without warmth, into the glade. Even the bustle of the cowpunchers closing in upon him conveyed no meaning to him. But here Hank Sherry pressed in before him, facing Captain Carney. And as he came in, Jack felt a slight tug at the rope which bound his hands together. He looked down in time to see the quick glint of a knife disappearing with open blade into the deep hip pocket of Hank's trousers. A deft backhand stroke had severed the rope in one place. It only remained for Jack to loosen and shake off the rest of the rope and he would be free. But in order to escape he would have to gain the back of Susan, it seemed, and since he had been dismounted only the moment before at command of Carney, while Steve was throwing the rope over the branch, the difficulty was almost insuperable. But the parting of the rope had roused an instant hope in him. A slight turning of his wrists caused the entire length of the rope to loosen. At any instant he could shake it off. But in the meantime he flashed a glance over the others.

No hand was near a weapon. They were rather intent upon the length of swinging rope and upon the plea of Hank Sherry. For the strange old man had thrown himself upon his knees beside Carney's horse, and reaching up both of his grimy hands, he was shrieking forth an appeal that they spare 'Charlie, my boy, the last that's left to me –'

Here a hand fell rudely upon the shoulder of Jack, and he looked up into the face of Lee Jarvis.

'Over under the tree,' said Jarvis, fairly trembling with fierce satisfaction. 'That's your place. That fool's howling won't save you!'

He thrust Jack forward and the latter went without resistance and took his place where the noose of the rope touched against his cheek. Around him stood the horses of the posse in loose circle. And beyond the horses, behind the big tree from which the rope hung, the mountainside rose at a sheer angle covered with a dense second growth. In the meantime, the voice of Hank Sherry had risen still louder.

'Say, Joe,' protested Carney, 'will you give me a hand to take the poor old devil away to his house and lock him up until this is over?'

Joe started his horse obediently forward. It passed between Jack and Carney, and at that instant Jack shook the rope from his wrist and sprang away for safety. There was no safe interval beween the horses immediately in front of him. Instead of attempting to slide through, he dived under Steve's horse, which stood with its side presented. And while the latter whipped out his revolver with a startled yell, Jack rolled to his feet on the very edge of the dense forest of second-growth trees.

Half a dozen guns exploded almost at the same instant behind him, but there was only a pin prick at his left shoulder and the next moment he had leaped behind the screen of leaves. Once there he ducked down and ran as close to the earth as possible, not up the steep hillside, but cutting across close to the edge of the clearing. And that maneuver saved his life for the moment, at least. Carney and Steve had sent their horses crashing up the mountainside through the saplings and, with the aid of the others, searched the ground before them with a steady fusillade of revolver bullets. A headlong flight would have ended, for Jack, in ten seconds. But running to the side the noise of his feet on crackling twigs fully covered by the shouting of the posse, the roar of guns, the snorting of horses, he skirted the clearing and came, in this fashion, to a point a hundred yards away.

There he looked out and saw Lee Jarvis gathering the reins of brown Susan. At least the big man knew a fine horse and had picked for himself the cream of the spoils of war. The sharp whistle of Jack brought Susan forward with a bound. The reins whipped out of the hands of Jarvis and tugged him forward. His toe struck a root and he toppled on his face while Susan came flying. She slackened her pace, but did not stop for Jack. There was no need. He sprang for the saddle, clung with foot and hand like a cat, and with a hail of lead whistling about him, gained the back of the mare and twisted into temporary safety among the trees at the same instant.

He looked back, as he flicked out of sight. The riders were storming across the clearing at full speed. Had they shot from a stand they must have riddled him with bullets. But they were following the lead of the old instinct which bids a man charge home and get to close quarters.

But they never sighted him in pistol shot again. Riding flattened to the back of Susan, letting her weave among the trees at her own will, Jack drew swiftly away until they came into an open natural lane among the trees, and down this the mare fled with arrowy swiftness. Once again, topping a bare shoulder of a mountain, Jack looked back and saw the others flogging their mounts ahead. But the random volley which they raised fell short and Jack turned in the saddle and waved a mocking farewell as he dipped out of sight again.

Twelve

He did not drive straight away from those unlucky mountains. No. Culver Valley and the worthy inhabitants thereof had by no means heard the last of Jack Bristol. He allowed Susan to travel on for less than an hour. Then he turned her to one side over a stretch of rock where she could not be trailed with any ease or speed, unbridled her on a grassy meadowland, and let her graze till noon without sighting any of the pursuers. Doubtless that first taste of the mare's running powers had convinced hard-headed Carney and the rest that a pursuit straight across the mountains would be worse than useless, so they had winded.

And when the sun hung high at noon, Jack bridled the mare again and turned straight back on the trail from which he had come. He wanted first to corner Sherry and learn from that mysterious-minded fellow exactly what had been going on in his brain. And after that there were certain duties which he wished to perform in Culver Valley. For they had made him taste all the agony of death; and against that heavy account he wished to pile up a balance.

He used little care during his approach to the Sherry house. He was reasonably sure that the disappointed posse would not wait patiently in the clearing. They would not dream that he dared return so soon. And they would go back to the valley to spread their unhappy tidings and warn the inhabitants along the Culver River to beware of the vengeance which was impending. It would be strange indeed if armed parties did not ride up and down the valley roads that night!

So he came back to the edge of the clearing and looked out from a gap in the trees. There was no sign of hostile life. Only a column of smoke rose lazily from the chimney. It was all so peaceful, with the noonday sun pressing hot upon the clearing, that it seemed impossible he had been a few seconds from death there that morning.

He cantered Susan boldly to the door of the cabin and dismounted. There stood Hank Sherry at the stove, a sack tied around his hips by way of an apron, frying meat, the fragrance of which rolled heavily to the nostrils of hungry Jack Bristol. The big mountaineer turned slowly, juggling a fork idly in his hand after the fashion of a cook. He nodded to Jack without the slightest sign of surprise.

'Sit down,' he said. 'Chuck is about ready.'

He pointed, and Jack saw that the table was equipped for two! He shied his sombrero across the room.

'Sherry,' he said, 'I ought to salt you away with lead. But by God, I ain't got the heart to pull a gun on you! I ought to cut that lying tongue of yours out of your head and nail it in the sun to dry. But the lies that tongue told this morning helped give me a chance to break away. There's only one bargain I'm going to strike with you: Tell me what hellishness was in your mind at the start of all this.

Will you do that?'

'And if I don't?' said the mountaineer, scowling terribly upon him.

'If you don't,' said Jack calmly, 'I'll stake you out on that clearing with your face turned up to the sun.'

The other shrunk back.

'I'm an old man,' he said. 'I'm a pretty old man, Jack. Would you treat me like that?'

'Has an old wolf got any call over a young wolf?' said Jack.

He was astonished to see the other nod and actually smile, as though he were pleased by the ultimatum which Jack had delivered.

'Sit down and eat,' he said mildly.

'Have I been asking you a question?' said Jack. 'Or maybe was it a chickadee singing on a stick?'

The mountaineer laughed uproariously.

'Son,' he said, 'you sure have a way with you. Well, I'll tell you everything you want to know. But sit down and eat first.'

'Why?' said Jack. 'I'll hear you talk before I eat.'

'You won't,' said the other with an equal firmness. 'Because what I've got to say will be bad enough to hear on a full stomach, but it'd sure get me a filling of lead if I talked to you hungry. Keep a bear's belly full and the bear ain't going to bother you none. I've handled game before, son!'

It was impossible, for some reason, to stand up before the assurance of the trapper. He stood with his hands resting on his hips, squinting out at Jack through his red-shaded eyes with an expression of exhaustless evil will.

So Jack Bristol sat down and took his place in friendly fashion opposite Sherry, his fascinated eyes never leaving the white cross in the forehead of the mountaineer, never ceasing to remember that the same brand was in his own flesh. And even against his will and against his conscious mind, it constituted a strong bond between them.

Not that he for an instant relaxed his guard. No, every instant he was sternly on watch for some trickery on the part of the older man. He sat in such a position that he could keep his eye upon the door. At any moment some unknown ally of Hank Sherry, he felt, might break in upon him. And yet, under the attitude of Sherry it was not violent hatred which he sensed. It was, rather, a profound determination to show a better side to him. The friendliness of the mountaineer surrounded him.

'Sherry,' said Jack suddenly, 'what do you expect me to do?'

'I got no expectations,' answered Hank calmly.

'What d'you mean by that?'

'I mean, I don't know which way you're going to jump. You may go at my throat, or agin you may sit there real sensible and eat what I'm cooking for you. I dunno which you'll do.'

In spite of himself, Jack felt a smile beginning somewhere in him. Only in waves, now and again, he recalled the old hatred of his former jailer. But the manner of Sherry seemed to banish all that had happened into the unimportant past. Again he told himself that he could not harm a man so much older than he; and also, he assured himself that to take revenge upon Hank Sherry now would be like taking revenge upon a wild beast for acting as nature teaches it to act. Opposed to this was a faint, but growing suspicion that Sherry was less beast and more man than he had suspected all the time he had been there.

'Hank,' he said at last, 'tell me what's been in your head and what you got planned for me now.'

The mountaineer shrugged his shoulders.

'What I got planned for you?' he queried.

'You knew what would happen to me when I left. What is your plan?'

'If I was to tell you the whole of it,' said Hank Sherry, 'it would be a lot better if I could show you what I was talking about. Suppose we climb up yonder and get a peek at the whole of Culver Valley?'

Jack Bristol nodded and followed up the mountainside. He was more and more profoundly amazed by the manner in which Sherry dominated him. He had every reason to wish to destroy the mountaineer. He had been tortured and branded and his very identity changed by this strange and terrible old man, but behold! he had just risen from the same table with Hank Sherry and now walked up the mountainside meekly submissive to the will of his leader.

While he turned these thoughts in his head, they struggled up the mountainside until they reached the crest. The climb had been as steep as a ladder, and they had risen to the bald summit above timberline. Unobstructed by trees, the vision swept clear before them over a host of lower peaks.

'And yonder,' said Hank Sherry, pointing, 'is Culver Valley!'

It was spread out neatly before them. The distance compacted it like a map so that the eye caught every feature at a single glance, and the marvelous clearness of the mountain air kept every detail clear. Culver Valley was funnel-shaped,

unning out from between loftier mountains near
t hand and extending toward lower and lower
ills as it grew wider until its mouth was lost in the
norizon mist far away. And in the center they saw
he bright streak of the Culver River twisting out
oward the plains beyond.

'There it is,' said Hank Sherry, 'there she lies —
old Culver Valley!'

Jack, looking at his guide in surprise at the
emotion in his voice, saw Hank Sherry raise his
nand and pass it slowly across his forehead, as
hough to shield his eyes from what they saw, or to
erase some torturing memory from his mind.

'It's the first time in all these years,' said Hank.
It's the first time that I've ever looked at Culver
Valley. But there ain't been a day that I ain't
thought about it. I've stayed down yonder in that
cabin and told myself that I'd forget all about
everything I'd lost. But it's a pile harder to do
things than it is to say 'em. Every time I've looked
up here at the top of this mountain, I knew damn
well what the mountain was seeing, and it was like a
mirror to me. I looked to the mountain and the
mountain showed me clear as glass all that I'd lost,
all that they'd robbed me of! And it ain't changed.
It's just exactly the way that I expected it to be.
There's Bleak Mountain standing north — my God,
I've seen Bleak Mountain on better days than this!
I've seen him wrapped up in rain-fog on the day
that my first boy was born. I've seen every tree on
his sides on the clear morning that I was married.
Yes, sir, there's old Bleak Mountain! Lord God,
son, it's a queer thing how we're all tied up with the
things that we've seen. I've looked at Bleak
Mountain so often that it seems to me that Bleak

Mountain must have eyes to look back at me. I'v
been happy and blue so many times, when I rod
under the shadow of Bleak Mountain that damne
if I ain't got to feel that the mountain was happ
and blue just the same as me!'

He paused and shook his head, while Jack Bristo
looked upon him with a deeper amazement tha
ever. A peculiar gentleness had come over th
voice and the eye of the veteran in this moment. H
lost in grimness; he gained in kindly dignity.

'Damn their rotten souls,' snarled Hank Sherry
'I'll see 'em all in hell one of these days if only
could help to put 'em there!'

The kindliness was gone; in a flash there wa
nothing but black malice in all his nature. But h
added after an instant, 'And there Culve
Mountains running south, and there's the ol
Culver River in the middle. Why, son, it brings m
jump into the middle of the days when I was .
youngster, younger'n you, spry as a linnet, full o
hell-fire and happiness!'

He stretched out his long, heavy arms and then
let them fall to his sides.

'That's finished,' he said. 'Well,' he added
turning to Jack with another alteration o
expression, 'I ain't brought you up here to tall
about scenery. I come up here to talk to you abou
the kind of folks that live down yonder in tha
valley!' He paused.

'Might it be,' he said as he began to speak again
'that when you were down yonder they told you
something about me and my boys and how we
come to be marked?'

'I heard that all from Lee Jarvis,' said Jack.

'Jarvis, and it was his father that done the

suggesting! It was his father that led the way and the rest of 'em followed. Well, I know that they told you – about the burning of the minister's house, and how they found out that my brother, Oscar, was the thief, and how they decided to mark the Sherrys and get rid of 'em, and how many years they'd stood for what the Sherrys had done in Culver Valley. They told you all of that?'

'They did,' admitted Jack, and he looked curiously at the big man, wondering what counter claim he could put up to justify his blood.

'When I begun to grow up,' said Hank Sherry, 'it wasn't hard for me to tell that other folks wasn't particular fond of me. If it happened that there was any whispering or noise-making or foolishness in school, the teacher didn't hesitate more'n a minute. She come straight down to my seat and yanked me up and licked me for what I'd never done. Same way through all the rest of the town. If anything went wrong they come looking for me or for brother Oscar.

'Well, son, you can't keep tar around all the time without getting dirty now and then. When I begun to get a little bit older and big enough to think for myself, I says, "As long as they think I'm bad, why not be bad? As long as they figure me to be a sneak and a thief and no good, why not get the fun of doing the things that they think I'm doing?"'

He paused again and walked a pace up and down the brow of the mountain, and still Jack stared at him with an immense curiosity. It seemed perfectly incredible that any moral considerations had ever influenced the brain beneath that slant and brutal forehead.

'Well,' went on the mountaineer, 'I begun to do

what they expected of me. My brother, Oscar, had started long before, and he showed me the way. For a couple of years I raised hell in one way or another pretty steady, but then I got a shock. I met up with a girl that had come new to the town with a pair of big, black eyes and a smile that stopped you up like a jerk on a Spanish bit and a laugh that kept echoing inside of you. Ever meet up with a girl like that?'

'Yes,' said Jack Bristol, and the picture of Nell Carney rose in his mind and took the place of the portrait which Sherry had drawn.

'I met that girl,' went on Sherry, 'and she knocked me loose from my old way of living. I didn't see nothing but her. She filled up the whole sky for me. I went to sleep thinking about her. I woke up dreaming about her. And I went hunting her, you might say. Well, she was new to the town, she hadn't hardly had a chance to learn the truth about me, and because she seen so much of me to begin with, she got to sort of liking me. Then along comes young Jarvis, that's the father of the Lee Jarvis that you know. He was the richest man in Culver Valley. And when he seen my girl he sure lost his head. Because all the Jarvis men go wild when they see a pretty face. And the first thing that skunk done was to go sneaking to her and tell her all about what the Sherry family stood for in Culver Valley!'

He ground his teeth as he remembered.

'It made her sick to listen to him, but the first thing she done after hearing was to come straight to me and tell me everything. And out of her telling me what she'd heard, and out of me admitting part of it and what not, the short of it was that we got married the same day, me because I loved the ground she walked on, and her because she thought she could save me from being what all my family had been before me.

'And she did save me, partner. We had four sons. I kept her comfortable and happy. I built a house; I got it fixed up; when I hired out to work I done more'n any two men. And when she died, I just kept right on because every one of them four boys had something of her in 'em. One had her happy way of talking and laughing all together, and another of 'em had the ways of her head and hand, and Charlie had her eyes. He had her eyes exactly!'

Here he paused again and once more made a turn up and down on the brow of the mountain, while Jack Bristol pitied him with all his heart.

'The boys growed up,' said Hank Sherry, 'and they got what I'd got before them. They got what everybody by the name of Sherry is always sure to get in Culver Valley. They was suspected when they did nothing. They couldn't go out and play in the street without having grown folks come out and keep an eye on 'em. And when the boys got a bit old it riled 'em bad to see the way they got treated. But I kept a stiff rein on 'em. I kept 'em straight, d'ye see? I worked like hell myself; I kept 'em working, too. They learned their lessons in school; they done their work; they didn't bother other folks. But still, in spite of that, nobody trusted 'em. Because there was the long years the Sherrys had always been bad, and there was my brother Oscar right then spending most of his time in jail.

'Then along come the time when the minister's house was burned. God knows I didn't have no

hand in the burning of that house. That minister
sure had the mercy of God in him. He was one man
in town that believed in me. He was the one man in
the whole of Culver Valley that would come and sit
down with me and wish me luck! When I heard the
fire alarm, I went and I worked with the first of
'em. It was me that stood first in the bucket line
until the heat of the fire peels the skin off of my
face. And then when I went off, near fainting, I
was so plumb done up, the roof crashed in and I
heard 'em say that the whole family was wiped out.

'It was as though one of my own boys had been
killed in that fire. I went home all sick inside. And
then they come and got us out of bed, all of us, and
me with the bandages still on my face where the
fire had burned me. They got us out and they told
us they'd hanged Oscar for the minister's death.
And then they lined up the boys and heated a
poker red-hot, white-hot –'

He stopped again and tore his shirt open at the
throat. Jack himself felt as though he were half
stifled.

'They took my biggest son first. They held him
down. And while he screamed they sent the iron
smoking on his forehead. And it was Jarvis who
held the poker. Oh, God, am I ever going to forget
that?'

He cast up his great arms as though with a
blasphemous defiance against the heavens.

'Then they heated the poker again and they got
the other three boys, one after another. Last of all
they come to Charlie. He was only a little shaver
then. I got down on my knees to them and begged,
but Jarvis damned me and branded little Charlie
with the rest. And then they come to me. But I

didn't feel the iron. There was too much pain on the inside of me to feel a thing like that. I saw the smoke of my own flesh roll in front of my eyes. That was about all. And then I looked at my boys and I knew that their lives were ruined.'

His voice changed.

'I still had a hope. I thought that I could make my boys grow up honest and straight. What was a mark in the skin, after all? Nothing terrible bad. Nothing that couldn't be lived down, I hoped. So I took them up here in the mountains and we built a house and lived by ourselves and trapped and hunted and got along pretty fine.

'And then one day a hunting party come up from the Culver Valley. And they come upon one of my boys in the hills. There was a pretty girl riding out ahead. When she seen the mark on his forehead she lets out a scream, and the rest of 'em come galloping up. They seen the mark on his forehead, too. They didn't ask no questions. They took it for granted that he'd tried to harm her, and they tied him to a tree and quirted him till the blood run down his back.

'He came back home. That night my two oldest boys sat down with him and they swore that they'd be even with the rest of the world for what had been done to 'em. I begged 'em not to try to fight odds of a million to one, but they went ahead, anyway. And one by one I lost 'em. Only Charlie remained. He was the best of the lot, and I thought that he'd get to be a fine man. And then you come, and he sees that mare and wants her more'n anything else on earth. And the end of it was that he starts in to finish you. Mind you, it wasn't that he was bad by nature. But every time he seen himself in the mirror he said to himself that he was damned, anyway, no matter what he done! He couldn't come to no good end. And so, when he sees your hoss, he says to himself, "Why not?" So he went in, and you know the end of Charlie.

'Not that I blamed you, but I said to myself, "If they put a mark on me and my boys, and a curse on us along with the mark, why can't I pass the curse along to one of them and see what happens?" And that's why I done what I done. It was a terrible bad thing to do, son. I ain't denying that. But I seen for myself that you were a tiger at fighting, and the thought of turning a tiger loose in Culver Valley sure warmed the inwards of me. So I put the mark on you – and there's the end of the story.'

He extended his right arm.

'Look down there. That's why I brought you up here. When Culver come here there was a Sherry with him. They split this valley in two and each took half. Along come the Jarvis folks. They cheated Culver out of his share. And now they've drove me out, and I'm the last Sherry!'

Thirteen

It was a singular story, Jack decided, because it left all of the truly important things unsaid. It gave all of the causes and hinted only in a general way at the effect. It was said that he hoped to loose upon peaceful Culver Valley a tiger in the person of Jack Bristol. To that end he had stamped Jack with the indelible identity of a Sherry. But how could he be sure that Jack would accept the rôle which was prepared for him? Of that there was no doubt, because no matter where he went, he would be followed, sooner or later, by the news that he was a Sherry. And then he must return, if he cared at all for human sympathy, human converse, to the one soul in all the world who understood that he was free from blame.

But though the mountaineer left these things unsaid, they were patent and clear to Jack. Suddenly he put the question bluntly to his companion.

'But suppose, Sherry,' he said, 'that I light out on Susan and strike out a straight line until I get a thousand miles from here? Where does your plan go then?'

The other merely smiled and shook his head. As usual, he failed to look into the face of Jack, but stared into the vague distance while he answered.

'Suppose a wolf,' said Hank Sherry, 'never got hungry. Then it never would kill calves and colts, eh?'

'I don't foller you,' said Jack.

'Well, they've rounded you up, ain't they?' said the mountaineer. 'They've had a rope around your neck, so to speak, ain't they? They've showed you what the Culver Vigilantes are, ain't they? Ain't they talked to you about the Culver Vigilantes that never yet failed to get a gent that they started after? And after they've pretty nigh hanged you, d'you mean to say that you could go away without getting back at 'em?'

'And suppose that I do?' said Jack. 'Lee Jarvis, I sure owe a grudge to. But after I get even with him, what's to keep me from leaving the valley and going on my way?'

'Why,' said the other, 'after you've started the game, maybe you'll find that it's too much fun to quit playing! But here's a chance for you to write all the lay of the land down in your head. If you was to go down into that valley, son, you'd have it alive and buzzing like a nest full of bees in a minute or two, son! They've got their telephones strung out everywhere. They shoot out of their alarms in a flock and they've got their damned vigilantes always ready to jump onto fast hosses with their guns and start out on a man hunt. They got a boast in Culver Valley that they don't need no sheriff. They take care of their own affairs' – his voice broke to a half-snarl, half-groan – 'like they took care of me and my boys! So if you got a mind to take a crack at 'em, write all the roads and all the lay of the land in your brain, Jack.'

There was no need to give that advice. Jack
Bristol had already memorized every detail which
could be seen in such a general survey. He was still
continuing that mental survey as he returned down
the hill with Hank Sherry. It was true. As Sherry
had said, the temptation would be great. And the
more he heard of the difficulty of the work, the
more determined he was that Culver Valley had
not yet heard the last of him. To be found in it
again, of course, would mean instant death at the
hands of whoever discovered him. To take that
chance by entering the valley meant that he might
have to shoot to kill in his own defense. But in spite
of all dangers there was still a luring bait in the
trap. Somewhere yonder in the valley was — yes, he
had been able to pick out the very site of the
Carney house — was Nell, filled with horror to this
moment by the thought that she had ridden alone
through the night at the side of a Sherry.

All that remained of that afternoon Jack spent in
grooming brown Susan and oiling a brace of
revolvers and a rifle to be carried in a long holster
under his knees when he rode. Hank Sherry paid
not the slightest attention to him, but devoted
himself to a continuation of his morning's labor of
wood-chopping. His ax rang merrily and steadily
until late afternoon with the sun just dropped
behind the western mountains, and then it was that
Jack Bristol set forth on his raid.

He had only a vague purpose. On the one hand he
must see Nell Carney and strive to convince her,
before he left, that there was no stain in his blood.
Then, having said farewell to her forever, he must
find out Lee Jarvis, whose cruel cunning had

brought him to the verge of death, find some means of striking at him a blow the rich man's son would never forget, and then ride on out of Culver Valley forever. As for the expectation of Hank Sherry that he could never disentangle himself from the pursuit of the Culver Vigilantes, he shrugged his shoulders at that evil prophecy.

Only in one respect had the mountaineer been right, and that was when he called the whole affair a game. A game it was, a truly wonderful game of chance. No game of cards was ever half so enthralling. For the stakes at cards could never run as high as life and death. He had played many a time for all his worldly possessions, but all of those former games were dull and stupid compared with this.

And as he went down the mountain pass into the upper levels of the Culver Valley, with the Culver River streaked down the center in a current of tarnished silver under the moon, a new happiness filled him. For there is no joy so keen as the joy of the fighter before he goes into battle. The ragged twinkling of lights in the lands below told him of so many homes, and in every home armed men ready to combat him. For he was the universal enemy. Yes, by the very fact that all hands were raised against him there was a suggestion that he possessed strength enough to combat them all.

Now brown Susan dropped into the smoother roads of the lowlands and the joyous rhythm of her gallop carried Jack on while the mountains rolled back farther and farther on either side; Bleak Mountain to the north and Culver Mountain on the south, rolling lines of summits dimly visible in the moonlight.

Hoofbeats drummed before him. Bobbing silhouettes of horsemen flocked on the road before him. But Jack Bristol kept straight on, sitting at an alert balance in the saddle, ready to flee, ready to fight. But by moonlight, who could recognize him?

The riders swept closer, dissolving from shadows into the distinct outlines of cowpunchers, with wide brims curling in the wind of their galloping, shouting to one another as they tore down the road. They had come in from some ranch among the hills.

They were starting for a 'time.' And speed was the best part of it all. They went by Jack with a chorus of whoops, and he answered them with shouts full as cheery. What would go through their brains if someone should tell them that they had just whipped past 'Charlie Sherry'?

That thought set Jack laughing to himself as he went on. He overtook a buckboard with a pair of down-headed horses jogging slowly out the road. The driver called to him. He called joyously back to the driver. After all, these were not a peculiarly evil people. They simply saw in him a Sherry, and in the Sherrys they saw a clan who had brought destruction and terror to the Culver Valley. If he were among them, he would have shared all of their prejudices. That he knew.

And the result was that half of the venom was taken from his thoughts before he turned to the side and came down the lane which led to the house of Captain Carney. If he could only ride into town, give himself up, and demand that they send to the south for means of establishing his identity; if he could only do that, how pleasant it would then be, with scarred or unscarred forehead, to settle down and live the rest of his days in beautiful Culver Valley? But if they sent to the south they would establish his identity, so he thought, as the slayer of Sheriff Harry Ganton. Therefore there was nothing to do but see the girl for the last time, and then flee. Somewhere farther to the north there might be safety for him; somewhere far in the north and east in a cold country. A shiver went through him at the thought.

He found that the Carney house was lighted only in a front room and that not brilliantly. Telephone lines had been established in Culver Valley but there was not enough power to wire the houses with electricity. Therefore the windows were soft with yellow lamplight. He left Susan in the center of a small group of trees near the house and slipped up to observe what went on within that lighted room.

What he found was Nell Carney talking seriously with no less a personage than big Lee Jarvis.

Fourteen

It was easy to see them and to hear. The shades were undrawn. He had only to ensconce himself at the side of the window opening upon the veranda in front of the house in order to both hear and see all that went on. And he eavesdropped shamelessly. Cruelty and bad luck had given him terrible handicaps in the matter of this girl. He felt that he could justifiably adopt somewhat shady methods in return.

' – and of course everything came out,' Jarvis was saying. 'The governor heard from a dozen sources about what had happened to me in my adventure with the Sherry blackguard. I waited in fear and trembling, Nell, upon my word! I thought that the old boy would descend upon me with lightning and thunder; because he was sure to guess that I was out to see you that night.'

He laughed at the thoughts of his own fears. But while his head was raised, Jack noted that a faint sneer shadowed the lips of the girl for an instant and then disappeared. But still it seemed to Jack that she continued to observe her companion with a hawk-like fixity.

'You can imagine how I felt,' ran on Jarvis, 'when the old boy came in to see me and blurted out at once that he'd changed his mind. Anything I wanted as badly as I apparently wanted you, he thought would be all right. And marry you I should! And so, Nell, in five minutes everything was arranged! Can you believe it? Just when I thought that disaster had come along, the skies cleared and the sun shone on me; and next week, my dear, we'll be married, eh?'

He sprang from his chair as he spoke and went to her. Jack Bristol looked down in sudden agony.

'Good gad, Nell!' he heard Lee Jarvis exclaim, and looking up again, he saw that she had not stirred from her chair. But one partially lifted hand had stopped Jarvis in mid-stride.

'What's up?' gasped the big man. 'You look cold as ice, Nell, confound me if you don't!'

'I'm sorry,' said the girl. 'I don't intend that. Only –'

'Well?'

'I don't know what it was,' said the girl. 'But when you came toward me like that I felt almost as if someone were watching us!'

She smiled faintly. Lee Jarvis, with an exclamation of annoyance, stepped closer to her. And looking up to him, she shrank back in what was almost absolute fear.

'Nell, what in the world has come over you? You look at me as though I were a stranger! You've acted like this ever since last night! Is it something I've done? Have I offended you? Don't be so infernally secretive. Try as I may, I never feel that I know more than the outer rim of your real nature!'

'I'm sorry,' answered the girl, her voice falling to such a pitch that Jack could barely make out what she said. 'I'm very sorry! But when you came toward me like that — well, Lee, I simply couldn't have endured it if you had taken me in your arms!'

He bit his lip.

'I know you've never liked that sort of thing,' he said. 'But good heavens, Nell, do you expect me to be a sort of old woman's companion and sit about and talk books, and what not?'

'I suppose that would be ridiculous, of course,' said the girl with acid sarcasm that made Jarvis crimson. But she added at once in a kindlier tone, 'Lee, we've always been more or less chums until your father sent you away to school. I missed you terribly when you were away. When you came back we were both so glad to see one another that don't you think we may have thought it was love, and after all there was not a bit of true love in our affection?'

His face was spotted with gray and purple, so sudden was the shock to him. One eye was now covered with a black patch. The other was discolored and squinting. For the instant his expression was one of devilish malevolence.

Then he turned on his heel and walked up and down the room for a turn or two without saying a word. And Jack could see that pride was battling in him and bidding him make no concession to her coldness. But his courage was not equal to his pride. He crumbled suddenly, and turning toward her cast out his hands.

'Good God, Nell, are you going to break things up?'

The girl rose in turn, and quickly, as though she had not realized until he spoke how very serious her last suggestion had been.

'I don't know what I've been saying, Lee,' she

said. 'I – I haven't meant to hurt you – but – I – oh, of course I don't mean'to break off anything unless you wish. I've given you my word, Lee, and my word is sacred. You surely know that!'

Lee Jarvis struggled with words that would not come, words which, Jack Bristol knew, should have assured her that he would never dream of holding her to her promise against her will. Then, on the gravel of the roadbed, there was a scattering of gravel and a horseman drew rein. Jack pressed closer to the side of the house, trusting to the shadow to conceal him. The stranger dismounted and came up to the front door.

'It's father,' said Lee Jarvis with an air of immense relief. He lowered his voice and said something which Jack could not hear. Then he opened the door and a man as tall as young Jarvis and of the same cast of countenance entered. It was the same face, but grown older. The square outline was more pronounced. The jaw more square, and at its base little ridges of muscle leaped out when he set his teeth. The cheek-bones were high and made prominent by a spot of color upon them. The eyes were deep-set and extremely steady in their gaze. The whole frame of the man was big, well-filled, athletic. He bore his later middle-age resolutely and lightly. One would expect him to ride or walk as far as any agile youth. An indomitable will was stamped upon him. His step, his incisive manner of speech, his gestures, his reserve, were all typical of one sort of very strong man. Withal, he was a handsome man.

He stepped into the room, smiling and nodding to the girl. He shook hands with her and kept her hand in his for an instant. It seemed to Jack that he was examining her as something which was about to pass into the possession of his family. Perhaps the girl felt the same thing and it was this which made her flush.

'And everything is settled and a date arranged?' he suggested.

Young Jarvis stared at his fiancée in a very horror of alarm, but she answered his father with a smile of perfect assurance, 'Next month is my lucky month, you see, and so we've decided to put it off at least as long as that.'

'Very good,' said the father, but there was a shadow on his face as he spoke. 'I am not one who favors sudden action at any time other than a crisis. I'm about to go back to town just now because we have just passed through a trifling crisis!'

They murmured polite questions.

'Yes,' said the elder Jarvis, his eyes sparkling, 'someone let it out that there is a heavy deposit in cash in the Dexter Bank. And this evening there was an attempt to blow the door of the safe –'

A chorus of exclamations stopped him.

'I was walking down the street after dark,' said the rich man of the Culver Valley, 'and I caught a glint of light in the bank. It seemed odd to me. So I slipped across the street, opened the door with a pass key, and, to make a long story short, I bagged my man in the middle of his work, with his "soup", and "soap" laid out and only a few minutes' work left to him. It –'

'You fought him?' asked the son.

'It was a short fight. I knocked the rascal senseless and then tied his hands. When I got him out to a good light I recognized him as young Frank Stroud; from beggar to robber seems to be only a step!'

'Young Frank Stroud!' echoed the girl. 'Poor fellow!'

The elder man turned sharply upon her.

'I presume that you have in mind,' he said, 'the story that I ground Frank's father between an upper and nether millstone and ground the life out of him, in the end. Is that's what's in your head, my dear? Let me tell you the truth. I found Frank Stroud senior a rich, but very foolish man. His business methods were slipshod. I often warned him against them, but he saw fit to go on his way disregarding my warnings. And the result was that when the crash came and I was in a position to clean him out, I did exactly that! I made him an example which will teach young men starting in business not to disregard advice!'

He stamped lightly as he spoke and set his teeth at the end of his speech so that hollows formed in his cheeks and a little wedge of muscle stood out at the base of his jaw.

'That's the story of Frank Stroud in brief. And now his son proves what the family is made of. The young wretch has turned into a professional safe-cracker. Well, he is lodged in the very front of the jail, now, and he can look through the bars at the bank which he tried to rob. The young fool begged like a dog to be let off. I laughed at him!'

And he laughed heartily, while Jack Bristol saw a flash of horror spread across the girl's face.

'But will you ride back with me?' suggested the father to the son. 'I'll give you a look at young Stroud.'

'I'd like that,' grinned Lee Jarvis.

He turned away, in his excitement almost forgetful of Nell. She came to the door and watched them hurry out to their horses, and then the gravel was scattered in a flurry of hoofs as the two rushed away on the road for the town of Dexter and wretched Frank Stroud.

That noise of hoofs died out in the distance, was heard again as the face of a hill caught the passing sound and flung it back, and then the blessing of silence spread once more over the Culver Valley, a silence so complete that when the girl sighed as she stood at the door, it seemed to Jack that the sound was at his very ear.

Fifteen

'Yes,' said Jack aloud, 'I'd call it hard talk.'

She gasped. The air swished around the door as she jerked it close. But it did not slam. Instead, she checked it and opened it again.

'Who is there?' she asked in a voice husky with fear.

'Somebody,' said Jack, 'who's on the outside of the house, and you're on the inside with fighting men ready to come on the jump the minute you call for 'em. Are you afraid?'

'Afraid? Who are you?'

'Think back,' said Jack.

'Ah!' cried the girl. 'It can't be you! You haven't dared come again!'

'D'you think it's as big a risk as that, lady?'

The door clicked. But it left her on the outside. She came straight down the veranda to him.

'Don't you know that the Vigilantes are watching for you? Don't you know that if they catch you there'll be no mercy?'

Jack Bristol laughed.

'I know all that,' he said, 'but it's worth the chance.'

'Worth it?'

'Why not? It's worth a lot to hear you warning

me of the danger. It means that I've got a friend in Culver Valley.'

'I pity you with all my soul!'

'Lady,' said Jack calmly, 'I sure got to differ with you on that. Maybe you think it's pity, but it ain't.'

There was an instant's pause.

'No?' asked the girl. 'Then what is it that makes me warn you?'

'Shame,' said Jack. 'You're plumb ashamed of the way you yelled out and started them after me the other night.'

'Yes,' admitted the girl after a moment. 'Perhaps that's it. They said – that you came within a hairsbreadth of being –'

'Yep. They had the rope hanging for me.'

'If that had happened, I should have despised myself forever!'

'Why?' asked Jack.

'Why? Because you had done me no harm.'

'Ain't there another reason?'

'Of what sort?'

'Lady, you knew that I wasn't Charlie Sherry!'

'What!'

'I say, you knew that I wasn't Charlie Sherry. When we rode through the dark talking, you knew that I was tolerable honest. Is that true?'

Again she paused, and finally she said, 'They told me how you denied the poor old man when he claimed you for his son. Are you ashamed of your own father and mother, Charlie Sherry?'

'My father and mother never carried that name. But call me Charlie Sherry if you want. That makes no difference.'

'I'm glad you confess your name!'

'I confess nothing,' said Jack Bristol. 'But no

matter what you say, there's something on the inside of you that tells you I'm not a Sherry. You wouldn't be talking to me here otherwise. There's a sort of a sense in a girl that tells her when there's danger. And you know that there's a pile less now than there was when you were talking to Lee Jarvis, say, inside of your own home!'

'You've listened to us? You've overheard us again?'

'It's a right I have.'

'A right!'

'They've double-crossed me and kept me out of a fair chance. I can't come by daylight, so I come by dark. Is there anything wrong in that? Suppose I hadn't come? I'd never have seen you turn your back on Jarvis.'

'Do you think I turned my back on him? You have sharp eyes,' said the girl curiously, 'but I'm afraid they see more than the truth.'

'Lady,' said Jack, 'when a gent takes a long chance on getting his neck stretched for the sake of seeing a girl, he most generally uses his eyes hard when he gets his look at her. I wasn't sitting here looking through the window at your face. I was looking right on through your mind and everything that went on inside you.'

She started. But she came a little closer toward him.

'You're the strangest of all strange men I've ever known!' she said.

'That's because I'm telling the truth to you.'

'And I think you strange for that reason?'

'Sure. I know the way men talk to girls. They act like the truth about things would be too much for a girl to understand. So they tell her just a little part of it, and dress the rest up in lies. I know, because I've done it myself!'

She began to laugh very softly.

'Charlie Sherry,' she said. 'I have to tell you to go away and never come back, for the sake of your own safety. But when you go I shall think of you a thousand times, I promise you that! You haven't been out of my head since I first met you last night.'

'And you —' began Jack ardently.

'Hush!' said the girl. 'I can guess that you were about to say something foolish. Isn't that true?'

'Whenever a gent lets go all holds and tells the truth about himself and the way he feels, why do people say he makes a fool of himself? Lady, I'm not ashamed. I came down here to see you once more. You've stayed in my mind like a picture I'd drawed myself. Ten times every hour I've been seeing the scratch and the spurt of that match Jarvis lighted, and then your face jumping out of the darkness, sort of scared and happy all at once. I came down here to see you once more, but now that I've seen you and heard you I know this isn't the last time. I'm coming again.'

'No!' cried the girl. 'If they caught you —'

Jack Bristol laughed.

'It's the greatest game in the world. I wouldn't miss a trick of it! There's only one thing in the world that's worth it, and that's Nell Carney; but she's worth a thousand times more!'

'Charlie Sherry,' cried the girl, and the name brought him up sharply, 'I shall never see you again, not if it means bringing you into such danger.'

'Why,' he broke in upon her, 'if I know that you care so much, there's nothing that'll keep me away.'

'But I understand,' she exclaimed in a different

tone, 'it's only taking the chance that brings you here. It's the gambling spirit. Just as it was the gambling spirit that made Frank Stroud try to break into the bank and steal.'

'And when Jarvis was telling about it,' said Jack, 'which did you like the most? Was it the thief or the rich man?'

'You have an uncanny way of looking into one's motives,' said the girl. 'And perhaps you're right. I remember poor Frank Stroud. His father was very well-to-do. And Frank was a happy, careless youngster. When Mr Jarvis crushed his father, Frank was able to do nothing but stay around and go to dances. And then his money gave out, and he disappeared; and here he is back, and ruined for life!'

'Has he done any worse,' said Jack, 'than Jarvis, when Jarvis smashed him?'

'Jarvis stayed inside the law.'

'Nell!' called the voice of her father from within the house. 'Oh, Nell!'

'Coming,' she answered. 'Charlie Sherry —'

'Are you going to stick to that name? Then, I'll do what you expect Charlie Sherry to do. I'll go down the valley for your sake and I'll let Frank Stroud out of the jail. Would that make you happy, Nell Carney?'

'You madman! You would be taken also. It wouldn't help Frank.'

'I say, would it make you happy to see Frank free?'

'Happy as a lark. But if you go —'

'Nell!' called the father, and his footfall began to come down the stairs in the house.

'If I set him free, you'll see me again?' asked Jack.

'Yes, yes — I mean no — oh, what shall I do and say?'

'Say good-by,' said Jack, 'for tonight, and remember that Lee Jarvis will have the face of his father when he gets to that age. Good night, Nell, and remember!'

Sixteen

He cast a circle around the little town of Dexter. Slowly, he sent the mare over the outskirts, jumping the fences one by one, sometimes riding a little way down one of the roads or lanes which focused in Dexter, and in short, examining at his leisure all the approaches – which were, incidentally, all the exits also.

And when that was done, he swung brown Susan around and cantered her straight down the main street along which all of the houses were grouped. It was a rash thing to do, when there were half a dozen men in the town who had actually seen him by the light of day, and while every other grown and armed man was on the lookout for him. But the very recklessness of it was his best safeguard. On the lookout though they might be, they would never dream of him actually galloping a horse through Dexter under the assembled noses of the Vigilantes so famous through Culver Valley. At least he went down that main street without interruption, even whisking through more than one bright shaft of light from window or open front door. And as he went he took stock of the town.

There was no doubt about the location of the jail

with its barred windows and the bank opposite. A little further down the street he passed a stable full of livery horses. Then, striking out onto the open roads beyond the town, he quickly made a detour to the left and curved back behind Dexter again, for he had framed a plan.

Evening is the front-yard time in a village. The entire population of the town was gathered along the main street, gossiping, joking. Jack Bristol, coming in from behind, found it comparatively easy to pick the most likely horse in the pasture behind the livery stable. He left Susan, stalked and captured the horse, and tethered it to the fence. Then he ventured closer, slipped into the main stable itself and without difficulty secured a saddle and bridle. So equipped he returned to the horse in the pasture, saddled the animal, and brought it out through a gate.

Next, riding Susan and leading the tough pinto of which he had made a prize, he went down the length of the town until he came to a point opposite the flat roof of the jail. Here he tethered the pinto behind a tree, left Susan beside it, and started in toward the jail itself.

But the moment he began his approach it seemed that the entire aspect of the town had changed. All the life had hitherto seemed concentrated solely along the main street, but now it appeared that the silence along the backs of the houses was merely a symbol that the houses were filled with watching and waiting men, ready to attack him when he drew closer.

That illusion passed in a moment. A man began to sing in the yard at the back of the jail. He disappeared inside, banging a screen door which jingled behind him, while his song trailed away into the interior. Even a jail seemed to possess cheerful and homely attributes in Culver Valley.

Jack paused in the rear of a convenient tree to make his last preparations. Even as he stood there an inner door behind the screen door at the rear of the jail was closed with a heavy jar. It was a steel door, barred above, solid steel below, as he could see. The screen door on the outside was simply to keep out flies and mosquitoes. Seen dimly behind this door, the jail was a dimly lighted room, entangled with a maze of steel.

Jack sauntered around to the corner of the building and, leaning there, rolled a cigarette. He did not light it, but the rolling gave him excuse to loiter while he scanned the front of the building narrowly and the street nearby. Down that street half a dozen young men, just past boyhood, were frolicking not a full fifty yards away. They possessed man power enough to crush him and his attempt if they caught an alarm in time. The rest of the street was vacant. This section, the bank on one side and the jail on the other, might be called the downtown district in Dexter. And at this hour people were at their homes.

As for the jail itself, the cell of Frank Stroud could be easily located through the description which had been given by the elder Jarvis. There were three windows looking out upon the street, but two of these were large – ample for the admission of sun and air. The third alone was narrow and tall, though all three were heavily crisscrossed with bars. But only that narrow one could open upon a cell. The others must open upon a central hall, or the office of the jail-keeper.

The observations of Jack completed in this fashion, he took out from his pocket a section of black lining cut out of his coat on the ride into Dexter from the Carney house. This he tied around the top of his head, having first sliced it across the front for eyeholes. He rolled the mask on the top of his head, settled his hat in place, and then stepped briskly to the door of the jail. A pair of young fellows strolled past as he waited, and when they paused his heart jumped. How small a thing was required to thrill the nerves when one defied the law! They went on again almost at once, and in the meantime steps approached the door from the inside.

Jack twitched the mask down from the inside of his hat. As the door swung wide, he jabbed his revolver into the stomach of a corpulent gentleman who stood gasping before him.

'Make this quick,' suggested Jack, and slipping inside, he closed the jail door behind him.

So doing, he shut out from the street the picture of the fat jail-keeper standing with his arms thrust up above his head. He dropped the revolver back to his side.

'Get your hands down!'

The other obeyed. Every cell in the jail was simply an openwork of bars. The gleam of that gun might catch the eye of the half dozen prisoners who lounged here and there in their cells; for the Dexter jail was the depository of criminals for all of the Culver Valley. There might be a riot in a moment if they suspected that there was a jail delivery taking place out of which they themselves obtained no advantage.

'Go back to your office,' warned Jack sternly, but

softly. 'Mind you, walk brisk. And don't try no queer motions with your hands. I'm watching you every minute. Step lively, old son! I'm right behind you!'

The fat man opened the door and led the way into an office at a table in which sat a wide-shouldered youth leaning over an open ledger.

'And about this McGuire; this G. McGuire that you've got wrote down here, Dad?' he inquired.

'Get me a pair of handcuffs,' said Jack.

The words brought the other bounding out of his chair. He was reaching for his gun as he landed on his feet. Then he caught the glint of Jack's leveled weapon. For an instant their eyes clashed. Then his hands came away and rose slowly above his head.

'That's good,' said Jack. 'That's mighty good! We pretty near had an accident happening, partner. Get those handcuffs, Dad.'

The jailer found them without a word. Jack brought the arms of the youth behind him and snapped the steel manacles over his wrists.

'Listen,' he said, 'I'm not going to gag you, but if I hear a whisper out of you, I'm going to come back here and feed you lead, understand?'

The other flinched and Jack, turning to the father, gestured to him to lead the way.

'We got the jail all peaceful, now,' he said. 'Just take your keys along. We'll have Frank Stroud out of his cell, old son! Just make that pronto, too.'

A wave of the gun made the jail-keeper start ahead with a grunt of haste. His heels struck heavily on the concrete flooring outside and that sound caused two or three heads to lift and turn toward them from the cots of the prisoners. Then they rose to their feet. The word passed. In five seconds every man in the jail was standing erect. They had not seen the revolver, for Jack now carried it in the pocket of his coat, but they knew that something was decidedly wrong; the air was filled with the scent of adventure.

Straight to the door of the cell farthest to the left went the jailer. Inside there was standing at the bars a big, blond man in the very prime of his late twenties. His big hands were gripping the steel rods before him. In the lock of his door the key turned. The jailer stepped back.

'Step easy. Take your time,' Jack cautioned the prisoner. 'Come out here into the aisle beside me!'

'What?' queried the prisoner.

'Go slow –' began Jack.

But as the door swung open he sensed danger at his side and turned in time to see the fat man reaching for a gun. Indeed the steel of the barrel was already glittering as he drew it forth. It needed only the touch of his trigger finger to wipe the fat man from his path, but instead, he drove his left fist into the pit of the jailer's stomach. He fell, gasping and wriggling. Jack picked the revolver out of his hand and gave it to Frank Stroud, who now stood excited beside him.

That fall had proven to the other prisoners that it was a jail break that they were witnessing, and a chorus of low voices began calling:

'You know me, Stroud. Give me a word to your pal!'

'Kid, listen to me! I can make you rich. I've got a turn that'll fix you for life.'

'Hey, black mask, for God's sake don't leave me

here in the hole when –'

'Let's let them out!' exclaimed Stroud. 'The more of us the better!'

'Let out nothing!' commanded Jack. 'I'm letting out one man and I've got one horse for him! Now sprint for that back door. I think there's only a latch holding it!'

Stroud waited for no more. He lit out at full speed with Jack at his heels and as they ran the low calls of the other prisoners changed to yells and imprecations of rage as they realized that they were not to be saved. Yonder on the floor lay the precious, glimmering bundle of keys which had fallen from the hand of the jailer. It had only to be picked up and tossed to one of them, and instead of that the two were fleeing to a selfish liberty.

The yell of the prisoners fairly split the roof of the jail. And when Jack and Frank Stroud threw open the rear doors of the building, the sound rolled loudly out with them, while the fat jailer, sitting up on the floor, began firing blindly in the general direction in which the pair had disappeared.

Seventeen

When the two fugitives sprang out into the night from the rear door of the jail, it was like leaping into the danger of an unwakened hive of bees. For the shouts from the jail had not raised a mere scattering of voices from the village. Instead, there was a literal roar of excitement and anger, and every voice that shouted in response was running at full speed toward the point from which the alarm had issued.

A frightened oath from Stroud asserted his alarm. When they reached the tree where the two horses were tethered, he flung himself into the saddle upon the pinto and plunged away at full speed. Quirt and heels drummed or lashed the flanks of the poor pinto until the durable little cowpony was throwing its head high in fear and bewilderment. Jack Bristol, ranging alongside at the effortless gallop of brown Susan, saw that his companion was wearing out his horse without even getting the full speed for a short distance out of the animal.

'Hold him in,' he cautioned Stroud. 'Let him hit his own gait. You're running him into the ground, partner.'

Another oath answered him. 'Hold him in? Why,

you fool, they'll have a dozen racers on our heels in a minute. They'll run us ragged inside of two miles!' He added, 'Listen! There they start. Good God, they must of been waiting for us all the time!'

As he spoke, there was a fresh outburst of shouts behind them, and then a shrill and wailing cry.

'That's Lee Jarvis, damn him!' groaned Frank Stroud. 'That's Lee Jarvis on his hunter.'

'What?'

'He's got a thoroughbred. Goes like the wind. We're done for. Jarvis and the rest must of been waiting for this to happen.'

Even while he complained in his terror, he beat at the pinto, wrenching at the poor beast's mouth because it was incapable of a greater burst of speed, and every wrench, of course, helped to stop the cowpony.

They were flying down the Culver River road, now, and close behind them a gun barked; someone had fired at a shadow. That shot proved how close the danger stepped on their heels, however. And Frank Stroud fell into another fury of quirting. Finally, in disgust, Jack reined close.

'Look here,' he said, 'you see this mare I'm riding?'

'I see it. She's lightning on wheels. Lord, Lord, what a stride!'

'She'll beat the best they have behind her,' said Jack. 'She'll beat any of 'em if you'll ride her straight ahead and not start feeding her the whip. Go gentle with her and she'll break her heart for you.'

'For me?'

'I mean it, Stroud. I gave a promise that I'd get you out of this and I'm going to do it.'

'Man alive —!' began Frank Stroud.

'We'll change horses. Mind you, make it a quick change. Then you ride straight down the road. When you get into my saddle you'll find a rifle in the case. Don't use that gun shooting at men. You promise me that?'

'I do.'

'One other thing, Stroud. When you get through with that hoss, tonight, ride her up through the mountains after you've shook off the Vigilantes. And leave her up at Hank Sherry's cabin. Then you can strike away through the mountains, and going north you'll make better time on foot than they could make if they lit out after you on hosses. Is that all clear?'

'All clear, partner.'

'If you don't leave that mare the way I say, why, Stroud, I'll find you in the end and tear your heart out!'

'Partner, if I don't do what you tell me to do, I'm the worst hound that ever lived. But if you take this damned pinto, what's going to become of you?'

'I'm going to play a game, that's all. I'm going to take a chance and win out. Don't you start worrying about me, son! Here we are. Now change!'

They drew rein in unison, and like practised horsemen, bounded to the road and up again into the opposite saddles. Before them was a dark lane, where the trees from either side wound their branches together above the way and made a solid canopy.

'Ride like hell,' said Jack. 'Just let the reins hang. She'll take care of the rest. She can jump any fence you come to. She's as sure-footed as a goat! And forget that you got a whip!'

This last advice was called after Frank Stroud, for the mare, once given her head, darted away to a lead of a dozen lengths in hardly as many seconds. She was fading away into the shadows almost at once. At the same time, the leaders of the Vigilantes entering the tunnel under the trees, set up a tumult of shouts and haloos as they heard the pounding of the hoofs of their quarry so short a distance ahead.

Jack Bristol saw, at once, that the pinto could not live for ten minutes ahead of this pace. And he ducked the cowpony to the side and brought him up short behind a tree trunk. It made by no means a complete screen to an entire horse and rider. He could only hope that the posse, plunging headlong after the heels of brown Susan, would never think of glancing to the side.

It was on this hope that he had dared to make the exchange of horses with Frank Stroud. Brown Susan with no great effort should be able to shake off the best horses of the Vigilantes. So there was no harm in letting the bulk of the pursuit thunder on after her. So he waited, pressing the pinto closer to the broad trunk of the tree, and leaning in the saddle, so that he could look around it and survey the hollow way.

The posse passed him in a rush of thundering hoofs, one flying horse bounding in the lead – that must be Lee Jarvis on his hunter – and then half a dozen riders on mounts which were only a whit less fast. That was the first flight of the pursuit. Behind came others. And still more followed. Forty armed horsemen were rushing on the heels of brown Susan. And at the sight Jack Bristol's heart leaped with envy. If he were only on the back of the matchless mare, he would make a mock of these fellows and their pride. He would play with them. No doubt the thoroughbred could walk around Susan on a straightaway, but over rough going and through the wear and tear of half a dozen miles of hunting, the indomitable strength and courage would begin to tell. But the pinto? Against such speed he had not a chance!

The last of the hunt rushed past. And then, as he reined the pinto back, the cowpony stumbled, snorted, recovered his feet.

That slight noise was a tragedy. It had caught the ear of the last of the riders, and now the fellow, with a shout to his companions in the lead, swerved his horse aound and came rushing back. So much Jack waited to see, and he saw, also, that other distant horsemen were swinging their mounts around. There were ample numbers for two hunts, this day.

As for Jack, he sent the pinto bolting through the woods, which stretched before him. There, at least, his training enabled him to put the fast roadsters of the others to shame. Accustomed to dodging hither and thither through the roundup at the heels of an agile calf, the pinto darted through the forest like a football half-back down a broken field.

A tumult of curses and shouts to the rear announced that the section of Vigilantes which had taken up this newer and hotter trail was driving ahead along it in spite of obstacles. Then the pinto came out onto a broad and smooth meadow. But Jack Bristol cursed both the extent and the smoothness. These were just the things the well-mounted men behind him wanted.

He cut along the edge of the woods for a short

distance and then twitched the pinto about and put him into the woods again. Would they hear him? Yes, he had fallen into a stretch of underbrush which set up a huge crackling, and when the Vigilantes came out into the open where their ears were not crammed by the racket which their own horses set up, they caught the noise at once and came after him with a cheer.

But they lost ground on that maneuver. They lost still more heavily in the second passage of the woods. But when Jack came onto the main river road once more, he knew there could be no more dodging back and forth among the trees. They would leave a guard on the outside and the inside of the grove, after this, and he would be running his head into a trap if he attempted to weave back and forth.

So he rattled off down the road at a round pace, never putting the pinto to his full speed, but keeping just inside it at a gait which the honest little horse could maintain for a great length of time. Would it be fast enough to hold off the flying Vigilantes, now that their own mounts had lost the keenest edge of their speed during the first brush?

He turned, as soon as he was clear of the trees, into the first rough field. He struck ploughed ground and gave it his blessing. Here the pinto was at home and the thoroughbreds and half-breds which the posse bestrode could break their proud hearts fretting through the heavy going. The pinto took it as a matter of course, laboring cheerfully ahead with pricking ears for which Jack's heart went out to him.

Then, looking behind, he saw the vanguard of the enemy take the fence with a rush. Lee Jarvis, had taught his companions the pleasure of jumping, and now they rode as to a hunt. They had spied their quarry actually jogging at a trot in the semi-distance of the moonlight. And they went for him with wild yells of pleasure. Hunting? Yes, and the fox hunt was nothing compared to the man-trail!

Jack looked back anxiously. He had not covered any great distance on that ploughed ground. Would it be an efficient barrier against the pursuit, even for a little time?

He saw the leaders strike the soft dirt. It made them flounder. It stopped them up almost as though they had struck a stone wall. A trot, as all men know, is the thing for soft ground; a walk, of course, is even better. But who could keep a horse back to a trot when a quarry was actually in sight? Not these youthful Vigilantes now that they could see their man.

They sent their horses ahead at a round gallop, though at what prodigious cost of strength and wind to their mounts, who could say? They gained rapidly, to be sure. They gained so far on the trotting pinto, that their leaders opened fire with revolvers. But it was impossible to fire with any accuracy from the backs of horses pitching along through ploughed ground. And the pinto went scatheless.

Beyond, he passed through an open gate and onto firm ground, and now he loosed the rein and let the pinto fly away at full speed. Every instant placed yards of precious ground between him and the posse. And they, seeing what had happened, with furious shouts spurred their mounts over the intervening stretch of the ploughed ground. They reached the compacted soil quickly enough, but they reached it with winded, exhausted horses. The first sprint out of Dexter down the road had been enough to set their lungs laboring. The labor through the trees had been an added burden. And now this crossing the ploughed ground had exhausted most of them. It was like trying to sprint uphill.

They galloped across the level and easy ground beyond, but the spring was gone from their striding. They gained slowly for the first mile. Then, as the pinto struck into the first of the rolling hills, the bigger horses behind him began to stop. The fact that they were entirely spent was proved by the beginning of heavy fire from the Vigilantes. And now the pinto began to gain rapidly, putting the yards behind him hand over hand. Safety was only the matter of another mile, at the most, before the beaten posse gave up the trail or else merely jogged on, entirely disheartened.

The older heads among the posse seemed to realize this, for now half a dozen of them stopped their horses altogether, dropped to the ground, and uncasing their rifles began to drop bullets around the fugitive. Revolver fire from the back of the running horse was one thing. Rifle fire from a rest was quite another. Jack Bristol began to weave the galloping little pinto back and forth, back and forth like a dancer, and then, in mid-stride, the poor pinto was struck to the earth with a bullet through his head.

Jack Bristol was flung head over heels. He rose with his head spinning. It seemed to his dazed brain that enemies were rushing upon him from every corner of the compass. Then he ran for a circle of rocks which crowned the nearest hill.

Eighteen

'My name,' said the brown-faced stranger, 'is Charlie Ganton. I been trailing this way to find a gent named Jack Bristol, riding on a brown mare that's called Susan – the slickest thing in the line of hoss-flesh that I ever seen!'

'I ain't seen him pass this way,' said Hank Sherry, after a moment of due thought. 'Come in and rest yourself while I fix you up a snack for breakfast. Nope, I ain't seen your man Bristol!'

Charlie Ganton threw his reins and dropped to the ground. He stretched himself, and then gave his body a violent shake. The sun was newly up. The mountain chill and the mountain freshness was in the air.

'I ate at sunrise,' he said, 'and I ain't hungry. But I'll trouble you for a cup of that coffee. It sure sounds good to me!'

And he sniffed eagerly as the fragrance of the vapor blew out to him.

The coffee was duly poured for him.

'If I might be asking,' said Hank Sherry in his most ingratiating voice and manner, 'might you of come far on his trail, this Jack Bristol that you been talking about?'

'About a thousand miles,' said Charlie Ganton

138

carelessly. 'Pass me some of that sugar, will you?'

'A thousand miles!' breathed the mountaineer. 'A thousand miles on one trail.' His eye grew cold and bright. 'That means murder, I guess. That sure must mean a murder!'

The other looked at Hank for the first time with a keen attention. For a moment he said not a word, but sipped his coffee thoughtfully.

'So's not to put you off on the wrong foot,' he said casually, 'I'll tell you that it ain't murder. And if you ever see him passing this way, you tell him that Harry Ganton ain't dead, that Harry's brother has been looking for him, and that if he wants to go back to his home town, everything will be hunkydory.'

'Not murder,' repeated the mountaineer. 'And Harry Ganton's brother is out looking for him. And if he comes back everything will be hunkydory.'

'Including the hoss,' put in Charlie. 'He gets the hoss, too. Because Harry allows that Jack pretty near raised that filly, anyways. It belongs to Jack by right of bringing up, he says. Though, speaking personal, I don't see how he figures it.'

The smile of Hank Sherry was so wonderfully bland that for the moment his face lost half of its ugliness.

'He gets a hoss and he gets let off for murder,' he repeated. 'That ought to sound like good news to him. Yep, if I was to meet up with him, I'd sure tell him what I know.'

'Look here,' said Charlie, 'if you got any queer ideas from what I've said to you, you might as well get over 'em right now. My brother is a sheriff and he's fixed me up with a start and what not to go up here as his deputy. I don't mind telling the rest of the yarn. There ain't any mystery. Harry got into an argument with Jack and they went for their guns, and Harry was the one that dropped. The boys give Jack a run for his money, but he got away on Susan. Meantime, Harry is getting well hand over fist and he figures that the only way he can make up to Jack for the long trail he's sent him on is to give him that brown mare. Though Susan would bring a thousand dollars or even two thousand out of more'n one man in Arizona!'

'Two thousand for a hoss!' breathed the mountaineer. 'Well, that's a considerable price. You folks down that way must be made of money. Set down, son, and tell me about your part of the country.'

'Just a minute,' said Charlie. 'How come this to be here?'

From the junk pile nearest the door he picked up a piece of leather twisted into a peculiar braid.

'How'd you get that?'

Hank Sherry took the thing and turned it in his hand.

'Don't exactly recollect,' he said calmly. 'Don't remember what that might of come from.'

'H-m-m!' said Charlie, his eyes bright with suspicion. 'Anything about it that looks queer to you?'

'Yep. I don't think I ever before seen a braid exactly like that one!'

'Maybe you didn't,' said Charlie, 'because the only man I ever knowed worked up a leather braid like that was the man I'm after now – Jack Bristol!'

'Well, well, well!' murmured the mountaineer, stroking his bushy beard while he wagged his head. 'You don't say, friend!'

'I do,' muttered Charlie Ganton, and finishing his

coffee at a draught, he stood up from his chair and fixed a keenly suspicious eye upon Sherry. At length, as though not able to see in what manner the other could profit by keeping the whereabouts of Bristol a secret, if he knew, he turned toward the door again.

'Which way had I better be going?' he asked the mountaineer.

Hank Sherry pointed to the east, away from Culver Valley.

'Hit out yonder,' he said, 'and you'll come into some good cow country. If your man come up from Arizona way, most like he'd be pretty apt to want to get into the cow country again, eh?'

'Most like,' nodded Charlie Ganton, and swung into the saddle again.

'So long,' he called, and waved his hand, but before his roan mustang had taken half a dozen steps, Charlie turned abruptly in the saddle and surprised a complacent smile of triumph upon the lips of Sherry. The latter banished the pleased expression at once, but not soon enough. Young Ganton, his brown face now darkened with suspicion and anger, wheeled his horse and came straight back.

'Stranger,' he said coldly, 'you know something. What's up?'

'Me?' said Sherry. 'Know something? How come?'

'Partner,' said Charlie Ganton soberly, 'lemme tell you this, the gent that I'm on the trail of is a wild one. He was always on the ragged edge of raising hell and doing something that he could never undo. Now he thinks that he's done a murder, and he's apt to do another if he thinks he's cornered. He's that tigerish kind that go to hell quick once they've started. That's why I ask you to put me onto his trail if you know it.'

'Sure,' said Hank Sherry. 'I'd do it in a minute. I sure would hate to see a gent cavorting around raising Ned. I'd sure hate to see that.'

And in spite of himself, his glance wandered toward the west, where Culver Valley lay beyond the mountains.

And as he glanced in that direction, it happened by rare chance that Frank Stroud came over the hill and showed against the horizon on brown Susan. But it was merely the exigencies of the chase and through following the easiest way out of Culver Valley that he had come toward Hank Sherry's house, not through a desire to follow his word as pledged to Jack Bristol. And when Charlie Ganton, with a shout of pleasure, galloped toward him, he drew up brown Susan and meditated flight.

For never in his life had he bestrode such an animal as the mare. She had carried him faultlessly all the night, she had baffled the best speed and the cleverest maneuvers of the hardest riders in Culver Valley. And he could not find it in his heart to give her up to Hank Sherry to be kept for the man who had delivered him from jail. As for the man who galloped toward him, he came alone, and it was Stroud's boast that he feared no one man in the world.

So he drew rein and waited. Charlie Ganton, in the meantime, slackened his pace when he saw that the horseman was not Jack Bristol. He drew down to a trot and then to a walk, while the roan pricked his ears at sight of Susan and neighed an eager greeting. They had known each other of old in the

Ganton pastures far south.

'Partner,' asked Charlie, 'where's Jack Bristol?'

'Never heard of him,' said Stroud truthfully.

'Never heard of him? Well, then, let me put it another way. Who'd you get this hoss from?'

'I raised her,' said Stroud. 'She was foaled right on my ranch.'

'Hell, man!' snorted Ganton in disgust. 'Look at the way she and this roan hoss of mine are rubbing noses. Don't that show they ain't strangers? I ask you again, where'd you get this hoss? I know her as well as I know my brother. It's Susan.'

'Look here,' said Stroud smoothly, though he shifted his hand so as to bring it nearer to the revolver which lay in the saddle holster. 'I've seen men that folks couldn't tell apart. And if that's true of men it's still truer of hosses. I got no doubt that you think the name of this hoss is Susan. But it ain't. The name of this hoss is Belle. I raised her on my own ranch.'

Ganton drew back.

'Partner,' he said, 'I sure hate to do this, but I got to. I've come all the way from Arizona to find the man that's been riding this hoss. Here's my badge –' he showed a star pinned inside the flap of his coat – 'and I got to arrest you, stranger, for appearing with property that looks to me like stolen property.'

'Arrest me?' echoed Frank Stroud, and his laughter was loud, though he kept his chin down and watched the other with a snarling earnestness. 'Son, you ain't got a chance. Get out of the way. I'm due on the other side of the mountains and – look out, damn you, keep your hand clear from your gun!'

'In the name of the law,' said Charlie Ganton with no little dignity, 'I arrest you for –'

'To hell with you and the law!' exclaimed Stroud. 'Get out of my way or –'

They went for their guns by mutual agreement, it seemed. The weapons leaped as though recoiling from springs into their hands. Frank Stroud was a shade quicker on the draw. His weapon exploded. But Charlie Ganton still sat his saddle. At the last instant he had both stooped and twisted sideways, and the bullet missed that moving and smaller target. His own bullet, discharged a fraction of a second later, struck squarely on the shoulder of Frank Stroud, jerking him far around. The shoulder bones were splintered by the ball. Clasping his left hand over the wound, he toppled to the ground with a cry of pain, while brown Susan, starting back in alarm, pricked her short ears and sniffed curiously at him.

Nineteen

The rocks to which Jack Bristol had run crested a small knoll and from this commanding position the onrushing Vigilantes recoiled and scattered into a circle, shouting their joy at having run the quarry to the ground. While they rushed for positions of strategic importance, however, Jack was busy as a beaver erecting a system of fortifications. The great stones which were heaped upon the crest he pried apart and rolled into a rough-shaped triangle. In the center of this he could lie with a fair degree of safety. So he crouched behind the barrier as soon as it was raised, and waited.

It was the end, of course. He might endure a siege here for a single day without food or water, but on the second day he must succumb. There was only one possible hope for escape, and that was through a rush under cover of the night to secure a horse from his besiegers and then break away across the country. But to steal out through the night in the face of such a circle of hungry-hearted manhunters and with the young moon shedding light over the hills would be merely a form of suicide.

Presently he heard a strong voice calling across the night from the top of an overlooking hill.

'Hellooooo! Stroud!'

'Hello!' cried Jack. Of course it was natural for them to think that this was Stroud.

'I'm coming down. Will you give me a truce to come by?'

'Come on, then! No tricks!'

A man appeared, looking gigantic in the faint moonlight and came upon the hilltop against the sky. He came boldly down into the hollow and then climbed the farther slope to the edge of Jack Bristol's fortification.

'Stroud,' he said at once, 'the jig's up.'

'Sort of looks,' said Jack, 'that it is.'

The other exclaimed, 'Who the devil is this? It ain't Stroud!'

'Why not?'

'I know Frank's voice. You're the other one, then? By God, it's Charlie Sherry!'

'How'd you recognize me?'

'We knew that one of the hosses we was following was your hoss. But it never popped into our heads that you'd swap hosses with Stroud. What happened? Did he take it away from you? And after you got him out of jail?'

'Sort of looks that way, eh?' said Jack.

'Sherry, what the devil possessed you to break into the jail and get Stroud out? Was he ever a friend of yours? I can't remember him that way!'

'What does all this lead up to?'

'It leads up to this, Sherry: Give yourself up and come along with me and we'll give you a fair and square trial and if there's a hanging at the end of it, it'll be a legal hanging, Sherry. Does that sound good to you?'

'Who gives you authority to offer me all of this?'

'They told me to say that to Stroud. It'll hold for you, too, I guess.'

'Go back and find out.'

So the other departed, but Jack Bristol knew beforehand that there would be no answer. The men of Culver Valley had too many things against Charlie Sherry. They had been balked by him once when he slipped through their hands; now, for half a night, he had played back and forth with them and only by sheer luck or a chance shot had they managed to come within striking distance of him. And now that they had him cornered they would finish him then and there.

He was right. The stranger did not return to renew the proposal in the name of the rest of the Vigilantes and when, a little over an hour later, a volleying of hoofbeats was heard in the distance, Jack knew that the rest of the posse had returned from their vain chase of Susan and had come back to join in the killing of Charlie Sherry.

They began to build little bonfires behind the hilltops. Now and then shadows brushed into his view. It was long range for a revolver, but had he wished to do murder, he could have dropped more than one of the youngsters whose shouts and laughter rang down to him. They were making a merry night of it while they waited for a chance to get their quarry. Once he thought that their noise making might indicate a lax watch and he slipped outside of his little fortress prepared for a dash for liberty. But the instant he began to run there was a solid volley of rifles. And he leaped back into his shelter with bullets flocking thick around him.

After that it was not long before pink began to

streak the east. And with the coming of light the bombardment began. Just north of him rose the highest hill. It looked down upon him at such a sharp angle that they could open a dangerous and close-plunging fire. They had followed his example and erected, with their many hands, an ample and strong barrier of rocks. Thrusting out the muzzles of their rifles through the interstices among the stones, they dropped slug after slug into the triangle of Jack's fort. Not a shot flew wild. It was a large target, and they had plenty of lead. So they amused themselves in fancy and freakish bits of marksmanship.

They chipped the points off the rocks. They placed their bullets neatly through the holes of his wall. They proved to him in a hundred ways that he had only to show himself in order to be riddled with lead.

He showed a small stick. It was only a streak of a thing to be shot at, yet it had not been exposed three seconds before the end was snipped off. He showed it again. Again it was severed, and the crowd on the higher hill yelled their satisfaction. He tossed a rock into the air and with a cheer the youngsters above him loosed a volley. That rock struck the ground unnicked. But the next one he threw was snuffed to powder when a bullet struck it. They had scarred and whitened the surfaces of the rocks on the farther side of his wall, but still they kept it up. Each one of them had a cartridge belt to empty, and each was doing his best to get rid of powder and shot. Yet it was not an altogether useless exhibition, for it kept Jack crowded into a corner, not daring to move.

The sunlight was beginning to slant and spill into

his fort when he heard a sudden shouting of dismay, and then warning cries. Peering out through a hole in the wall, he saw Nell Carney galloping at full speed across the hollow, while a score of voices were vainly warning her away. To Jack Bristol she came like a hope of heaven to one damned. When she drew near, he rose to meet her. Of course there were expert riflemen looking on, but would they dare to draw a bead, no matter with what skill, when Nell Carney was so near the target at which they aimed?

They did not dare. There was only an excited and enraged clamor of voices. And then Nell Carney had reined her horse beside him and was commanding him, in a voice hysterical with fear, to get back into shelter. He did not stir. She dropped out of the saddle and stood beside him so that her nearness could more effectually shield him.

'Oh, why, why have you done it?' she cried.

'Because I promised you to get him out, and he's free now, I guess.'

'You held up the jail-keeper. You gave Frank your own horse. Was there ever such a generous madman in the world?'

'Lady, not a crazy man, but a gent that did what he told you he'd do. It looks like I throwed myself away. But you see, it was only the luck that broke against me. They nailed my hoss with a lucky shot. They nailed that poor old pinto hoss that I was riding. And that was sure an honest hoss, if ever an honest hoss stepped. He worked like a trouper. Never let up till he had all of them fast-stepping hosses dead-beat!'

'And you spend your time pitying the horse you rode when – when you're in a place like this?'

'Nell!' cried a voice from the top of the hill.

Jack looked up and saw Lee Jarvis recklessly exposing himself and calling to the girl to go from the hilltop at once, for otherwise terrible things were apt to happen. Jack raised his hand, and the figure on the hilltop dropped out of view behind his barricade.

'Doesn't take soothing syrup to quiet him,' said Jack, grinning at the girl.

'Leave you?' she answered the demand of Lee Jarvis. 'I'm going to stay until they've promised to let you have law.'

'You're wrong,' said Jack. 'you've got less'n a minute to stay.'

She shook her head.

'It was I who brought you into this. And I'm going to stay until you're out of danger.'

'That's like you,' said Jack thoughtfully. 'A gent could see that you'd be as square as that. But it don't work, lady. I'm not going to hide behind a woman's skirts. That's ten times worse than dying. You see? But before you go I'm going to ask you one thing: You believe me when I say that I'm not Charlie Sherry?'

'I believe you,' she answered, with great tears glistening in her eyes. 'Oh, I knew all the time that you couldn't be he. But the scar seemed proof. I knew all the time. For there was something which made me believe what you said, and not what my eyes told me.'

'Then one more thing,' said Jack, 'whatever happens to me will you keep in your mind that Lee Jarvis ain't worthy of you? Nell, I've heard him lie about a man that licked him in a fair fight. And a man that'd lie about that ain't worth his salt.'

'I'm only waiting to face him alone and then I shall tell him,' said the girl, grown stern and savage for a moment.

'And that's all,' said Jack. 'Good-by.'

'I told you before and I tell you now, I'm not going.'

'Nell, in my part of the country a gent that hides behind a woman is called the worst hound in the world. If you don't go, I'm going to walk down that hill right into their guns. I swear I am. I'll fight this out without a woman's help!'

'No, no!'

'I mean it!'

She threw out her hands toward him, then checked the appeal.

'I'll go back up the hill and make them swear to give you a legal trial. Will you surrender then?'

'When they agree to a legal trial, yes,' said Jack, and swallowed a sardonic smile.

But the girl, with a cry of triumph, was into the saddle, and as he dropped back into shelter, she turned in the saddle and kissed her hand to him – in full view of all those armed watchers on the hill!

There was something so gay and so gallant about her that it stopped his heart and, raising his head a little too recklessly a bullet jammed the hat off his head and flicked away a lock of his hair.

And after that, the steady bombardment was resumed. There was no more heard of the girl. They had taken her by force and led her away, as he knew that they would. They had led her away and, new men pouring in every moment from the surrounding farms, fresh belts of ammunition were beginning to empty toward the little fort as though they actually planned to shoot away the stones to powder.

In the meantime the pressure of a new and even
more terrible enemy began to be felt. It was the
rising sun which, as it sloped up toward meridian,
heated the stones until they were difficult to touch,
while the direct rays scorched the motionless body
of the fugitive. If he could have raised his head
above the wall to meet the breeze, but then there
were bullets waiting. And he must endure all the
long day until night. What time was it now? Not
more than ten, at the most.

He amused himself looking out through the
holes among the rocks and watching the arrival of
newcomers until, close to the intolerable heat of the
noon hour, he saw a rider coming on a horse whose
liquid gallop was vaguely familiar. Yes, all in an
instant he knew that it was Susan!

Had Frank Stroud come to give himself up in
return for the freedom of the prisoner in the fort?
No, in another moment his heart sank still more,
for he had made out the bronzed features of
Charlie Ganton, who would add to the list of
charges against him that of murder After this he
could expect no mercy, indeed.

And, suddenly, he decided that he had endured
long enough. It was useless to wait until his last
energy was exhausted. Better, far better to die
while he still had the strength to die fighting. He
loaded his revolver, saw that it was in good working
trim, drew up his belt to the last notch, and
prepared to rise to his knees, but as he did so,
Charlie Ganton rode over the brow of the hill
above. To lead a charge?

No, he came with his hand raised, and behind
him man after man was rising and waving; they

were even calling what sounded like friendly words.

He listened in a daze. And when Charlie rode up, he rose, hardly knowing what he did. He found his hand gripped in a strong grasp. He felt himself clapped on the back.

'By God, Jack,' Charlie was crying, 'I've come at a lucky hour. But the trouble's over. I've come to tell you that Harry is not dead. That bullet only sliced him across the breast, the lucky devil! He's not dead, and he's sent me a thousand miles after you to get you out of mischief. And he's throwing in Susan, here, for full measure to make up for the distance you've traveled.'

The brown mare thrust her head between them and poked her wet muzzle into the face of Jack. He patted her between the eyes, but still he was dazed, too utterly bewildered to understand. Other men were coming. Was it a trick, after all? No, they could not assume such smiling faces; they were not actors enough for that!

'I've cash to pay the man who owned the pinto. And I've left Frank Stroud – the skunk! – at Hank Sherry's, that old fox. They can get Stroud and bring him back to the Dexter jail whenever they want. If they want to go the limit and hold you for breaking into the jail, I have a warrant here from Harry to arrest you on another charge for something you done first. But that warrant will never be served, Jack, except to get you out of this mess!'

And then the whole truth burst on him like a flood of light, not out of the words which he had heard kindly Charlie Ganton speak, but because he saw Nell Carney come galloping over the hill while

Lee Jarvis rode downheaded in the opposite direction.

He saw her sweep into the hollow like a bird. He saw her spur at full speed up the slope again. And before the others she was before him and stood on the ground facing him and laughing. But all the while that she laughed the tears were coursing down her face.

'Oh, Jack Bristol,' she cried, 'I'm the happiest person in the world. Because you knew all the time that you were an honest man; but I could only hope it!'

'Nell,' he answered, 'I never knew until this moment that I would die an honest man!'

That was the speech which Charlie Ganton carried back to the southland; but it was a speech which the townsmen in Arizona could not quite believe. They are still waiting to see the name of Jack Bristol in a headline.

For that matter, so is Mrs Jack Bristol, but she expects to see her husband's name in print for far other reasons; for Culver Valley has decided that it needs a sheriff. The Vigilantes are a matter of the past. So completely broken is their power that Jack Bristol could bring old Hank Sherry back into the valley with all of his crimes and all of his sorrows upon his head. And there he lives by the verge of the river in a hut whose front door looks out toward the blue Culver Mountains.

THE ROCK OF KIEVER

MAX BRAND

"Brand practices his art to something like perfection."
—*The New York Times*

Here are three of Max Brand's classic short novels, all carefully restored from Brand's own manuscripts, and collected in paperback for the first time. In "Range Jester," Barry Home, once a free-spirited cowboy, now an ex-convict, returns to the small town of Loomis. "Slow Bill" is the story of young Jim Legrange, who leaves home for an abandoned gold rush town where he runs into an old prospector who has a photograph of Jim's father. But he calls the man in the picture Slow Bill and says he was once his partner. And in "The Rock of Kiever," Texas Ranger Charlie Stayn swears vengeance against his best friend's killers and defies the ranger code, heading into the Kiever Mountains to track them down.

___4719-5 $4.50 US/$5.50 CAN

SOFT METAL
MAX BRAND

Collected here for the first time in paperback are three of Max Brand's greatest short novels, all restored to their original splendor, just as the author intended. In "The Red Bandanna," Clancy Morgan returns to town to warn his best friend, Danny Travis, that Bill Orping is heading there, looking for a confrontation. But when he gets there he finds that Orping has arrived before him and was shot in the back—and it looks like Danny was the killer. "His Name His Fortune" is the story of a young gambler who falls in love with the daughter of a wealthy rancher who despises him. And in the final short novel, "Soft Metal," Larry Givain, fleeing from a posse, meets a beautiful woman at a deserted cabin belonging to one of the men in the posse. Her brother is also holed up in the cabin, pursed by a notorious gunfighter. With death drawing ever nearer, Givain realizes his life will never be the same again.

___4698-9 $4.50 US/$5.50 CAN

Dorchester Publishing Co., Inc.
P.O. Box 6640
Wayne, PA 19087-8640

Please add $1.75 for shipping and handling for the first book and $.50 for each book thereafter. NY, NYC, and PA residents, please add appropriate sales tax. No cash, stamps, or C.O.D.s. All orders shipped within 6 weeks via postal service book rate. Canadian orders require $2.00 extra postage and must be paid in U.S. dollars through a U.S. banking facility.

Name_____

Address_____

City_____ State_____ Zip_____

I have enclosed $_____ in payment for the checked book(s).

Payment <u>must</u> accompany all orders. ❏ Please send a free catalog.

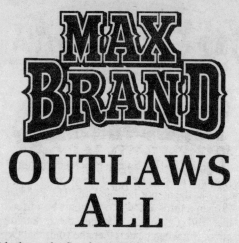

OUTLAWS ALL

From Alaska to the Southwest, Max Brand, the master of the Western tale, brings the excitement of the frontier to life like no one else. His characters live, breathe, struggle and triumph in a world so real you can hear the creaking of the saddle leather. Gathered in this collection are three classic short novels by Brand, all filled with the adventure and heroism, the guts and the gunsmoke, that made the West what it was.

___4398-X $4.50 US/$5.50 CAN

Dorchester Publishing Co., Inc.
P.O. Box 6640
Wayne, PA 19087-8640

Please add $1.75 for shipping and handling for the first book and $.50 for each book thereafter. NY, NYC, and PA residents, please add appropriate sales tax. No cash, stamps, or C.O.D.s. All orders shipped within 6 weeks via postal service book rate. Canadian orders require $2.00 extra postage and must be paid in U.S. dollars through a U.S. banking facility.

Name_____
Address_____
City_____ State_____ Zip_____
I have enclosed $_____ in payment for the checked book(s).
Payment <u>must</u> accompany all orders. ☐ Please send a free catalog.
CHECK OUT OUR WEBSITE! www.dorchesterpub.com

MAX BRAND

THE LEGEND OF THUNDER MOON

Thunder Moon was born white. But as a boy he was captured by a mighty Cheyenne brave who needed a son, and was raised in the ways of his father's tribe. As Thunder Moon grew, he learned Cheyenne culture and sought honor through warfare and hunting to overcome the stigma of his light skin. Yet there are some traditions Thunder Moon cannot accept. One of these is the self-torture of the Sun Dance, the major rite of passage to adulthood for braves. He has to find another way to prove himself worthy in the eyes of his adopted people. His chance comes in a test so daring, so courageous, that no man can doubt his manhood. Thunder Moon will lead a raid against the Cheyenne's fiercest enemies, the scourge of the Plains—the Comanches!

___4583-4 $4.50 US/$5.50 CAN

MAX BRAND

SAFETY McTEE

Here, in paperback for the first time, restored from his own typescripts, are three prime examples of Max Brand at his rousing best. In "Little Sammy Green," a son has a difficult time living up to the reputation of his gunfighter father, until fate forces him to prove himself. "Black Sheep" is the extraordinary story of a nine-year-old tomboy who comes up with a scheme to win an outlaw his freedom, even though it puts her own life in jeopardy. And "Safety McTee" tells of a gunfighter who earned his nickname by merely wounding, not killing, his opponents. But when he's forced to shoot an old man in self-defense, he finds himself hunted by a lynch mob that doesn't appreciate his past mercies.

___4528-1 $4.50 US/$5.50 CAN

Dorchester Publishing Co., Inc.
P.O. Box 6640
Wayne, PA 19087-8640

Please add $1.75 for shipping and handling for the first book and $.50 for each book thereafter. NY, NYC, and PA residents, please add appropriate sales tax. No cash, stamps, or C.O.D.s. All orders shipped within 6 weeks via postal service book rate. Canadian orders require $2.00 extra postage and must be paid in U.S. dollars through a U.S. banking facility.

Name_____
Address_____
City_____ State_____ Zip_____
I have enclosed $_____ in payment for the checked book(s).
Payment <u>must</u> accompany all orders. ❑ Please send a free catalog.
        CHECK OUT OUR WEBSITE! www.dorchesterpub.com

MAX BRAND

THE QUEST OF LEE GARRISON

As a young man, working as a line rider on a great ranch in the Southwest, Lee Garrison spends hours reading tales of the knights of the Round Table. His life will never be the same, though, after a dying Indian stumbles into his line shack. The Indian traveled hundreds of miles in search of the magnificent mustang known as Moonshine. After burying the Indian, Lee catches a glimpse of the mustang and takes to the trail. The chase will lead him across thousands of miles, and before his quest ends, Garrison will learn the meaning of hope and the cost of dreams. And he will be forced to make a terrible, shattering decision.

___4558-3 $4.50 US/$5.50 CAN

Dorchester Publishing Co., Inc.
P.O. Box 6640
Wayne, PA 19087-8640

Please add $1.75 for shipping and handling for the first book and $.50 for each book thereafter. NY, NYC, and PA residents, please add appropriate sales tax. No cash, stamps, or C.O.D.s. All orders shipped within 6 weeks via postal service book rate. Canadian orders require $2.00 extra postage and must be paid in U.S. dollars through a U.S. banking facility.

Name_____

Address_____

City_____State_____Zip_____

I have enclosed $_____ in payment for the checked book(s).

Payment <u>must</u> accompany all orders. ❏ Please send a free catalog.

CHECK OUT OUR WEBSITE! www.dorchesterpub.com

TROUBLE IN TIMBERLINE

"Brand is a topnotcher!"
—New York Times

Barney Dwyer is too big and too awkward to be much good around a ranch. But foreman Dan Peary has the perfect job for him. It seems Peary's son has joined up with a ruthless gang in the mountain town of Timberline, and Peary wants Barney to bring the no-account back, alive. Before long, Barney finds himself up to his powerful neck in trouble—both from gunslingers who defy the law and tin stars who are sworn to uphold it!

_3848-X $4.50 US/$5.50 CAN

THE WHITE WOLF

MAX BRAND

"Brand is a topnotcher!"
—New York Times

Tucker Crosden breeds his dogs to be champions. Yet even by the frontiersman's brutal standards, the bull terrier called White Wolf is special. With teeth bared and hackles raised, White Wolf can brave any challenge the wilderness throws in his path. And Crosden has great plans for the dog until it gives in to the blood-hungry laws of nature. But Crosden never reckons that his prize animal will run at the head of a wolf pack one day—or that a trick of fate will throw them together in a desperate battle to the death.

_3870-6 $4.50 US/$5.50 CAN

Dorchester Publishing Co., Inc.
P.O. Box 6640
Wayne, PA 19087-8640

Please add $1.75 for shipping and handling for the first book and $.50 for each book thereafter. NY, NYC, and PA residents, please add appropriate sales tax. No cash, stamps, or C.O.D.s. All orders shipped within 6 weeks via postal service book rate. Canadian orders require $2.00 extra postage and must be paid in U.S. dollars through a U.S. banking facility.

Name_____

Address_____

City_____ State_____ Zip_____

I have enclosed $_____ in payment for the checked book(s).

Payment <u>must</u> accompany all orders. ☐ Please send a free catalog.

RONICKY DOONE'S TREASURE

MAX BRAND

"Brand is a topnotcher!"
—New York Times

A horsebreaker, mischief-maker, and adventurer by instinct, Ronicky Doone dares every gunman in the West to outdraw him—and he always wins. But nothing prepares him for the likes of Jack Moon and his wild bunch. Hunting down a fortune in hidden loot, the desperadoes swear to string up or shoot down anyone who stands in their way. When Doone crosses their path, he needs a shootist's skill and a gambler's luck to survive, and if that isn't enough, his only reward will be a pine box.

__3748-3 $3.99 US/$4.99 CAN

Dorchester Publishing Co., Inc.
P.O. Box 6640
Wayne, PA 19087-8640

Please add $1.75 for shipping and handling for the first book and $.50 for each book thereafter. NY, NYC, and PA residents, please add appropriate sales tax. No cash, stamps, or C.O.D.s. All orders shipped within 6 weeks via postal service book rate. Canadian orders require $2.00 extra postage and must be paid in U.S. dollars through a U.S. banking facility.

Name_____
Address_____
City_____ State_____ Zip_____
I have enclosed $_____ in payment for the checked book(s).
Payment <u>must</u> accompany all orders. ☐ Please send a free catalog.

TIMBAL GULCH TRAIL

"Brand is a topnotcher!"
—New York Times

Les Burchard owns the local gambling palace, half the town, and most of the surrounding territory, and Walt Devon's thousand-acre ranch will make him king of the land. The trouble is, Devon doesn't want to sell. In a ruthless bid to claim the spread, Burchard tries everything from poker to murder. But Walt Devon is a betting man by nature, even when the stakes are his life. The way Devon figures, the odds are stacked against him, so he can either die alone or take his enemy to the grave with him.

_3828-5 $4.50 US/$5.50 CAN